T0285573

A Lethal Walk
in Lakeland

Books by Nicholas George

A Deadly Walk in Devon

A Lethal Walk in Lakeland

Published by Kensington Publishing Corp.

A Lethal Walk in Lakeland

NICHOLAS GEORGE

KENSINGTON PUBLISHING CORP.
kensingtonbooks.com

This book is a work of fiction. Names, characters, businesses, organizations, places, events, and incidents either are the product of the author's imagination or are used fictitiously. Any resemblance to actual persons, living or dead, events, or locales is entirely coincidental.

To the extent that the image or images on the cover of this book depict a person or persons, such person or persons are merely models, and are not intended to portray any character or characters featured in the book.

KENSINGTON BOOKS are published by

Kensington Publishing Corp.
900 Third Ave.
New York, NY 10022

Copyright © 2025 by Nicholas George

All rights reserved. No part of this book may be reproduced in any form or by any means without the prior written consent of the Publisher, excepting brief quotes used in reviews.

All Kensington titles, imprints, and distributed lines are available at special quantity discounts for bulk purchases for sales promotion, premiums, fund-raising, educational, or institutional use. Special book excerpts or customized printings can also be created to fit specific needs. For details, write or phone the office of the Kensington Special Sales Manager: Attn. Special Sales Department, Kensington Publishing Corp., 900 Third Ave., New York, NY 10022. Phone: 1-800-221-2647.

KENSINGTON and the KENSINGTON COZIES teapot logo Reg. US Pat. & TM Off.

Library of Congress Control Number: 2024944017

ISBN: 978-1-4967-4529-3
First Kensington Hardcover Edition: February 2025

ISBN: 978-1-4967-4531-6 (ebook)

10 9 8 7 6 5 4 3 2 1

Printed in the United States of America

A Lethal Walk
in Lakeland

From Chase's Journal

A member of my walking group was murdered tonight. What's worse is they told me it would happen.

"We look like such a loving family, right? Don't let that fool you, Chase. If the others had a chance, they'd do away with me in a hot minute. Trust me. Each and every one of them wants to see me dead."

I couldn't have gotten a clearer warning. So why didn't I do anything to prevent it?

Sure, I kept my senses on alert, but that wasn't good enough. I need to clear my conscience—work with the police, find the killer, and bring them to justice.

Chapter 1

Saturday
St. Bees Bay, Cumbria, England

Outside the window of the Northern Line train, the northeastern coast of England flashed by in quick bursts—hawthorn and beech trees, power lines, weathered cottages. Beyond lay the North Sea, the sun playing upon its gray waters, filtering down through a wash of clouds.

Some might consider the view sobering—depressing even—but to me it was as welcome as a sunrise. I was back in my favorite country, and about to be reunited with the man I'd met on my last English walk, the man I couldn't get out of my head.

Before me on my tray were the morning's London *Times* and a tall iced coffee. It had been a long day—I'd endured a tedious, ten-hour flight from Los Angeles—but I knew a reward was awaiting me at the train station in Workington that would make it all worthwhile.

That's when my cell phone chimed. A text message had just come through:

Emergency came up. Won't be able to join you on walk. So very sorry. Call me when you get a chance. Mike.

Damn!

My spirits sank as quickly as the proverbial lead balloon. As if to underscore my mood, the sun vanished completely behind a cloud, dimming the inside of the train car. I tried calling Mike, but the cell coverage on the train was too spotty.

With no way to discover the type of emergency that had befallen him, the next forty-five minutes were pure hell. When I finally stepped out onto the platform at Workington, I tried calling again. This time Mike answered.

"What's going on?" I asked. "What's happened?"

His frustrated sigh came through loud and clear. "Chase, I can't tell you how sorry I am. There's been an unexplained death down here. Some kind of food-borne contagion, it looks like. There's a fear that it might spread. I just can't get away."

Mike was the coroner for North Devon. It wasn't unusual for urgent matters to come up, but why at that moment, of all times?

Maybe this wasn't as bad as I feared. "Can you join me tomorrow? Or the day after?"

"I'm afraid not," Mike responded. "This doesn't look like it will be resolved that quickly."

I closed my eyes, cursing my luck. I'd been looking forward to the week's walk, without question, but spending time with Mike had been my main reason for coming on this trip.

"What if I bail on the walk and come down there?" I suggested. The train ride to Devon would be another four hours, but I would do it if that's what it took.

"Sorry, but that won't work either. I'm going to be slammed over the next few days. Even if you were here, we wouldn't have much time together. No, I insist that you stay there and take your walk. It's only a week, right? I should have my arms around this situation by then."

It was me I wanted his arms around. I thought hard for other options, but came up blank.

"I'm as broken down about this as you are, Chase," Mike said in a tone that convinced me he truly was. "Please don't be angry with me."

I watched the train I'd just deboarded pull away. "Of course I'm not angry. Just disappointed."

"We will be together," he said. "Just not quite as soon as we'd hoped."

I felt just as hollow as I did when Carlton Fisk, a popular Boston Red Sox catcher and World Series hero, left Boston to sign with the Chicago White Sox. Even though the news sent me into a weeklong sulk, I recovered, and I would this time, too. To Mike I said, "Okay then. I guess I'll see you in a week."

"We'll talk in the meantime. I want to hear how your walk goes."

Oh, that's right, the walk. "Of course. But watch out for yourself, will you, please? I don't want you coming down with whatever disease seems to be going around."

He laughed. "No worries. In my profession, you learn to take all the necessary precautions."

As we bid each other a wistful goodbye, I struggled to say the L-word. Why was that so hard? By the time I'd worked up the courage to tell Mike I loved him, he was off the line.

I'd met Mike Tibbets the year before, on another walking trip, along the northern coast of Devon. A man in our group had been killed, and as coroner, Mike was called to certify the cause of death. At the time, I was still wrestling with the recent passing of my long-term partner, Doug, and finding a new romance was the last thing I expected—well, other than murder. But it happened. Mike and I were attracted to each other instantly, and once the killer was identified (thanks, I admit with all modesty, to my efforts, in conjunction with those of the local police), we spent a glorious week together exploring southwest England.

After I returned home to California, Mike and I stayed in contact through texts and video conversations. It became increasingly apparent there was something special going on between us, and we both realized we needed to be together physically, not just virtually. So, despite the budget concerns that usually governed such a decision, I began planning my return to England.

After hearing me repeatedly praise the wonders of country walking, Mike agreed to accompany me on a guided walk. I found Rovers North, a tour organizer in the Lake District (an area I hadn't yet explored) and signed us up for an abbreviated six-day walk along the Coast to Coast trail. I also checked with my friend Billie and was thrilled she could join us as well. As the day of departure grew nearer, though, I grew anxious. Would Mike still feel the same about me when we were together again, in the flesh?

Standing on the deserted train platform, I resigned myself to the fact that I wouldn't be learning the answer to that question for another week. I grabbed the handle of my suitcase and trudged out of the station toward the waiting taxis. Fifteen minutes later, I arrived at the small hotel in St. Bees where the walking group was due to assemble that evening.

I trudged into the lobby, and my spirits lifted when I saw Billie perched on a chair, thumbing through a tourist brochure. Her dark gray hair was in its usual frizz, and she wore one of her trademark self-knitted sweaters. She looked up and broke into a smile.

"Chase! You made it!" she said, rising to give me a hug. "So good to see you, you rascal!"

Billie, a Yank like myself, had been a close friend since we met on a walk in Northern Ireland many years before. We'd wanted to tackle the Coast to Coast path ever since. Now we were finally getting around to it.

"It's great to see you as well," I said. "When did you get in?"

"Last night. I like being at the meet-up point early, as you know, to get the lay of the land. But wait a minute." She looked around. "Isn't Mike supposed to be with you?"

I nodded grimly and told her about the change in plans.

"What a shame! But apart from that, how has the long-distance romance been working out?"

I sat on the chair beside her and shrugged. "How would you expect? We get together over FaceTime, but it's not the same as being together in person. I was hoping we could work out a better solution over here. I even suggested that he move to the US, but he's still a couple of years from retirement."

"Move in together? That's a pretty big step, Chase."

Sighing, I said, "I don't see any other solution."

"You could move here, you know. You're already retired. And you love England."

She was right, of course. Since Doug passed away, I was free to go wherever I pleased. But combining households was, as she pointed out, a big step; and even though Mike meant a lot to me, I wasn't sure I was ready for that big a change at this point in my life.

"Have any of the others in our group arrived yet?" I asked.

"I haven't seen any, which is strange. Usually I'm not the only early bird. Anyway, you're here, and that's all that matters. We can head out on our own if worse comes to worse."

"Hello!" a voice rang out. We turned to see a genial white-haired man walking toward us, smiling broadly. "Are you Rovers North folks?"

We said that we were. The man introduced himself as Charlie Cross, our walk leader. I was pleased to see he was a cheerful and exuberant chap. A medium-sized English springer spaniel stood at his side, looking at us with a broad doggie smile.

"Can't have you sitting out here waiting for the cows to come home," he said. "Follow me and Ramses to the bar, and we'll enjoy its libations!"

We went with him and his dog into the hotel bar, a compact, wood-paneled space with small tables and a broad counter lined with beer taps.

Charlie stepped up to the bar and turned to us. "What's your pleasure? This round is on Rovers North."

"I'd like the house's best bitter," I said. Walking was my passion, but British ale ranked a close second.

"Same for me," Billie echoed. We found a table, and once I sat, the tension in my shoulders started to ease. There's nothing like a pub—even a slightly faux one in a hotel—to improve my spirits.

Charlie returned with three glasses topped with foam. He sat and was about to propose a welcoming toast when a voice said, "Excuse me, are you here for the walk?"

We looked up to see a fresh-faced, brown-haired man in his mid-thirties.

"We are indeed," Charlie said.

"I'm Joe Scarbun. Pleased to meet you." He already had a beer, and he placed it down on the table as he sat.

"Did you just get here?" Billie asked Joe. I hadn't noticed him on my train, which was the only means of reaching the small town, outside of driving.

He gave an acknowledging smile. "A few days ago, I flew into Manchester, rented a car, and spent a couple days getting up here. Mostly to acquaint myself with the country. I'm a birder, and I'm dying to see some of the species in this part of the world." He looked around. "Are the others in our group here, too?"

"Not yet," Charlie said. "The others are the Uptons, all members of the same family. I received a text telling me they've been delayed due to missing their flight from America. They were able to get on a later one, though, and should arrive this evening. They assured me they'll be alert enough to start off on our walk tomorrow morning."

This was disappointing. I always look forward to getting to know my fellow walkers over dinner on the first night. That's harder to do while walking.

"They're all from Texas, aren't they?" Joe asked.

Charlie nodded. "Yes, they're all from the western part of the state, I gather. El Paso and some place called Lubbock."

This was another disappointment. For this walk, I'd wanted to be among Brits and not be constantly reminded of home. That's why I selected a small British tour company that catered primarily to locals. I was surprised when the others on this walk all turned out to be Yanks—or Canadian, in Joe's case.

We chatted for a while and finished our beers. Charlie suggested we get settled in our rooms before reassembling at the hotel restaurant. As Billie and I walked to the front desk, it seemed her enthusiasm at seeing me had decidedly dimmed. She seemed distracted. We checked in, obtained our keys, and headed to our rooms.

My room, a small space at the end of the hallway on the second floor, was what could be called serviceable at best. The décor wasn't going to win awards, but its basic bed-chair-floor lamp setup would be fine enough for one night. The sole window looked out on the hills to the north, resplendent in their springtime greenery. I changed into fresh clothes and headed downstairs to the restaurant, a warmly lit room where Billie was already seated with Joe and Charlie. Ramses was on the floor at Charlie's feet. Through the windows I could see night coming on.

A server came in to take our drink orders.

"I've already had a beer, but I think I'll have another," I said.

"Do you mind if I take a look at the bar?" Joe asked. "I'm about to start my own microbrewery in Toronto and have been looking forward to seeing what they offer over here."

Charlie offered to accompany him and give recommendations.

As the two walked off, I turned to Billie. "Are you all right? You don't seem to have the usual verve you do at the start of a walk. And don't tell me that's because you feel bad that Mike didn't come. Where's your knitting? You usually carry your needles and yarn with you everywhere you go. Even at dinner."

Billie's eyes shot to her side. "My God! How did I forget to bring those down?"

I leaned toward her. "What's up, Billie?"

She chewed on her lip for a moment. "Chase, you know I hate burdening others with my personal problems. But . . ."

"Out with it."

"To be blunt . . . I might be homeless when I get back to Vermont."

"Homeless! How on earth could that happen?"

She hesitated again. "Frankly, it's mortifying. Just before I left, I got a phone message from my bank. They went to make the usual withdrawal for my monthly mortgage payment and found that my retirement account had been completely emptied. I tried calling my investment advisor, and lo and behold, it seems she's fled the country."

This didn't seem possible. Billie was an intelligent woman. How could she not have done the due diligence necessary to secure a trustworthy investment professional?

"I know what you're thinking," she said. "What kind of fool am I, right? But Marie's a close friend and has been managing my investments for years. She was almost like family! Last month, she told me about a can't-miss opportunity, something involving investing in certificates of deposit somewhere overseas . . . was it the Mariana Islands? I can't remember. She said I'd get a minimum annual return of twenty percent."

"Twenty percent?" I said. "That's impossible."

Billie nodded grimly. "So I've found out. But I'm terrible with money matters, and I've always trusted Marie completely. That's why I granted her access to my accounts. I can't believe she'd do this to me!"

"But . . . what about your pension?"

"Oh, I still have that, and Social Security, but it won't be enough to maintain my current lifestyle. I literally don't have any other assets. Librarians aren't exactly known for stashing away piles of money, you know. If I can't make my mortgage payment, where am I going to live? Things will go from bad to worse. As James Baldwin said, 'Anyone who has struggled with poverty knows how extremely expensive it is to be poor.'"

Her eyes moistened, and her lip trembled. I saw Charlie and Joe head back to our table, holding our pint glasses. "We'll work something out," I said to Billie. "Trust me on this." There was recourse for people who'd fallen victim to financial fraud, but I kept silent, not wanting to raise any hopes.

Despite her news, Billie turned into her usual amiable self as the four of us began chatting, sharing stories of our lives. Charlie told us that he lived locally and was a veteran walk leader, mostly guiding groups through the Lake District. His preferred route was the full Coast to Coast, but he offered the abbreviated version for those pressed for the time, stamina, or cash.

When it came time for me to talk about myself, I glossed over my past career with the San Diego Police (that always provoked a flood of awkward questions) and simply said that I had worked for the city for many years. Billie divulged, also without elaboration, her background as a small-town librarian. Joe confessed he had quit his job a few months before in the hopes of becoming an artisanal brewer. I asked what kind of work he'd been doing. When he responded that he'd been a portfolio manager in an investment management firm, I flashed Billie a raised eyebrow. Could he be of help with her problem? I made a mental note to pursue that later.

Our drinks arrived, and Charlie's mobile phone gave a chirp. He checked an incoming text message. "It appears that our Texans have finally arrived in London. They're taking an evening coach up here."

"Don't expect them to be too chipper when the walk begins tomorrow," I said.

"Perhaps they'll catch some sleep on the bus," Joe said.

Over a surprisingly tasty dinner—I devoured a juicy Cumberland sausage and chips—we continued discussing our coming walk, the local countryside, and, inevitably, more personal matters, such as our relationship status. Charlie was married, but Joe was single. I mentioned that I was seeing someone but didn't get into details. Billie made a small joke about enjoying the life of a spinster. Her spirits had improved, perhaps assisted by the wine we were all sharing in large proportions. When we reached the dessert course (dandelion flower parfait), we felt comfortable enough with one another that I decided to pull out my mental note.

"I have a question about investments," I said to Joe.

"Chase, no," Billie warned.

"Well, I can't give any personal advice," Joe said. "But go right ahead."

"Canadian laws are probably different than those in the US, but what protections are there for someone who has been swindled by a financial advisor?"

Joe took a sip of wine before responding. "That depends on a lot of things. To begin with, we'd have to know if the advisor was a licensed fiduciary and if the assets were in a protected account. Our two countries have similar laws on the books about this type of thing. Most first-world countries do, given the global nature of investing these days."

Billie confessed that she didn't know the answer to Joe's questions but promised to find out. She didn't sound hopeful, but his expertise was something to keep in mind, at least.

Noting the time, I announced that I should call it a day. "The first night in England is always the hardest," I said. "Time change and all that."

"You come over often?" Joe asked.

"Chase and I have been on several long-distance walks in England together," Billie said.

"Is that so?" Charlie said. "Which was your favorite?"

"That's hard to say," I replied. "Each has had its own special attraction."

"Except the last," Billie said. I shot her a warning glance, but she was already into the details of the murder on our Devon walk.

"My word!" Charlie said. "You know, I heard something about that. It seems there was an ex-police detective in the group who helped the police find the killer."

"That was Chase!" Billie said. So much for keeping my background hidden.

"Wow," Joe said. "Lucky thing you were there."

"The CID did most of the heavy lifting," I said. "Needless to say, Billie and I aren't looking for that kind of excitement this time."

"No need to worry about anyone being done in on one of my walks," Charlie said. "In the unlikely event that they should, however, it's comforting to know we have a policeman with us."

He was clearly joking, yet the idea of encountering another murder made me uneasy. What were the odds there'd be one on this walk? Probably astronomic. I trusted the rest of the walking group would prove to be as easygoing and placid as Joe. Who could imagine him as a killer?

Chapter 2

Sunday, 9 a.m.
St. Bees Bay, Cumbria, England

The next morning, I was gathered with the others on the beach at St. Bees, tightening the laces on my walking boots and looking out to the dark roiling waters of the Irish Sea. With each crash of the waves, the wooden bench beneath me shook. Gusts of sea-sodden wind blew in from the north, thrashing my face and soaking my beard.

My long-anticipated week's walk in England's fabled Lake District was starting off on a decidedly dreary note.

"We're supposed to walk into that?" Billie, seated beside me, asked as she surveyed the water. She's always prepared for the weather, and that day was no exception. She wore a waterproof jacket over one of her thick self-knitted sweaters, its bright pattern of squirrels and acorns barely visible beneath the jacket's folds.

"We just have to stick the toe of our boot in the water," I said. "If we do it quickly enough, we should be all right."

Around us our fellow walkers, eight of them, were also preparing their boots and eyeing the sea nervously. Perhaps they were wondering why the British walking tour they'd signed up for was going to begin with a plunge into the ocean.

Yet this "christening of the boots" was a time-honored ritual for anyone about to tackle England's Coast to Coast path, which spans nearly two hundred miles across the north of England to Robin Hood's Bay on the North Sea.

"Everyone ready?" asked Charlie. We all murmured a reluctant affirmation. Beaming a broad grin, he didn't seem fazed in the least by heavy surf or wind. "Very good," he said. "Come on, Ramses!"

His dog, the only one of us eager for a dip in the water, followed him down to the sea. We trailed behind.

"Are you sure it's safe?" asked the slight, grayish-blond-haired woman in front of me. "It looks dangerous to me." She then let loose a sneeze that almost sent her into the water. I remembered her as Jenna, the wife of the tall man walking beside her. Even though we'd been introduced only an hour before, though, I'd forgotten his name. Rock? Spock?

We reached the lip of the sea, waves lapping at our feet. How far out did we need to go? Charlie looked at the water's turbulence as if he were looking at a placid pool. "Nothing to worry about. Just do as I do!"

He marched forward, his trousers rolled up past his ankles, just as a mammoth wave slammed into him, drenching him completely. He remained standing, though, and laughed it off. Ramses was beside him, immersed in the water, and loving every second of it.

"You don't need to come all the way in," he shouted to us, his voice barely audible above the roar of the surf. "Just dip the toe of your boot in the water, not the whole boot as I just did. Nothing's worse than walking in wet socks." He walked back to the shore, where he bent to pick up a small pebble.

"And don't forget to collect a stone," he instructed. "You'll be carrying it with you, to toss into Robin Hood's Bay when our walk concludes."

Despite the demonstration, none of us had yet entered the water.

"Come on, then," Charlie prompted. "Do you wish to begin, Mr. Chasen? Miss Mondreau?"

Billie and I gave each other a what-the-hell look and walked briskly toward the surf, dipped the toes of our boots in the water, scooped up stones, and hurried back to the sand before any rogue wave attacked us.

One by one, the others timidly did the same, led by Carole, a short, plump dark-haired woman in her late thirties. She wasn't as lucky as Billie and I; a large wave thundered into her. She let loose an ear-piercing squeal and landed on her bottom in the foam. Her friend Fiona, a striking, young auburn-haired woman, helped her to her feet.

"Hot spit and monkey vomit!" Carole hooted. She bent to pick up a stone and scurried out of the surf, her hair hanging in wet strands. "My butt hasn't been that cold since the commode froze in our outhouse!"

Parker and Pratt, lanky men in their forties (and identical twins), went forward next, in tandem, barely letting the water lap at their boots before picking up pebbles and returning.

The tall man—Brock, that was his name!—grasped his wife's hand and proceeded a couple of feet into the surf just as another giant wave threatened to smash into them. They rushed back to shore, not bothering to gather pebbles.

"We didn't pick up stones!" his wife said. "Won't that bring us bad luck? Should we go back?"

"Maybe you'd better do just that, Jen," Pratt said in a mocking tone. "Lord knows, we don't want you getting struck by lightning or eaten by a bear on the first day of our walk."

"Don't listen to his teasing, darling," Brock said to his wife. "You'll be fine. Stop being so damned superstitious."

The remaining member of our group who hadn't yet christened his boots was Joe. He happily stomped into the water, gave a loud yell, picked up a stone, and galloped back to the shore.

"Now we're committed to reaching the other side!" he announced, holding up his stone. The others shouted and hooted in agreement.

They were a rowdy bunch, all right. I found myself regarding them like a ball club manager reviewing his opening-day roster. Whatever lay in store for us on the trail, I felt certain that, with this group, the journey wouldn't be a dull one. Nevertheless, I couldn't help but regret that one particular walking partner would not be joining us.

Billie sensed my dismay. "Come on, Chase," she said, as we began following Charlie back up the beach. "Don't think about Mike right now. A new walking adventure awaits us!"

She was right. I looked up ahead of me and saw one of the most enticing views known to man: an unexplored trail stretching out ahead, leading to possible hidden worlds and wonders. This particular one led up the beach and into the flat-topped green coastal hills. As I started walking, I began whistling Hank Williams's "My Bucket's Got a Hole in It" (his tunes always put a spring in my step), and soon we approached a large sign announcing the official start of the Coast to Coast path. It displayed a map showing the route of the path, which doesn't, as some mistakenly believe, cross the country at its widest point. Still, it's a formidable trek, and I was somewhat disappointed that we would only be walking a fraction of it in the next six days. Traversing the entire path (as many people do) takes more than two weeks. Nevertheless, we would still be taken by van to the terminus on Robin Hood's Bay, to throw our stones in the North Sea.

"Hey, why don't we mark this occasion with a photo?" Joe suggested. He pulled off the camera he wore around his neck and recruited a passing local to snap a picture of us. He joined us as we obligingly stood by the sign and did our best to smile, although most of us were still wet and none too happy about it.

Beside me, Carole shivered. "It's hard to believe we're so far from home. All of this just to settle a score."

I was intrigued by her comment. "Settle a score?"

She flashed me a look of surprise, as if she hadn't realized she had spoken. "It's nothing," she said.

We began the slow climb up the hill that circled the bay. The trail was a clearly worn path through natural grass, passing through gates denoting boundaries of the fields (the land was private, but the trail was public). The breeze became less damp, and our clothes and boots began to dry off. This was more like the walk I'd envisioned—dry and moderately challenging. I relaxed and put my arms and legs on autopilot, moving without conscious thought. At the top of the first bluff, we paused to collect our breath and look out at the slate-gray sea. A fence protected us from the three-hundred-foot drop down to the sandy beach.

"We're now on the Coast to Coast," Charlie announced. Everyone applauded as if we had completed the walk rather than just begun it. He pointed outward. "Note how red the cliffs are. They're made of sandstone particular to this region. You may have spotted houses made from it."

We gazed down at the shore upon which we had been walking only a few minutes earlier. It already seemed a world away. To the south rose the buildings of the small town of St. Bees, some indeed red from the sandstone, but many paneled in brilliant white, providing a cheerful counterpoint to the overcast morning.

"Let's move on," Charlie said. "We're covering nine miles today. At the village of Sandwith, we'll stop for lunch, and later, at Moor Row, we'll board the van for our hotel near the town of Ennerdale, which will be our starting point tomorrow."

As we resumed walking, I again checked out my new companions. There had been little chance to get acquainted with the Uptons at breakfast that morning, and I tried to remember all the relationships. Fiona, Brock, and the twins, Pratt and Parker, were siblings—Brock clearly the oldest and Fiona the youngest. Jenna was family by virtue of being married to Brock and didn't appear to share their boisterous Upton temperament. Carole was a childhood friend of Fiona's but considered part of the clan as well. They were a close group, but I hoped not too insular; over breakfast, there had been a fair number of in-jokes and shared references.

My experiences on previous walks taught me that we'd all likely become good friends by the end of the week. Enjoying a long outdoors walk was a unique bonding experience. I was curious as to what had motivated these people to take this particular walk—perhaps they had seen it in a film or read about it in a magazine—but I was willing to bet that none fully grasped what they were about to experience. Walking long distances over six days would strengthen their limbs, of course, and maybe take a few pounds off, but it could change them in other, more profound, ways. They might not get bitten by the English walking bug, as I had been, but once we reached the North Sea, I knew that none would be the same.

Charlie, his dog faithfully trotting at his side, led us north along the hilltop path. Pratt walked directly behind, just ahead of Billie and me. At least, I thought it was Pratt—he and his brother were practically indistinguishable from one another; they even wore identical dark blue parkas—but I'd noticed that Pratt was the more lively and vocal of the two. His brother, Parker, was more reserved and had hardly said a word since breakfast.

Pratt also wore a distinctive gold neckband, something I rarely saw on men.

Behind us, Carole and Joe walked together, chatting amicably, followed by Brock and Jenna and, lastly, Parker. He walked almost robotically, looking down at the ground rather than the view around him, his arms swinging in an awkward rhythm.

It was a shame he wasn't enjoying the view, because it was incomparable. To our left, over the water, shafts of sunlight sliced through the clouds and danced upon the sea. To our right, a squat yet stately lighthouse perched in a field dotted with red wildflowers, seabirds darting from behind its round, lattice-capped white tower. The wind gusted in fits and starts, bracing but not too cold. The contrast of this landscape to the parched, dry hills of my native Southern California was striking—and invigorating.

Charlie kept us moving at a brisk pace, which was just what I liked. The others were keeping up, even Brock, who looked to be the least fit of the group; a hefty paunch loomed over the waist of his walking pants. He seemed to be enjoying himself, but I wondered how he would fare when we tackled some of the more challenging ascents to come.

"Sizing up our companions, Chase?" Billie asked with a sly glance. "I can hear your mental wheels turning."

I returned her smile. "It's always interesting to study those whom we'll be spending time with. It's like a baseball team at the beginning of the season. Everyone is wondering about the new players—whether they'll be an asset or a liability."

"Have you come to any conclusions?" she asked, knowing that, although I was retired, I couldn't shake off the habit of assessing others. It was one I had often employed in my police career.

I pondered Billie's question. Carole's cryptic comment about "settling a score" came to mind, but I didn't want to indulge in idle speculation based on such little information. I said, "I'm here to enjoy a walk, not put together psychological profiles." Actually, this was a small, white lie; I had formed an initial impression of the group. From what I'd observed so far, the Uptons didn't seem to be enthused about this walk. Their hearts weren't in it.

Part of my heart was missing as well. Mike's absence was palpable. I had to remind myself to be in the moment and not dwell on what might have been.

As we continued, Billie looked out to the coast, which curved northward toward Scotland, and to the others walking in front of us. "This seems like a nice group to me," she said. "I think it's sweet when families do things together."

I grunted in agreement, but even though I didn't really know them, "sweet" wasn't a word I would have chosen to describe the Uptons.

The trail descended to a small pebble beach at the bottom of a cleft between two hills. Parker, with his peculiar gait, caught my eye. He was taking carefully measured steps, focused intently on his legs and feet.

Suddenly, a flock of geese appeared overhead, flying low and honking noisily. Most of us stopped to look up at them. I was reminded of the fleets of bombers that flew over England during the Second World War. I hadn't been there, of course, but I remembered the images from old films and newsreels.

That image sent me into one of my "deep focus" moments in which time seems to stand still. These spells began when I was a child and were partly responsible for my nickname (fellow cops would tease me about getting lost in thought and chasing something down the rabbit hole.) At these times, my vision intensifies, telescoping into the world around me like the slow-motion lens of a sophisticated camera.

In that particular instant, I saw everyone at once. Charlie was standing beside a large rock with pronounced red striations, keeping his eye on the group. Several feet away, dressed in the same type of pants and jacket as Parker, Pratt was turning his head toward his brother. Brock was nearest to me, his legs and walking stick in motion. Jenna was behind him, her eyes cast downward. Carole and Joe were paused, in the middle of an exchange of words. Fiona was looking at Charlie. Billie, her hand raised, was wiping a strand of hair from her eyes. Beyond our group, the sea stretched to the horizon and meshed nearly imperceptibly with the blue-gray of the sky. Around us, lupins dotted the headland, their bright purple contrasting sharply with the mottled greens and ochres of the surrounding gorse and gravel.

Yet it was Parker, with his rigid walking posture and vacant gaze, who attracted my primary focus. It was as if . . .

Suddenly, in a flash, everyone was in motion again, walking along the beach to the next upward bend of the path. The wind buffeted my face; gulls screeched above; Ramses ran and yipped at them.

But one of us was missing.

"We're moving, Parker!" Pratt called out. His brother was still frozen, several yards behind us.

"For God's sake, go get him," Brock said.

Pratt ran over and gripped his brother's shoulder. Parker shook it off. Pratt grabbed him again, shaking him, and Parker fell to the ground.

"Yipes!" Billie said. "What's that all about?"

Pratt reached out to help his brother up, but Parker shot to his feet and pummeled his fist into Pratt's jaw, sending him flying backward to the ground. Brock dashed over and, as if he were tackling a quarterback on the thirty-yard line, barreled into Parker. Both men fell on top of Pratt, and the three soon became a scrambling, fighting jumble. Fiona and Carole screamed for them to stop. Ramses ran around them, barking wildly.

Somebody had to put a stop to this, and a quick look at Charlie—watching wide-eyed and gape-jawed—told me it wasn't going to be him. I ran over, reached down, and yanked up an arm that turned out to be Pratt's. "You," I said, pointing straight at him, "stay there and don't move a muscle." I turned toward the other two, who'd stopped scuffling.

"Stand up and move away from one another," I directed. Brock and Parker slowly got to their feet, regarding one another warily.

Charlie walked over. "What on earth are you doing?" he asked the Upton men.

Pratt turned to his brother and surprised me by flashing him a big grin. "It's just ol' Park here. He tries to behave, but sometimes he can't control himself and needs to be reined in a little." My surprise heightened when Parker smiled back.

"I don't want any fighting on this walk," Charlie said.

Brock snorted out a laugh. "Don't get your tights in a tangle. It's just us Texas boys letting off a little steam." Turning to Parker, he said, "Isn't that right, Pecker?"

"Don't call him that," Fiona said.

Parker looked mostly dazed. I put my hand on his shoulder. "Are you okay?" I asked.

He looked up at me and gave a small nod.

Fiona came and put her arm around Parker, then faced me and Charlie. "Parker has behavioral issues. Nothing to worry about. He takes meds to keep them under control."

Autism, I wondered? Asperger's? Whatever. If he was taking medication, it wasn't doing a good job. From my limited exposure to autism, I knew one of its symptoms was a difficulty in quickly switching activities—such as from walking to standing still and back again.

"Sometimes you gotta rough Park up a bit to bring him around," Pratt said. Parker nestled his face against Fiona's shoulder.

Charlie said, "I'll state again that I won't tolerate fighting on my walk. It had better not happen again, or I'll boot you out, the lot of you." He gave the Uptons one final glare to show them he meant business, and started leading us up the hill on the other side of the ravine. I followed, although not quite with the bounce I had had minutes before.

Beside me, Carole said, "Hoo-boy! You didn't know what a crazy bunch you were getting in with, did you? If the Uptons make it through this week without killing each other, it'll be a miracle!"

Chapter 3

Sunday, Midmorning
Cumbria Coast, North Head

After the brawl, Charlie tried to reestablish his authority and move us forward, but I could tell he was rattled; there was none of his usual tour-guide patter. When we scaled the next rise, he closed his eyes for a couple of moments to calm himself.

"Very well then," he said, looking out on the horizon. "Out there is Feswick Bay. It's the dividing point between South Head, where we've been walking, and North Head, which is where we're heading now. We'll pass some bird-observation points, so keep your eyes open. There's a chance you'll see a few black guillemots. This area has England's only colony."

"Fantastic!" said Joe, fondling his camera. A pair of small bird-watching field glasses dangled from his neck.

The view was commanding, but I was still puzzled by Parker. There was more going on there than just behavioral quirks. As we followed Charlie up a slightly steeper and rockier stretch of trail, I asked Billie, "Still think the Uptons are sweet?"

She gave me a sly, confident grin. "Don't let them shake you. I think that's part of their strategy."

I didn't want to worry about anyone's "strategy." Instead, I focused on my walking. Feeling the welcome strain on my calf muscles, I inhaled deeply, invigorated by the crisp air and its hint of saltwater. I had misgivings about spending a week with this group, but if anything could get me centered again, it was the soothing movement of my limbs and the indelible charm of the English countryside.

My reverie was broken by a voice at my side.

"I've never seen anything like this back home. It's like being on another planet."

It was Fiona, her long raven hair swinging beneath her walking hat. I was about to ask her what had tempted to her to travel to another planet when she added, "Don't mind my brothers, okay? They all got fire in their blood. They inherited it from our daddy, who was a real pain in the behind, if you know what I mean. Poor Parker's got it the worst. He served with our forces in Afghanistan, and it did a real turn on him. He was screwed up to begin with, and that only tightened the noose. Pratt's the only one who can get through to him, and even then, it's touch and go."

"What is Parker's problem exactly?" I asked. It didn't sound like a simple case of PTSD, if there was such a thing as a "simple" case.

Fiona chuffed a laugh. "Who knows? The medicos come up with all sorts of explanations, but the one that seems to stick is bipolar disorder. Course, who in the hell knows what the hell that means? It covers a multitude of sins, as my gramma used to say."

We reached the top of another hill and paused for those behind us to catch up. The last to arrive was Brock, breathing heavily as he struggled to extract a water bottle from his backpack. He took a large gulp, coughing some back up. Pratt went and gave Brock an enthusiastic slap on the back. I was expecting another fistfight, but Brock just glared at him.

"This walk will do you wonders, bro," Pratt said to Brock,

amazing me by completing a full sentence. "You'll be a new man by the end of the week."

"I like the man I am now," Brock replied. "And don't call me 'bro.' You know I hate that."

"Sorry, old man."

"I don't like being called 'old man' either," Brock shot back. "You're not that much younger than me."

"But I am younger," Pratt said, dancing around Brock. "And I always will be!"

Parker approached. "I'm young too, aren't I? That's great!" He executed a similar dance move to Pratt's

"Quit mincing around, Pecker," Brock said. "You and Pratt look a pair of fruits."

Fiona stepped up. "Stop teasing him! Show some respect, will you?"

Parker gave what I interpreted as a thankful smile to Fiona, but his face melted back into a sullen and trancelike state. I was concerned about the epithet Brock had used. Was I going to spend the rest of the week with a homophobe?

Joe raised his field glasses and surveyed the horizon. "I think I see a couple of terns," he responded. He let down his glasses, lifted his camera, adjusted the lens, and snapped a few quick shots. Turning to me, he said, "When we get inland, I hope to spot a great tit. That's the prize I'm after."

I waited for someone to make a lewd comment.

"Wish I'd brought my shotgun," Brock said. "Those birds wouldn't stand a chance, let me tell you."

Joe regarded him coldly. "I don't approve of people who get pleasure from killing other creatures."

"Oh, don't get all tree-hugger on me. I'm not going to shoot anything. It's Jenna you really need to worry about. She's a much better shot than I am." Standing a few feet behind him, she smiled and bowed her head modestly, then braced herself for another sneeze. It was a doozy.

She blew her nose and said, "Sorry. For some reason, my allergies are really kicking up here." She held up a small bottle. "I hope my medication holds out!"

John Updike once called Fenway Park, home of the Boston Red Sox, "a lyric little bandbox of a ballpark." He wrote that the ubiquitous Dartmouth green that binds the park together brings everything into "sharp focus, like the inside of an old-fashioned peeping-type Easter egg." I'd only been to Fenway once, when I witnessed an unfortunate trouncing of the Sox by the Cleveland Indians, but I instantly felt the organic pull of the ballpark; it had burrowed immediately into my soul.

I've always felt the same about the English countryside. This was the first time I'd been in the English northwest, standing on the bluff overlooking the sea, but I felt completely at home. A frequent question came to mind. Had I lived there in some past life, buried deep within my DNA?

Whatever the reason, as I stood on the mostly barren clifftop, dotted here and there with wildflowers and occasional shrubs (but no trees), a comforting reassurance permeated me. At that moment, this was where I belonged; it made me happy. I call Southern California my home, but as I took in the full view of the sea and coastline, I wanted to linger. Billie may have been correct. Perhaps moving over here wouldn't be such a bad idea.

The group was preparing to move on, however, so I started walking and fell into step with them.

As we proceeded forward, the trail narrowed, forcing us to walk in single file. Charlie was at the head of the pack, of course; Pratt and Parker walked behind him, then me. The twins were laughing and conversing, a stark contrast to their behavior not long before. I figured that when it came to the Uptons, and Parker in particular, I could count on sudden mood swings.

Okay, indulge me for a bit. I'm a Red Sox fan, and as I watched Parker with his brother, another analogy came to mind.

Jimmy Piersall was one of the most colorful players in the Boston team's history. He was a solid infielder, but was best remembered for his clownish antics—he was always in motion, arguing with umpires, joking with teammates, running bases backward, making fun of his own mistakes and those of others. In the ninth inning of a game against the St. Louis Browns, Piersall imitated legendary pitcher Satchel Paige's every move to rattle him, resorting to flapping his arms like a chicken and squealing like a pig.

Fans loved Piersall, but not everyone else did. After one incident, in which he spanked the four-year-old son of a teammate in the Red Sox clubhouse during a game, he was demoted to a minor league team in the South. Even there, he was ejected from the team on four occasions because of his behavior.

Finally, he was institutionalized to receive treatment. The official diagnosis was manic depression, what we today call bipolar disorder. Piersall was given electroshock therapy, which reduced his immediate symptoms, such as paranoia and severe mania, but also affected his memory. He remembered very little of what had prompted him to receive treatment in the first place.

Amazingly, he played with the Sox for fifteen more years and was employed in the baseball world for twenty years after that. He knew his reputation was as an out-of-whack kook, and he regaled in it. "Probably the best thing that ever happened to me was going nuts," he once said. "Who ever heard of Jimmy Piersall before that?"

For years, he took medications, such as lithium, to stabilize his mood swings and control his condition. As I watched Parker—walking with a bounce and laughing with Pratt, a stark contrast to his somnolent state not long before—I wondered what medications he might be taking.

"Chase!" Billie called out from behind me. I froze and saw that while I'd been lost in thought, I had strayed dangerously close to the edge of the bluff. Moving forward again, I kept my eyes on the trail. After a half mile, it curved inland at an abandoned stone quarry.

Charlie asked us to gather around.

"You've just had your first taste of the Coast to Coast," he said. "What a glorious beginning, don't you think?"

Carole was breathing hard. "That last climb was a doozy! A few more of those and I'll need to learn to yodel."

"Be thankful you don't have a full kit on your back," Charlie said. He turned toward the sea and pointed. "That land you see out there in the distance is the Isle of Man. And up there to your right, you can make out Burrow Head, in the Scottish Southern Uplands." The green-topped outcropping was barely visible in the distance.

Facing us, he said, "From now on, we turn our sights to the east, on what I consider to be the best long-distance footpath in England. I'm not sure how much you know about the history of the Coast to Coast. It actually is a relatively new walk. Although segments of it have been popular with walkers for years, it was Alfred Wainwright who brought it all together and gave it a huge boost when he wrote about it in 1973."

I did a quick mental calculation. That year, I was twenty, studying police science at San Diego State. Even then, I'd fallen in love with walking, frequently traversing the desert, mountain, and seaside trails in Southern California on weekends. It wasn't until much later, though, that I had the resources to travel abroad. I was in my thirties when I made my first visit to England, tackling part of the Cotswold Way outside Bath. I was immediately hooked.

"As you know," Charlie continued, "we'll only be walking sections of the path, as the entire thing would take us approximately two weeks. But never fear, we will be sampling what you might call the path's 'greatest hits'—the Lake District, Yorkshire Dales, and North York Moors. We'll be passing through storybook villages, green pastures, and the ruins of castles and abbeys. On the final day, we will repeat this morning's ritual by dipping our boots and tossing our stones into the waters of the North Sea at Robin Hood's Bay."

Fiona raised her hand.

"Yes, Mrs. Swain?" Charlie asked.

"The walk won't be too . . . tough, will it? I mean, most of us have never hiked this much, and—"

"Speak for yourself, Fi," Pratt spoke up. "I've done tons of hiking. Mexico, Utah, Colorado . . ."

"Give it a rest, Pratt," Carole said. "You don't have to remind us what a stud you are."

Charlie said, "Mrs. Swain's question was a good one. I won't pretend that this walk will be easy. It is rated at the highest level of difficulty in our marketing brochure, as I trust you noticed. But it's not as if we'll be climbing the Himalayas. Leisure walkers tackle the Coast to Coast all the time. You all seem fit enough"—he darted a cautious glance toward Brock—"but if, at any time, any of you feels you are not up to walking, just let me know. You can always ride in the van with our driver."

"We all came to walk, and that's what we're going to do!" Pratt said with the enthusiasm of a Little League coach. Carole and Brock shouted in agreement.

Charged up by Charlie's talk, we headed off again. I fell in beside Joe, his camera and field glasses swaying against his chest. I inadvertently began whistling "Howlin' at the Moon."

"What's that song?" Joe asked. "Sounds familiar, but I can't place it."

He didn't place it even after I told him. "Hank Williams," I said. He confessed that he was a fan of the Canadian rock band Nickelback. No comment from me.

A few moments later, he said, "These Uptons are a handful, aren't they?"

Despite my misgivings, it was too soon to pass judgment. I simply said, "They're high-spirited, that's for sure." I asked Joe if he'd done much long-distance walking.

"I pretty much have to when I'm out birding. Far-flung spots are where I can spot the rare ones. But I really came over here to meet with local brewers. I'd like to learn some of the secrets these guys have. They really know their stuff."

"I admire anyone with the guts to start a business," I said.

"Thanks," Joe said. "For years, I worked a nine-to-five job in a downtown Toronto high-rise. Earlier this year, I lifted my head from my PC and looked out the window—something I never did—and saw the most vibrant rainbow I'd ever seen. I took it as a sign: *Follow your heart.*"

That sounded like good advice to me. "Well, you came to the right place for brew. British ale is second to none, in my opinion."

The path narrowed, bringing the group closer together. In the distance, we began to see the houses and shops of a village I surmised to be Sandwith.

"That's where we're going to have lunch, isn't it?" Carole asked. "Thank goodness. I'm pooped."

"Pooped?" Joe said. "This little stroll was just a warm-up!"

"They usually start us off easy on the first day," Billie noted. "Six miles isn't bad. Over the next few days, we'll average about ten or so."

"And people do this for fun?" Carole said.

"Well, I'm having fun," Fiona countered. I couldn't help noticing how much she had seemed to be enjoying herself on the trail—breathing deeply, energetically swinging her arms, looking up at the sky and letting the sun bathe her face. She really was a beautiful woman, there was no denying it.

Pratt went up to her and placed his hand on her shoulder. "That's why we came over here, isn't it? To cheer you up?"

I leaned toward Carole. "Why does Fiona need cheering?"

"You don't know, do you? Her husband, Steve, died a couple months back. Lymphoma. We all figured she needed a change of scene." She moved close to me. "Well, some of us thought that. Don't fall for this grieving widow act she's been putting on. Truth is, Fi couldn't be happier that Steve is dead. When he kicked the bucket, she practically threw a party."

Fiona didn't appear to be putting on an "act" of grief; so far, she'd been all smiles. What was Carole implying?

Chapter 4

Sunday—Lunch
The Horse & Quail

When we reached Sandwith, Charlie led us up a side street to a small pub called the Horse & Quail. Billie eyed the hinged sign, depicting a quail perched on the horse's mane, warily. "Good grief! I hope those aren't the specials on the menu."

Charlie instructed us to leave our walking sticks and packs by the front door and seat ourselves around a reserved table at the back. As Ramses followed his master inside, Jenna said, "Wait a second. Is that dog going to eat with us?"

Charlie paused and gave her a smile. "My dog is part of the group."

"But it's . . . unsanitary."

He gave her a shocked look. "There's nothing unsanitary about Ramses. Dogs are always welcome into pubs if they're well-behaved."

Jenna scowled, looking down as Charlie and his dog walked past her. Brock took her arm. "You're just going to have to get used to the way they do things over here, honey." She reluctantly let him take her to the lunch table.

Once we were all seated, the hostess directed our attention to the day's lunch menu on a chalkboard: local smoked trout, toad in the hole, meat pies, and duck legs.

Carole gave out a hoot. "We're supposed to just eat their legs? What about the rest of 'em? What do they want us to do, starve?"

The hostess picked up on Carole's accent and asked if she was from America.

Carole laughed. "Lordy, all it takes is for one word to leave my lips and y'all can tell I'm a Texas gal faster than a sneeze through a screen door."

Charlie reminded everyone that he had earlier taken our lunch orders so all we had to do was figure out what we wanted to drink.

"This is the fun part," Joe said, eyeing the large taps lining the bar. I spied familiar names like Jennings, Thwaites, and Old Speckled Hen, but saw nothing local. When the red-haired lass from the bar came over to take our drink orders, she confirmed that the Horse and Quail served no local craft ales. I assured Joe we would encounter plenty of them in country pubs later in the walk. We ordered from the national brands, which were all unfamiliar to Joe and the Uptons anyway.

When the server left, Billie turned to Pratt. "I'm curious. What made all of you travel halfway around the world to walk in northern England?" I listened closely. His response should be interesting, I thought, remembering what Carole had told me.

Pratt grew somber. "Fiona's husband, Steve, passed on early this year, and she's taken it hard. I got everyone together and suggested we bring her over here to get her mind off of it. She was practically raised on the Beatrix Potter books. What better place to heal a broken heart than the land of Peter Rabbit? We're going to visit where Potter lived when we're through with the walk."

He looked at Fiona, who looked down at the table. Was she "faking" her grief?

"There's nothing too good for my baby sister," Pratt added. Carole's face was a passive mask.

"You used to read me the Peter Rabbit books," Parker said to Fiona. "Then when I got old enough, I read 'em myself."

Fiona grinned. "Whenever I was feelin' down, I'd look at the books and imagine I was in that beautiful place where Peter Rabbit lived. I kept telling everyone that I'd go there someday."

"The Coast to Coast doesn't go through Beatrix Potter country exactly," Billie noted. "She lived near Windermere, farther south. But we will be going through Borrowdale, where she spent some of her time."

"Why didn't you just go to Windermere instead of taking this walk?" Joe asked. The same question was on my mind as well. The Uptons looked at one another—uncomfortably, I thought—waiting for someone to answer.

"I want to see the Taj Mahal," said Parker.

"Oh, here we go," said Carole.

"Listen, pinhead, we've told you," Brock said. "The Taj Mahal isn't around here. It's on the other side of the world."

"Still want to see it," Parker said. "I'm saving up. Can I have French toast?"

"You ordered a burger," Brock said. "Just eat it and shut the hell up."

"Ease off, Brock," Fiona said. "One of the ground rules you agreed to was not to rag on Parker."

"Can't help himself," Parker said. "He hates me."

"Now you listen here—" Brock began to rise, but Pratt grabbed his arm. "Let's all be nice to each other and remember why we came, okay? Fiona gets to have her childhood dream come true, and we all get to spend some time together as a family again."

I was expecting Brock to make another snarky comment,

but instead he took a deep breath and picked up his glass. "Pratt's right," he said. "Here's to being a family!"

The others—including Parker—all chorused "To the family!" before sampling their ales. The gesture seemed genuine, yet I wasn't convinced. The Uptons weren't very good actors.

Brock set down his beer, made a face, and said, "Yuck. This damn stuff is as warm as cat piss."

"That's how they serve it over here," Joe said. "It bothers some people, but serving these ales cold would dull the flavor."

"I like it," Fiona said. "Nice and smooth. Yum!"

A small ding sounded, and Carole picked up her cell phone. She checked a message and said, "Well, good heavenly days! Listen to this, Fi! The airline found our bags. They'll be at the hotel when we get there."

Fiona gazed upward. "God bless you, Saint Anthony!"

Carole dug into her backpack, extracted a pill bottle, and downed one with her beer. She turned toward us. "That damned United brought Fi and me over here and sent our bags somewhere else. Can't believe they found 'em so fast. I'd-a sworn they'd turn up months from now at the North Pole."

Pratt started defending the airline (apparently, he'd worked briefly in the industry), and soon he and the others were engaged in another debate. Fortunately, lunch arrived, and we all focused on the food, most of the dishes new to the Texans. Carole had ordered toad in the hole and gave a loud laugh after her first bite.

"This is yummy!" she squealed. "It ain't real toad, though, right?"

"It's beef sausage," Joe said. "You think they would serve you an actual toad?"

"Hell, why not? They eat snails in France, don't they?"

"Toads, too," Billie said. "Well, frogs, technically."

Charlie put a small portion of his steak-and-kidney pie in a small bowl and placed it on the floor for Ramses. Jenna, reaching over to accept her plate from the server, looked down disapprovingly at the dog and brushed her hand against a salt shaker, sending it to the floor. She gave a small shriek and jumped up.

"I've got it, Jenna," Parker said, reaching down to pick up the shaker. "It's just a little spilled salt. No big deal."

"Yes, it is!" she said in a panic. "It's a sign. We never should have come over here!"

Billie and I exchanged concerned glances.

"Jenna, just throw some of the salt over your shoulder," Pratt said. "Isn't that the way it works?"

Brock stood and took Jenna's arm. "Pratt's right, honey. That spilled salt business is just a silly superstition. Sit down and eat your lunch, okay?"

His words had a calming effect. She managed a small, apologetic smile and sat down.

Fiona leaned close and whispered, "You'll need to get used to Jenna. When it comes to superstition, she's as crazy as a bullbat."

Soon we all were focused on our meal. The morning's walk had given us all an appetite. My steak-and-ale pie was tasty, but I was still trying to get my head around the Uptons. Was Jenna's jumpiness just because of superstition? What really was wrong with Parker?

As we ate, I surveyed the others. Brock and Jenna were chatting, her anxiety over the salt incident apparently behind her. Parker and Pratt were enjoying their meals and chatting between bites. Billie and Charlie were conversing. Carole was paying more attention to Joe than her food. At one point, she let out another yelp of a laugh. Someone should record that laugh of hers, I thought, and use it to get people's attention during emergencies. Fiona was the only one of us not involved in a conversation. I turned to her and said, "Your friend is quite a character, isn't she?"

Fiona did not look amused. "Oh, C.W. can be funny, all right. But she can also be a terrible flirt." After a pause, she added, "Don't get me wrong—we've been friends for ages, but she sorta invited herself along on this trip. Pratt was the one who agreed to have her join us. He thought her being here would be good for me."

"That was thoughtful," I said.

She nodded. "He's always been protective of me. Since our folks died, he's felt it's his responsibility to be my guardian angel. I gave him his nickname, you know. His real name is Patrick, but when I was a little girl, I kept pronouncing it 'Prattick.' So everyone shortened it to 'Pratt.' Kinda fits him, don't you think? Pratt the Brat. Always looking for that get-rich-quick payoff. I can't begin to tell you all the trouble that's gotten him into."

I was always amazed at how little prodding it took to get some people to begin spilling out intimate family details. "Prat" is also a British slang word for "idiot," but I chose to keep that little bit of trivia to myself.

After taking another a healthy swallow of beer, Fiona said, "Listen to me! Here I am, airing all the Upton dirty laundry. Come on. You need to tell me a secret about your family so we'll be even."

I thought of my small family circle—my sister Allison, a maiden aunt, and a few others in the farther recesses of the family tree. "I have a great uncle who collects antique andirons," I said.

"What's an andiron?"

"That thing you put beside your fireplace to hold wood. The point is, every family has its oddities."

She laughed. "What you really mean is black sheep."

Soon everyone had finished their lunch, and Charlie announced that it was time to get back on the trail. As we rose to leave, Brock saw Fiona pause to finish Parker's beer. "Enough, Fiona! For God's sake."

"I was just finishing Parker's since he was just gonna leave it there. Jesus, Brock, stop acting like my dad!"

"Someone has to," he said. "You know your limit. I don't want to have to pick you up off the floor."

Fiona glared at him defiantly and reached down to grasp another nearly empty ale glass. She swallowed it and gave her brother a triumphant smile before walking away.

Chapter 5

Sunday Afternoon
Clearhaven Farm

Fortified by the lunch, everyone was ready to get back on the path. The stretch leading out of the village was at first muddy and overgrown, but became easier to handle when it turned into a gravel lane that wove its way through a narrow valley. The friction among the Uptons seemed to have evaporated. Fiona chatted with Parker, Carole shared a laugh with Pratt, and Brock appeared placid as he walked beside his wife.

I should have been relishing the moment—appreciating the stunning vistas of the distant fells—but I couldn't get the Uptons off my mind. There was something about them that didn't go together, and if there's one thing I hate, it's an unsolved mystery. Of course, I knew little about the family, and they could have a history of mercurial moods. I'd had my share of experience with people like that, professionally as well as personally. Doug's sister Cara is bipolar with a capital B, frantic and abrasive one minute, calm and sweet the next. She's extremely disquieting to be around for any prolonged period, and I generally avoid her, but when I'm with her, I try to focus on her good points. Parker was like Cara in that respect, but not others. I was still waiting to discover his good points, other than his dashing good looks (he didn't have his twin brother's broad, sexy smile, however). Well, it was still early days, as they say over there, and no doubt I'd have an opportunity to chat with him at some point.

As if reading my mind, fate stepped in to arrange precisely that. The path took a sharp turn, and I found myself walking beside Parker. He was proceeding more naturally than earlier, walking in comfortable, easy strides. Had he taken his medication? I suppose I was studying him too obviously, and he noticed it.

"Do you believe it?" he asked.

"Believe what?" I replied, curious.

"What they say? About me?"

I certainly wasn't expecting this question. "What do they say?"

" 'Poor Parker.' Problem child. Black sheep."

Black sheep is precisely what Fiona had called him.

"Nobody has said anything like that to me."

He looked at me with a fresh eye. "Your name Rick?"

"That's right, although most everyone calls me 'Chase.' "

"I like nicknames. Chase is a good one."

"What's yours?"

He gave a short, derisive laugh. "Brock has lots. Don't like any of them. Fiona calls me 'Scoot.' I like that best."

"That's an unusual nickname. Where does it come from?"

A pause. "You'll have to ask her."

We traded questions back and forth, in a casual, strangers-getting-to-know-one-another kind of way, but his responses were guarded. He told me he lived outside of El Paso, and liked ice cream and John Wayne movies. When I asked if he had a job, he said, "I like fixing things."

"What kind of things?"

Another pause. "Broken things."

I wondered how far I should probe. "Your sister tells me you were in the army," I said. "In Afghanistan."

At first, it seemed as if he hadn't heard me. He kept walking, looking at the ground. Perhaps my question was too unsettling, bringing back ugly memories. When I figured that silence was one of those vagaries of his "condition" and I could expect no reply, he said, "Helmand Province." After two steps, "Mortar rounds." Another two steps. "My friends died." Two steps. "I got angry." A pause. "But not angry enough."

I certainly didn't want him to relive old battles. "Your family must love you, though," I said.

Again, I waited for an answer. "We all got problems. Our folks got killed. We lost the ranch. Pratt's always broke. Steve got sick and died. I trust God. He's got a plan. But sometimes I'd like to know. What it is."

"Your parents were killed?" I asked.

"Drowned. Car went off a bridge. Fi was with 'em. She doesn't remember."

"Your sister was in a car with your parents when it went off a bridge? How old was she?"

"Seven. They died. She got out okay."

"How horrible."

"Stuff happens."

I was reminded of a similar incident when I was eleven. My father was driving us home after visiting friends. He'd drunk too much, something too common with him, and he ran a red light. It triggered one of my multiple-perspective moments: I saw cars veering and swerving to avoid hitting us—my mother yelling at my dad—Alison beside me, her eyes wide with horror. It was a miracle we didn't get hit, let alone killed.

Parker noticed my attention was elsewhere. When I snapped back to the present, I saw him studying me the way I had studied him earlier. "The scientific term for brain freeze is *sphenopalatine ganglioneuralgia*," he said.

Where had that come from? Did his "condition," whatever it was, give him some freakish kind of ability to sense the mental states of others? There was no question: Parker was a conundrum, and an unsettling one at that.

After that, he sped up his walking pace and moved ahead of me, perhaps distressed over the turn in our conversation. Frankly, I was relieved. His halting, staccato-like speech and puzzling statements were exhausting. Were they signs of autism or some other mental condition? Despite my familiarity with Jimmy Piersall, I wasn't as well-versed on such disorders as I should be.

Yet something else was bugging me about Parker. There was something in his voice's rhythm, its cold steadiness . . .

I was reminded of another voice. Sometimes I think I'll never stop hearing it.

"There'll be more. You can't stop me, Detective Chasen. Can't make me stop."

Vaclav Cerny was the very image of a nondescript man: fortyish, average in stature, his face unremarkable, neither unattractive nor attractive. He had an unexciting job, working as a quality-control inspector for a firm that made safety masks for factory workers. He had emigrated to the United States from Czechoslovakia with his parents when he was fourteen, but apart from that had led an unexceptional life: no scholastic or sports achievements, no close personal relationships, not even a dog.

But there was one thing about Vaclav Cerny that was unusual: his hobby.

He liked to kill young women—and not just any young women. He targeted those he perceived to be "loose": prostitutes, call girls, porn actresses. Sometimes he would expand his criteria to include strippers and adulteresses. There was an additional bizarre requirement for his victims: the young women needed to have been born between October 23 and November 21. That was how he became known as the Scorpio Killer.

By the time I was assigned to the team investigating his killings, there had been three, although we hadn't yet discovered the astrological connection. We knew the crimes were committed by the same person because a similar note was left on each body: "She was wanton and died in atonement of her sins of lust."

When I was named the lead detective on the case and my name began to appear in news reports, I started receiving calls from Cerny himself, taunting me and daring me to catch him. He was careful never to call from a number that could be traced. His clipped manner of speaking—and the occasional bizarre non sequitur he would unleash—was distinctive but proved to be a dead end when it came to identifying him. I met with behavioral experts who offered a wide range of theories, which all boiled down to the basic belief that Cerny was nuts. More helpful was his accent, still noticeable enough to be identified as Czech. That helped us make headway in the sex-worker community, and eventually we amassed enough leads to create a profile of Cerny and, ultimately, find him. When I was present at his arrest, he gave me one of those soulless smirks I had seen from fiends in slasher films. It sent a chill down my spine.

Cerny killed himself in his prison cell four days later, hanging himself with his bedsheets.

My thoughts of the past were jarred away when the path took a few sharp, upward curves. Eyeing Parker ahead of me, focusing carefully on his steps, I almost had to laugh at my comparing him to Vaclav Cerny. His manner of speech might be off-putting, but he certainly did not strike me as a serial killer.

The path soon straightened, and Parker's walking became more relaxed. Billie and Carole, who'd been several lengths behind, were now beside me.

"I was telling Miss Mondreau here that I feel awful about what you've had to put up with from our little clan," Carole said. "The bickering and all."

"Chase and I don't mind, do we?" Billie said. "Families are bound to have problems." She was making light of it, but I suspected she was as bothered as I was.

"They just like to rile each other up," Carole said. "They'll settle down once they get over their jet lag." She went on to talk about growing up with the Uptons as a second family.

Carole was a chatterbox, and I decided to float a question that was on my mind. "I still don't understand why they brought Fiona over here if, as you say, she isn't really grieving."

Carole sighed. "The answer is simple—grieving or not, it's always about Fi. She's the Elmer's glue that holds all the Uptons together. They either love her or hate her, but they'd fall apart in a million pieces if it wasn't for her."

"What's behind the animosity?" Billie asked.

"Ya gotta understand the Uptons," Carole said, as we carefully maneuvered around some large rocks and stones. "It took me years to do that, Lord knows, and I ain't sayin' I'm an expert on them by any stretch. But once you figure out that all their problems come from good old Bobby and Paloma, it becomes easier."

"Bobby and Paloma?" I asked.

"Their folks. They were royally screwed up. Bobby wanted kids with a hot passion and Paloma didn't. No, wait, that's not quite true. Bobby wanted a son . . . an heir to carry on the family name. So he was proud as a peacock when Brock came along—Brock's real name is Robert Upton the Second, by the way. Well, thanks to Bobby's on-and-off approach to birth control, Paloma cranked out three more kids. Bobby didn't give a hang about any of 'em—he had his precious Brock, and that's all he wanted. As for Paloma, she'd have drowned Pratt and Fiona in the washbasin if she could have gotten away with it. But when it became clear that Parker was a different kettle of fish, he melted her heart. She saw him as some sort of wounded little bird who needed a mother's love. As if the other two didn't! She doted on Parker, and the other kids resented her for it."

"I understand the parents died in a car accident," I said.

Her head swung toward me. "Who told you that?"

"Parker." Was this supposed to be some big secret?

She faced forward again. "Yep, they did. Real tragedy, it was. But be careful with Parker. Don't believe everything he says."

"What's his problem exactly?" Billie asked.

Carole let loose a bark of a laugh. "Depends on who you ask. Some of the doctors say low-scale autism, some say it's trauma from his war experience. Truth is nobody really knows. He's a decent sort, but Lord knows he's been dealt a bum hand of cards. His momma smothered him too much, and his daddy ignored him."

Billie asked, "With Parker's medical history, how was he ever accepted by the army?"

"He made a big show about wanting to serve his country. He's good at putting on an act sometimes. It bugs the hell out of the others. Brock hates that Parker was his mother's favorite, and he's certain that Parker plays up his condition to get sympathy. The others are harder to read when it comes to Parker. Sometimes Jenna is on his side, sometimes not. Pratt's the one who looks after him—he lives not far from Parker, and it makes sense, them being identical twins—but he gets fed up with him from time to time too. The only one who loves Parker wholeheartedly is Fiona. She'd do anything for him."

Carole flashed us a guilty look. "Listen. I talk too much. I don't mean any disrespect to Fi. She's my best friend, she really is. But . . . well, let's just say she coulda been a better wife to Steve in his final days. He needed her love then more than ever, and she wasn't around a lot to give it. She liked to go out to the bars."

We were entering personal details that I felt uncomfortable exploring further. But Carole couldn't stop talking.

"Fi likes to have a good time, and you can't blame her, can you? With her looks?"

"She's attractive, yes," I said.

Carole eyed me. " 'Attractive'? What are you, gay or something? She's a knockout! She could make any farmer plow right through a stump."

Billie said, "As a matter of fact, Chase *is* gay."

"Oh!" Carole said. "Goodness! I'm sorry. I meant no disrespect. Some of my—"

"—best friends are gay," I said.

She laughed. "Don't mind me. All the others will tell you I'm a big blabbermouth. It's true! I'm all that and a bag of chips."

A sign proclaiming CLEARHAVEN FARM appeared to our left, and soon we were passing by large fields dotted with cattle and sheep. At one point, we came across two men, dressed in farm clothes, crouching within a group of lambs. The men looked up as we passed.

Charlie walked over. "How are you doing this fine day?" he asked.

"Not too well," said one farmer. "There's a virus loose among the sheep in this area. We thought it had been wiped out, but there's been two or three cases just this past week."

"I heard about that," Charlie said. "There's a vaccine for it, though, isn't there?"

"Aye," the man said. "If we get to the animals early enough."

One lamb trotted over to the fence. Fiona reached over to stroke its fleecy coat.

"Careful!" Pratt warned. "You might catch that virus."

"No need to worry," the farmer said. "The disease can't be transferred to humans through that kind of contact." I wondered if this had anything to do with the "food contagion" Mike was investigating.

We continued through a vale, its rocky outcroppings looming above the fern-dotted slopes on either side. Although nature can play dirty tricks, such as releasing deadly viruses, it could also create vistas like this. The bright afternoon sun bathed everything in its glow. This was the kind of intrinsically English setting—that distinctive juxtaposition of the untamed with the tame—that fueled my stride. For a few minutes, I was able to dismiss the Uptons' problems and enter a state of detached contentment.

When we passed through a gate and came upon a fork in the trail, Charlie stopped us. "We'll take the path to the right, down through a tunnel beneath the rail line, and on through a couple of fields. That stretch can get confusing—you'll be tempted to take the path leading into a small forest, but just stay behind me."

As we headed down to the tunnel, Billie said, "Good thing we've got a guide, isn't it?"

"You can say that again," I said, knowing only too well how easy it was to become disoriented on British trails. Despite the English passion for rambling, the country's paths are often erratically signed, and even the most detailed map can't save you when a way marker is missing.

Sure enough, if left to my own devices, I certainly would have taken the path leading into the forest. But I stayed with the others as we followed Charlie across a small stream and over a wall stile. We then climbed a stairway carved into the hill, up to a disused railway in the process of being reclaimed by nature. Swatches of purple and gold wildflowers sprouted around us.

A sharp birdcall rang out, and Joe whipped up his field glasses to canvass the sky. He raised his camera just as a brightly colored bird swept overhead. He snapped a few photos and turned to me with a smile. "Can you believe it? A spectacled tyrant!"

Carole stepped up. "You're really into birds, aren't you? That's so sweet!"

Joe smiled at her. "They're fascinating creatures when you get to study them." He looked up and handed her his field glasses. "There's a red kite up there. Want to take a look?"

Carole raised the glasses to her eyes and followed the bird across the sky. "Wow! We don't have birds like that in Texas."

"Sure you do," Joe said, taking the glasses from her. "People just don't take time to notice them. I'll let you know when I see some rare ones. Would you like that?"

Carole smiled at him. "I'd love it!"

Charlie called for us to move on. The path veered from the rail line toward a narrow road, which we followed to a small caravan trailer where a vendor was selling tea and scones.

"We'll rest for a bit and have our afternoon tea," Charlie announced, easing off his rucksack. "How does that sound?"

"To be honest, I could use some coffee," Fiona said.

"Tea is more of a midafternoon meal over here," Billie told

her. "You haven't lived until you've had a freshly baked scone dripping with raspberry jam and clotted cream."

We put down our packs and walking poles and sat at two small café tables. The proprietress, a young woman in a pink apron, brought out trays of scones and the fixings as well as full pots of tea.

"There's always a debate about how to properly prepare a scone," Charlie said as he poured the tea. "Some say to put on the cream first and then the jam, while others prefer to do it the other way round. I'm a cream-first man myself."

He demonstrated by dipping a small spoon into the jar of clotted cream and slathering it on his scone, then doing the same with the bright red jam. The others followed suit.

"I remember how to do this now," Fiona said, as she picked up her spoon.

Billie took her first bite and smiled in deep contentment. "My word, this is good!"

"It almost beats Jenna's red velvet pie," Fiona said.

"Her dead fly?" Brock asked.

"Her red velvet pie, Brock," Carole said. "When are you gonna get a hearing aid?"

"There's nothing wrong with my hearing," he said. Turning to Jenna, he said, "Everyone loves your pie, sweetie." She smiled and playfully elbowed him. Then her eyes widened, and she let out a sharp scream.

"Jenna, what is it?" Fiona asked. She followed her sister-in-law's gaze and saw a large blackbird perched across from us on the back of an empty chair.

"It's another omen, that's what it is!" Jenna wailed. "A sign of death!"

The bird looked more interested in our scones than anything else. He was quite striking, with a bright yellow beak and eyes ringed with yellow that contrasted with his coal-black feathers.

Jenna dropped her spoon and stood, backing nervously from the table. "We need to stop all this foolishness and get back home. Right this minute!" She turned and started walking away.

"Don't worry, I'll calm her down," Brock said as dashed after her.

The blackbird flew off.

Chapter 6

Sunday, Late Afternoon
Moor Row

Jenna's outburst popped the frothy bubble of our afternoon tea.

Charlie managed a half-hearted smile. "Actually, it's the white birds over here that folks associate with death," he said.

"Don't expect Jenna to know anything about that," Carole said, unflustered as she took another bite of scone. "She looks for doom and gloom everywhere she goes. Sometimes I'm surprised she has the courage to get out of bed in the morning."

"She's not as bad as all that, C.W.," Fiona said.

"I'm not so sure," Pratt said. "Jenna's been into that astrology and tarot card crap for years, but it's only recently that she's become this freaky about everything."

"Maybe she's going through the change?" Carole offered.

Any speculation about Jenna was put on hold when she and Brock returned. She still looked spooked and sat without comment. Brock placed a scone on her plate and helped her apply the jam and cream. She took a couple of small bites before losing interest. Soon we had all finished ours.

"Anyone for seconds?" Charlie asked.

"No," Parker said. "The sky is out of date."

"For God's sake, Pecker, why can't you ever talk sense?" Brock said.

"Brock, why can't you lay off him?" Fiona said.

Parker looked unfazed. "I need to pee. Where's the men's room?"

Charlie nodded toward the caravan. "There's a loo round back."

Parker grabbed his knapsack and headed off behind the trailer. Brock stood and stretched. "We all know Pecker. He'll be in the head forever." Turning to his wife, he said, "Darling, what do you say we walk over and have a look at what fish they have in that pond over there?"

Jenna gave a small smile as Brock took her hand and led her to a small garden pond that most likely contained no fish. When they were out of earshot, Joe said, "He's really something, isn't he? Why does he pick at Parker like that?"

"It's a long story," Fiona said.

"It's not that long a story, Fi," Pratt said. "The truth is that Brock doesn't really like any of us, but he especially hates Parker."

"That is so not true!" Fiona said.

"Sweetie, you know Pratt's right," Carole said. "If it were up to Brock, he'd have been an only child. He never thinks the rest of you measure up."

"In what way?" Billie asked.

"Brock inherited our folks' ranch after they died," Pratt explained. "He couldn't wait to unload it. That's when he bought his first Chevy dealership. Now he's got two of 'em. We used to joke that Brock could turn on the phony charm like a car salesman, and then he became one."

"A very successful one," Carole pointed out. "Used to be you couldn't turn on late-night TV without seeing a cheesy commercial for Upton Chevrolet."

"I don't understand," I said. "Why did Brock inherit everything?"

"Because he was the oldest," Pratt said. "That's the way the old man's will was written. It's easy to be a success when you're handed millions. Any of us could have done the same thing if we'd been in his shoes."

"Brock's a smart man," Fiona said. "His success isn't just because he got our folks' money."

"Quit defending him, Fi," Pratt said. "All of us are smart."

Carole gave a laugh. "It's like the old saying, Pratt. 'If you're so smart, why ain't you rich?'"

"I might be real soon, C.W.," Pratt said. "You know that big deal I've been talking about? I'm waiting to hear about it paying off any minute."

Fiona chuckled. "Is that like the start-up you financed that sold different flavored toothpastes from around the world? Or the combination child and dog day-care centers?"

"Those were solid ideas!" Pratt said. "Was it my fault their timing was off?"

"Whatever this is, it's just another of your pipe dreams," Carole said. "Anything to keep you from doing an honest day's work like the rest of us."

Pratt swung toward her. "You call answering phones all day while filing your nails work?"

Carole's eyes flared. "You take that back, Pratt Upton! You know damn well I'm a highly trained medical administrator!"

It looked like it was time again to turn a hose on the smoldering fire that was the Uptons. "Why don't we start thinking about getting back on the trail?" I suggested.

Charlie checked his watch. "By Jove, you're right. We must keep to our schedule." He called over to Brock and Jenna to join us so we could get ready to leave.

"I'll check on Parker," I said, getting to my feet. "I need to make a pit stop also."

"Make it quick," Charlie advised.

I reached the rear of the caravan just as the door of the small, stand-alone privy swung open. Parker, his knapsack slung over one shoulder, walked out while rolling down the sleeve on his right arm. My presence jolted him.

"We're about to get started on the trail again," I said.

"Great!" he said with a broad smile. "Love the trail!"

The pathway to Moor Row, the terminus for that day's walk, ran alongside a narrow country road that had, thankfully, little automobile traffic. A stream gurgled as we strode past broad pastures, and beyond lay the green Cumbrian hills. Charlie pointed out Scaffell, in the distance, saying it was one of Alfred Wainwright's favorite peaks. I felt momentarily humbled that, in all my sixty-seven years, I'd never made a list of my favorite peaks.

Joe raised his field glasses to survey the view, and when he lowered them and raised his camera, I figured he'd spotted another bird. He snapped a few shots and turned to me.

"Willow warbler," he said. "Did you see it?"

"Didn't see a thing," I said. "You must have a good eye."

"You learn to be observant when you take up birding."

Or when you've been a detective, I was tempted to add. I turned my attention from the passing countryside to our group. Joe and I were toward the rear of the pack. Only Brock and Jenna were behind us. Pratt was far ahead, in front of everyone, including Charlie.

I began to hear something in the distance that sounded like . . . people singing.

"Listen!" Joe said.

The singing—which it clearly was, coming from multiple voices—grew louder.

Val-de-ri, val-de-ra, val-de-ri, val-de-ra-ha-ha-ha

We paused as nine young, stalwart blond men and women in matching hiking shorts and shirts marched toward us, their voices as vigorous and vibrant as their walking.

I love to wander by the stream
That dances in the sun
So joyously it calls to me
Come join my happy song!

They smiled at us broadly as they passed. They reached the "val-de-ri, val-de-ra" refrain again as they headed away, and Carole picked it up. "Val-de-raaa! Val-der-ra-ha-ha-ha-ha-ha!"

"Stuff a sock in it, C.W.," Pratt said.

"You're no fun," she said, as everyone continued walking. "I feel like I was just dropped into a scene from *The Sound of Music*!"

The hikers were a bit too Aryan Youth–like to lift to my spirits, but they had an energizing effect on the others, who strutted along with more verve than before. Joe surged ahead of me, and before I knew it, I was walking beside Brock. Jenna was a few steps behind us.

"I can't believe I'm enjoying this," Brock said. "When Pratt came up with this walking trip idea, it sounded like as much fun as diving into a barrel of pig slop. But you know what? There may be something to it."

I gave him a smile. "Walking is one of the best activities you can do. It helps bring our bodies in line with our minds. Most people don't do it enough, in my opinion. It's the most basic of human movements, and if you avoid it, everything else begins to go."

He gave a whistle. "That's pretty deep. But I must say it's doing me good. I might not need to take so many blood pressure pills when we're through."

I decided to take advantage of Brock's positive mood and

probe a little bit. "It was nice of you to come all this way for your sister," I said.

"For Fiona? Hell, I'm not doing this for her. She should have been a better wife to Steve. He was a fine man, but she didn't stand by him in his darkest hours. Don't believe any of that hooey about her being grief-stricken."

That went along with what Carole had told me. I said, "She's had a challenging life, though, right? Losing both parents at such young age. Is it true she was in the car with them when they had their fatal accident?"

Brock turned his head toward me, brows furrowed. "Somebody's been airing the Upton dirty laundry, haven't they? Most likely that blabbermouth Carole. Yes, Fi was in the car with them that night. The others all think Daddy was plastered and that's why he drove off that bridge. I don't believe it for a moment. Fi probably distracted him. She was a little terror as a kid."

"Was there an official ruling on the cause of the accident?"

Brock walked several strides before answering. "If you ask me, the police didn't handle that very well. Sure, they tested my father's blood, and it showed he'd been drinking. So what? He'd just eaten dinner, after all, and he liked his beer. The report said his drinking was a 'factor' in the accident. But it was pouring rain that night, Fi was probably acting up, being the little fussbudget she always was, and Daddy wasn't familiar with the road . . . well, the truth is, we may never know what the cause really was. Fi's always claimed that she doesn't remember a thing about it."

I thought about this for a few moments. "That's not surprising. She was just a child, and losing your parents that way had to be pretty traumatic. It's no surprise that a child would block it all out."

Brock gave a short laugh. "Oh, I think that memory is in there somewhere. It just needs to be shaken loose."

"How would you do that?"

"Oh, I don't mean actually shaking her. That's only something I would try with Parker."

He said this with a smile, but his contempt for his brother was no laughing matter. "Why are you so hard on him?" I asked.

"Hard on him? Yeah, I guess I am. You know why? It's because he's got everybody fooled. Fiona and Pratt think he's this fragile little bird, and they bend over backward for him. But he's a phony, and they flat out don't see it."

"A phony? In what way?"

"All this baloney about how 'damaged' he is, and how we all have to tiptoe around him because of his 'condition.' What a load of bull manure."

"Isn't it true that he suffered some sort of breakdown in Afghanistan?"

"I can't understand why he enlisted in the first place. Where did he think the army was going to send him, the French Riviera? If you ask me, the whole thing was just an excuse to get access to drugs."

Drugs had crossed my mind also, especially when I saw Parker leave the lavatory with his sleeve rolled up. I might as well ask straight out. "Does Parker have a drug problem?"

Another pause. "His biggest problem is that he wants everyone to feel sorry for him. I won't play that game." He walked along for a few moments in silence and then fell back to walk beside Jenna, who had been closely—and silently—listening to us the whole time. I wondered what she made of her husband's opinions about his brothers and sister. Perhaps, I thought, I would get a chance to chat with her later. Walking provides plenty of opportunities for that.

Charlie stopped us where the trail crossed the stream. To get to the other side, we needed to walk single file over a large log balanced on two rocks.

"Mind your balance as you go across," Charlie said. "The best approach is to walk steadily and not stop." He demonstrated by walking purposefully across the log in five long strides. He made it look easy enough, but there was a three-foot drop into the water beneath, and while the fall wouldn't seriously hurt anyone, it was intimidating.

Joe crossed next, followed by Carole, who was a bit shaky and paused halfway. A word of encouragement from Joe propelled her to the other side. Parker started across in small, halting steps. Brock followed a couple of feet behind, holding his arms out to each side as if he were walking a tightrope. He began to flail and darted forward to grab hold of Parker's shoulder. Parker swung around, sending Brock down into the stream. He gave a yell as he toppled into the water.

"Brock!" Jenna screamed. She rushed down the slope toward her husband, but lost her footing and slid into the water as well. This sent Ramses into a barking frenzy.

Soon all of us were scurrying down to the stream to pull them out. After Charlie helped Brock to his feet, Brock turned to Parker and yelled, "I'm going to kill you, you deranged monkey!" He lunged forward, and before Pratt and I could hold him back, he punched his brother in the jaw, driving him into the water also. Parker shot back up on his feet and was about to go after Brock when Joe grabbed him. I held back Brock before he could react. He squirmed and tried to release himself from my hold, but gave up when it became clear that he wasn't getting anywhere. He might have had an advantage over me in years, but I'd kept myself in shape.

Fiona marched up to Brock. "Can't you behave yourself for once? Parker didn't mean to push you into the water. It was an accident, for heaven's sake!"

"He meant it, all right! He's been waiting for the right time."

"Bull crap, Brock," Carole said. "I'd have whipped you into the soup too if you'd grabbed me that way!"

"You stay out of this," Brock hissed. "This is a family matter, and you certainly ain't family, C.W. You're nothing but cheap white trash."

Carole glared at him. "I've had just about enough of your lip, Brock. It's time for you to paint your ass white and run with the antelopes!"

Brock told her to shut up, Pratt railed at Brock, Jenna screamed at Pratt, Carole shouted at Jenna, and Fiona attempted to outshout everyone and make peace.

In the loudest voice of all, Charlie bellowed, "Enough!" He stepped into the cluster of Uptons. "What is it with you lot? You're all behaving like children. I meant what I said this morning. If there is one more outburst like this, I'll cancel the bloody walk and not refund one shilling of your fee." He let his threat sink in. "Does everyone understand me?"

There was a chorus of grudging assents. Joe released his hold on Parker, who fell to the ground like a limp rag doll.

"What happened?" Joe asked, wide-eyed. "What did I do?"

Jenna knelt beside Parker, unzipped his backpack, and extracted a small metal box. From it, she pulled out a pair of green latex gloves, a small vial, and a hypodermic needle. She began to unwrap the needle—agonizingly carefully, I thought—before positioning it over the vial and loading it up. Finally, she inserted it into Parker's right arm. Perhaps it was because Parker was in such need of help, but her studied ministrations were frustrating.

"You okay there, honey?" she asked Parker. Moments later, his eyes fluttered open.

"What was that all about?" I whispered to Fiona.

"Parker gets spells," she whispered back. "It's a good thing Jenna used to be a nurse. She knows just how to handle him."

Jenna slowly got Parker to his feet and assured Charlie that he would be strong enough to continue.

After putting Parker's medicine back in his kit, Jenna joined Brock, who said, "I need a heart pill, honey." With more speed than she had demonstrated with Parker, she fished a small container out of Brock's pack and handed it to him with his water bottle.

The others were doing the same thing. Pratt extracted a small pouch from his pocket and tapped a pill of some sort into his palm.

"I'd kill for a Xanax," Carole announced, digging into her knapsack's side pocket.

"Got one for me, too?" Fiona asked.

Soon all the Uptons were downing their pills of choice with gulps from their water bottles.

Billie came to me and murmured, "I think we're seeing the solution to managing the Uptons. Keep them medicated."

Chapter 7

Sunday, Early Evening
Broadmoor Hall

The rest of that afternoon's walk was free of drama, but I still found myself on the alert should some petty issue or comment flare into a fight and I would need to intervene. Of course, I could have ignored that if it happened, but I'm not the kind of guy who can stand aside while others are squabbling. Call it bravery or call it butting in, but enduring that kind of pressure is fatiguing. Why couldn't I have been blessed with normal walking companions, easygoing folks focused on appreciating the countryside around them rather their airing petty grievances?

Better yet, why couldn't Mike be there with me? We had such a wonderful time bumming around southwest England together after my last walk, visiting his favorite secret hideaways in Devon—a small crystal-blue pond at the end of a hidden glen, a surprise vista overlooking the moors, an off-the-beaten-path seaside cove. I was pleased to discover he was quite the outdoors type and a good walking companion.

Now I was stuck with the Uptons for another four days, like it or not. Thank goodness, Billie was with me or I would have bailed on the whole thing.

Before long, we entered the small village of Moor Row, where a van was waiting to take us to the hotel that would be our base for the next three days.

After the previous night's run-of-the-mill accommodation, I wasn't prepared for the grandeur of Broadmoor Hall. The two stone griffins at the foot of the front drive tipped me off that this was not going to be a two-star affair. But I was still blown away when the structure itself came into view, a gray-stoned fortress with battlemented parapets and leaded windows, all framed with blooming wisteria. The whole thing looked like the set of a Gothic movie.

As the van pulled up, Pratt let out a whistle. "Damn! This place puts Palomino Acres to shame, Brock!"

"What's Palomino Acres?" Joe asked.

"That's what Brock calls his tacky spread back home," Carole said.

"It's not tacky, C.W.," Fiona said.

Carole put her hand to her face. "Well, excuse me! I guess everybody's front parlor has a mechanical bull and a chandelier made out of bullet casings."

The inside of the hotel was every bit as impressive as the outside. Instead of a traditional reception area, a petite French provincial desk was positioned at the threshold of a great room filled with antiques, frayed rugs on a stone-flagged floor, piles of books, and a haphazard scattering of well-worn sofas, vases of garden flowers, and modern art mixing with old sepia-toned photographs. The place exuded a "staying with old-money friends-in the country" vibe.

"Now, this is a place after my own heart!" Brock said, crossing to a wall-mounted cabinet displaying several rifles. "Take a look at these babies. I wonder if they loan them out." Inside the case were seven long- and short-stock walnut-clad hunting rifles, in pristine condition.

"I believe they're antiques, Mr. Upton," Charlie said. "Probably not in working order."

We heard a cheery "Good afternoon!" and turned to see a smiling, middle-aged, red-haired woman wearing a floral blouse and trim black skirt.

"Welcome to Broadmoor Hall. I'm Lavinia Cooper, the day manager. You are the Rovers North group, I presume?"

"Indeed we are," said Charlie. He set to work with Mrs. Cooper to check us in and distribute our room keys. While waiting, Jenna noticed a copy of the local paper on a nearby table.

"Look at this, Brock," she said, holding up the paper. A headline proclaimed LOCAL SHEEP FALL VICTIM TO INFECTION.

He took the paper from her. "Good gravy! Hey, Charlie."

Charlie went over, and Brock handed him the paper. "That sheep disease is on the front page. Should we be worried?"

Charlie gave the article a quick scan. "It looks as if the authorities have everything under control, Mr. Upton. It's a disease borne by insects, and sheep are particularly susceptible. The chance of human beings getting infected is practically nil."

Brock snorted. "'Practically nil' doesn't mean it can't happen. We're not having sheep for dinner, are we?"

Charlie assumed his most reassuring smile. "Every night you will have a choice of dinner entrées, which may include lamb, yes."

"But aren't they cooked in the same kitchen?" Brock asked. "I know how these diseases spread. We've had 'em in Texas. It only takes one tainted dish in the kitchen and before you know it, everything's tainted!"

Charlie struggled to maintain his composure. "This virus is all perfectly under control, I assure you. Ovine diseases occur regularly and are quickly addressed by health officials and the veterinary community. Don't let one newspaper story frighten you."

Brock was about to say more when Mrs. Cooper asked for his name so she could check him in. He and Jenna went to her desk.

Billie leaned close to me and said, "I hate to admit it, but that sheep disease is giving me the creeps too."

"If there were really a problem, the authorities would be on it," I said. "They're pretty good about reining in that kind of thing over here. Sheep are a large part of their economy, after all."

My assertion seemed to put Billie at ease. Perhaps she was still shaken by her financial situation. That was likely the case, and it was something I was determined to help her with.

Then Jenna found something else to complain about.

"Oh, hell no, Brock," she said, her voice strained. "Ain't no way we're staying in that room."

Her husband looked at their room key, bewildered. "What's wrong with it? You haven't even seen it yet."

She pointed to the key. "Room Fourteen. Don't you know what that means? It's really Room Thirteen, but they didn't want to call it that!"

Sighing, he checked with Mrs. Cooper, who reluctantly affirmed that there was no actual Room Thirteen. "It's common practice in the lodging industry not to assign that number, Mr. Upton," she said. "Some people have crazy superstitions, you know."

Jenna was about to object when Brock said, "Yeah, I get that. But please give us another room, will ya?"

Her eyes darted to the guest ledger. "I'm afraid we're at capacity this evening."

Seeing that Jenna was again about to go off the deep end, I stepped forward and offered to exchange their room with mine. Brock thanked me, although it was clear he was getting as annoyed at his wife's superstitious fixation as the rest of us. Astrology, salt shakers, blackbirds, the number thirteen . . . what was next?

"Looks like we're sharing a room again, Park," said Pratt as he took his key from Mrs. Cooper. "Just like when we were kids, right?"

"Marshmallow dreams," Parker said with a smile.

Pratt turned to me. "He would dream about food a lot as a kid," he said by way of translation.

My room and Billie's were adjacent on the second floor. Despite its unlucky number, my room was calm and secure-looking, with a small fireplace and a mixture of antiques and quirky modern pieces. The small bath boasted a roll-top tub and a marble wash basin. Thick curtains framed a leaded window, through which I glimpsed a broad lake in the distance that I knew as Derwentwater, one of those that gave the Lake District its name.

I set my suitcase on a small stand and zipped it open. Over the years, my late partner, Doug, had taught me (and sometimes harangued me) to pack properly, by folding or rolling shirts and pants so they took up as little room in my case as possible and putting smaller items such as underwear and socks into plastic bags. Doug felt this would make me feel organized, which it has, but it also feels overly fussy.

Thinking about Doug made me think about Mike. I sent him a text telling him we'd arrived at the hotel, and I checked my wristwatch. Dinner was two hours away. After I finished unpacking, I contemplated a bath but instead took a shower, put on a fresh dress shirt and slacks, and headed in search of the hotel bar. It turned out to be in a small room connected to the main house, brightly lit and paneled in blond wood. An array of bottles was displayed on shelves lining the wall behind the polished counter. Billie was already there, perched on a barstool, a full beer glass before her.

"Imbibing already?" I asked as I sat beside her.

"Give me a break, Chase! You make me sound like a lush. After today's adventures, we both deserve a tipple."

I asked the barman for his best bitter. He nodded and promptly filled a pint glass from a nearby tap. I took a satisfying sip and sat beside Billie. "Now that we're finally alone, let's let down our hair. You've had another day of walking with the Uptons. Are you still willing to continue?"

She curled her hands around her glass. "They're lively, I'll give them that. Never a dull moment. But I'm good. How about you?"

I thought a moment. "I'm not sure. Something isn't right. They've told us a lot about themselves, but . . . I don't think they're telling us the most important stuff."

"This is just a walking trip, not one of your investigations. These people don't owe us any explanations."

I gave an acknowledging nod and took another swallow of ale.

The twins appeared in the doorway. They were both wearing green-checked shirts and blue slacks; I could identify Pratt only by the gold band around his neck and his big, black cowboy hat. Why had he brought that with him?

Billie was having similar thoughts. "What's with the matching outfits?" she murmured. "You'd think they were a singing group."

"Talking about us?" Pratt asked as he sat beside us. Parker took the remaining empty stool.

"We were wondering how you tell yourselves apart," Billie said.

Pratt smiled broadly. "That's easy. I'm the handsome, incredibly sexy one."

This earned a rare smile from Parker. Its hint of modesty made him look more distinctive, less a carbon copy of his brother. The truth was they both were exceptionally good-looking, with rugged yet perfectly proportioned features and mesmerizingly blue eyes. My thoughts started heading in a dangerously erotic direction, and I sought to redirect them.

"Want some beer?" I asked. Holding up my glass, I said, "I recommend this one. Bluebird Bitter, I believe it's called."

"Sounds good," Pratt said. "What about you, Park?"

Parker said, "I want a Shiner Bock."

Pratt laughed. "They won't have Texas beer over here, dummy. You need to try some of the local stuff, like Mr. Chasen here."

I signaled to the barman, and he promptly set down two pint glasses, full to overflowing, before the twins. Each took a healthy long gulp, after which Parker emitted a small belch.

"British ale is sneaky," I said. "If you're used to American beer, it will seem stronger-tasting but less potent. Before you know it, though, you're hooked. You never want to drink anything else."

"You obviously don't know how Texans feel about their Lone Stars or Shiners," Pratt said. "It's a pretty strong bond."

Billie and I smiled. The brothers were in a good mood.

"I know what you're thinking," Pratt continued. "What are these two hayseeds doing so far from their precious beer over here in Jolly Old England? Well, it's true that Fi is the main reason we came. But honestly, we all needed a break. This past year's been rough on us, what with Steve dying, Parker fighting his PTSD, Brock having that mini-stroke, and me with my . . . business problems."

"What kind of business are you in?" Billie asked.

"I'm what you might call an entrepreneur. You heard Carole and Fi making fun of some of my ideas. For a few years, I ran a nightclub outside of El Paso called Hillbilly Hacienda. Kind of a Tex-Mex mash-up to reflect the local culture. But the timing wasn't right. Too much competition. I had to liquidate a few months back."

His face fell for a moment, but he snapped back into a smile. "I'll be on top again soon, just wait and see. A sure investment I made is just about to pay off."

I saw a cloud pass over Billie's face. Had Pratt's comment reminded her of her own "sure" investment?

"That neckband you're wearing is certainly impressive," I said. "Where did you get it?"

Pratt put his hand to the gold band, as if he'd forgotten he was wearing it. "Oh, I got this years ago. It's similar to one my dad used to wear. His was a pair of ancient Mayan gold discs he got when he worked in Mexico right after college. Mine isn't that valuable, but it reminds me of him."

The band certainly looked valuable to me: large, thick gold squares linked together. I wonder if he ever removed it.

"Texas has arrived, y'all!" shouted a throaty voice from the bar entrance, followed by a whoop. I didn't have to turn around to see that it was Carole, wearing a glittery blouse and giant hoop earrings. Fiona was right behind her, dressed in a more demure outfit that nevertheless showed off her figure.

"Dial it down a notch, will ya, C.W.?" Pratt said.

Carole struck a mock pensive pose. "Sorry, Pratt, but I can't imagine what on earth you mean." She laughed and wedged herself between me and Pratt at the bar. As she began asking the bartender questions about the beer selections (the look on his face suggested that he could have benefited from an interpreter), I suggested we move to a larger table.

Soon Carole was carrying over a bowl-shaped glass filled with a red fizzy liquid. "Can you believe it? I asked him for a po-teet martini, and this is the closest he could get. I'm almost afraid to taste it."

Brock and Jenna came in. I was half-expecting him to be wearing a Stetson as well, but his denim jeans and big belt were the only giveaway that he wasn't a local. When they took their seats, Fiona said, "I need a drink too."

"What would you like, sis?" Pratt asked. "Your wish is my command."

"Something strong."

"Fiona," Brock said. "Take it easy on the hard stuff tonight. You know how you get."

She gave him a withering glance. "Take it easy? If there ever was a time I need a drink, it's tonight."

As Pratt walked off to get Fiona's drink, Carole held up her glass and said, "You know, this is pretty decent! It's not what I wanted, but damn, it carries a helluva wallop."

"Pratt!" Fiona called out. "Bring me what C.W.'s having."

Carole turned to us. "Did Fi tell you all? We got finally got the bags the airline lost. Well, all but my cosmetics case. Good thing I packed some basics in my carry-on."

Joe walked in, and Carole motioned him to sit by her. Clad in a polo shirt and slacks, he looked like more of an urbanite than any of us.

"I'm going to get a beer first," he said and headed to the bar. A few moments later, he returned, followed by Fiona and Pratt with their beers.

Charlie was the last to arrive, this time unaccompanied by Ramses. He got a beer, took the one remaining chair, and said, "Does everyone have his or her drink of choice? Very well, then. Let's raise our glasses. Here's to an invigorating week of beautiful walks, beautiful scenery, beautiful food, and"—he added with a sly grin—"beautiful drink!"

We cheered and clicked our glasses together.

"Let me tell you a bit about tomorrow," Charlie said. "We'll start by taking the van to the small village of Cleator, near where we left off this afternoon. From there, we'll head back in this direction, through a forest and over a small hill. The next part will be the steepest climb of the week, up Raven Crag. But then we descend to a river trail that will take us to Low Cock How Farm, where we'll have our lunch."

Carole was in the process of squeezing drops into her eye from a small plastic bottle, and paused. "Wait, wait, back up a bit. What's that about the steepest climb?"

"Nothing you can't handle, I assure you," Charlie said. "In the afternoon, the walk will be shorter and much less taxing. We'll pass through a small forest and then through the town of Ennerdale Bridge. We'll stop for refreshments and then walk to Ennerdale Water, one of the smaller lakes in the Lake District. That's where the van will pick us up and bring us back here. We should get back early enough for you to explore the hotel garden and grounds."

The Uptons looked at one another, the conviviality of a moment before gone. They looked somber and uneasy.

"When we reach Ennerdale Bridge, will we be going to the bridge itself?" Brock asked.

Charlie chuckled. "It would be hard not to. There's not much else in that little town."

The group remained silent.

Charlie checked his watch. "Why don't we make our way over to the dining room?" he said. "You can bring your drinks."

Everyone got to their feet. As we followed Charlie, I pondered Brock's question. That wasn't the first time a bridge had come up in conversation that day. Another had been mentioned—the bridge the Uptons' parents had driven off, to their death.

Chapter 8

Sunday Evening
Broadmoor Hall Dining Room

We entered a private dining room just off the hotel restaurant's main room, precisely the kind of elegant chamber I expected. Ornate wall sconces blazed above framed paintings of Lakeland scenes. The antique, polished oak dining table was set for nine.

There were no place cards, so we were free to sit where we pleased. I sat near Charlie at the head of the table and asked why Ramses wasn't joining us.

He laughed. "The little blighter ate earlier. He's up in our room, most likely sound asleep by now."

Jenna and Brock sat to my side, while the other Uptons mixed with the rest of us.

Fiona sat on my other side and swept her gaze around the room. "Now, this is class."

Two servers—a young man and woman, both wearing waistcoats in the hotel's trademark indigo color—entered to distribute the menus.

Charlie clinked his wineglass with his spoon. "Welcome, everyone! We're especially privileged tonight because this establishment has recently earned two Cumbrian florettes."

"Is that good?" Pratt asked.

"Extremely," Charlie responded. "That is how the local epi-curean society rates restaurants in this region. This establish-ment is particularly known for its locally grown or foraged produce, as well as lamb, milk, and free-range eggs."

As everyone studied their menus, Brock said, "I'd stay as far away from the lamb as you can get."

"Then what will you have, old man?" Pratt said, studying the offerings. "I don't see any ribs or Frito Pie on here."

"You can't go wrong with any of these dishes," Charlie said.

"What is hogget?" Jenna looked over the menu.

"The meat of a young sheep," Charlie answered. "Just over one year. Anything younger is technically a lamb."

"I say, stay away, honey," Brock said sternly.

"It's very tender and very flavorful," Charlie added.

Fiona set down her card. "Then that's what I'll have."

"Really?" Pratt asked. "With that sheep disease going around?"

"I can assure you again there's nothing to be concerned about," Charlie said. "All this meat has been rigorously in-spected."

"You see?" Fiona said, turning defiantly toward the others. "I say the hell with it! I didn't come all this way to eat the same stuff I do at home."

Most of us wanted a cocktail or wine with dinner. The server took our orders and quickly returned with the drinks. He had difficulty remembering who'd ordered what, and there was a bit of confusion as glasses and goblets were traded and passed around, but eventually everyone got what they requested.

Billie raised her glass. "Here's to Charlie and a walk we'll never forget!"

"Hear! Hear!" everyone echoed, with glasses raised. As we all took a drink, Charlie gave us a humble smile.

The server returned to take our meal orders. Other than

Fiona, most opted for the salt-aged duck or Cumbrian beef. The rainbow trout sounded good to me.

The starter course—a sweet cabbage soup—was soon brought out. Fiona pensively sipped a spoonful and laughed as she saw the others do so as well. "I still can't believe my brothers came all the way over here and are eating strange food."

"It's because they love you," I said.

She paused before taking another sip. "Perhaps."

"I'm sorry to hear about your husband. My own partner, Doug, passed away a couple of years ago. I can't say my grief is equal to yours, but I know it's hard."

Fiona reached and lightly placed her hand on my shoulder. "I'm so sorry for you. Steve had been sick for a long time, so it wasn't like a total shock or anything. Still, you're right. It's . . . hard. Harder than anyone realizes." Her eyes, dark green and soul-deep, began to well up with tears.

I didn't want to get into a discussion about dead husbands, but it was hard to get Doug out of my mind.

Fiona straightened up and wiped her eyes. "You're a good-lookin' man, Chase. You won't have trouble finding someone else."

Of course, Mike flashed to mind. "You'll find someone, too," I said.

"Just won't be you, right?" she said with a laugh.

"Afraid not."

"Listen, I hear that you used to be with the police. So, tell me. How long does it take after a crime is committed before it can't be punished?"

The spoonful of soup I was raising stopped halfway. "What kind of crime are we talking about? That would make a difference. Many crimes can't be prosecuted if too much time has passed since they were committed, but others—such as murder—have no such restriction."

"Murder? Good Lord, no. I'm not talking about murder."

"It also depends on where the crime was committed. In the States, there's a five-year statute of limitations on most federal crimes. But individual states may treat other violations differently. And, of course, laws in other countries can be different as well."

She took in this information—meager as it was—silently as she finished her soup.

Her question was so odd I couldn't leave it hanging there. "Does this have anything to do with your parents' death?" I asked.

"What? No, of course not. There was no crime committed there. At least, not that anyone knows."

I hesitated before asking, "You were in the car with them when it happened, weren't you?"

She nodded. "Yes, but I don't remember anything about it. That night has always been a complete blank. Brock and Pratt have always thought someone else was at fault. They think that if they took me back to where it happened, it might make me remember. But, honestly, what good would that do? That's all water under the bridge, isn't it?"

Considering the car went off a bridge, that seemed a strange analogy.

Fiona took a sip of her cocktail and gave a chuckle. "You probably think we Uptons are all nuts, don't you? Fighting like cats and dogs, and me asking weird questions. Well, you wouldn't be half wrong. But it's not as bad as it looks."

I didn't want to appear nosy, but I asked, "Is it true that they brought you here to lift your spirits?"

She raised her brow. "Have you been talking to Carole? She'll tell you it's all hogwash because I don't have any spirits to lift."

I didn't know how to respond.

"The truth is I honestly did love Steve. He was no saint, I

can tell you that. Sometimes he could be a hard man to love, and I'll confess that I could have been a better wife to him, especially at . . . at the end. I'm no hussy, but I did step out a couple of times. Steve found out and took it bad. I'm having a hard time forgiving myself. Carole hasn't forgiven me at all. She had a thing for Steve herself."

That was interesting information, but it didn't answer my question.

"I need another drink," she said, motioning over the server.

The bowls were cleared, and the entrées brought out. I took a bite of my trout. It had a delicate taste of lime, garlic, and something else I couldn't quite identify. Fiona appeared to be enjoying her hogget.

"How is it?" I asked.

"It's delicious," she said. "I never had anything like it. Not too tough and not too tender. The mint sauce is heaven. And the parsnips! I didn't know they could taste so good." She took another bite and then finished her cocktail.

As we ate, I realized I'd forgotten that Jenna was seated across from me. I praised her quick action when Pratt fainted and asked her how she was enjoying her slice of beef.

She gave me a sweet smile. "Beef is always a hit with us Texans. And this is very tasty."

"Glad to hear it."

She thanked me again for switching rooms. "You must think me a silly old fool, but there have been so many dark portents! The universe is communicating something in a big, big way. Unfortunately, it's already too late, I think."

I didn't want to encourage her delusions, but I couldn't resist asking, "Too late for what?"

She calmly sliced another forkful of beef. "To prevent the tragedy to come." She leaned closer and said, "There's a strong indication one of us won't be leaving here alive."

Did she mean leave the dining room? Or England? I was

getting used to Jenna's dire pronouncements. She came across as reasonable, then let loose with what Pratt called "doom and gloom," so it was clearly a pattern.

"Is the universe telling you anything more specific?" I asked.

She looked at me as if I had questioned her character. "It's not that simple. I can read the signs up to a point, but to fully understand them takes a special gift. Only a few have that talent."

I figured it was best to leave this matter alone. My tolerance for fortune telling was limited, and I didn't want to encourage her. Around me everyone was engaged in other conversations. Across the table, Carole and Joe were chatting quietly, laughing and smiling. I would have been blind not to see a romance forming. Well, why not? They were both young and single. Good for them. If Mike were there, I'd hoped we'd be doing the same thing.

I pictured him, hundreds of miles away, toiling over dead bodies. My trout, with its open eyes staring at me vacantly, started to look not so tempting.

"Where's the waiter?" Fiona said loudly, holding up her cocktail glass. "I need a refill."

Perhaps Brock was right to warn her about drinking too much. She shoved her chair back and shakily got to her feet. "Don't want to wait. I'll go get it myself."

"Fiona, sit down," Brock commanded. As she started around the table, he leaned toward me. "She's over her limit."

Fiona wobbled and grabbed Joe's shoulder to keep from falling. Instead of letting go, she took hold of his other shoulder and leaned close to his ear. "You're kind of cute, you know that?" she said. He squirmed uncomfortably.

"For lord's sake, Fi, behave," Carole said.

Fiona went to face her. "Joe's not your property, C.W. He might like to see what it's like to be with a real woman."

"You mean someone who was such a real woman that her husband confessed that he would have rather been with me?"

"Don't you believe her," Fiona said to Joe as she curled her arm around him.

Joe politely lifted Fiona's arm off his shoulder and moved his chair away from her. Because she was holding on to it to keep her balance, she fell to the floor with a scream.

"Good lord," Brock said, going over and pulling Fiona to her feet. "Didn't I tell you to lay off the sauce? Now you're making a spectacle of yourself."

Fiona yanked herself away. "You get your filthy paws off me! How many times do I have to warn you not to touch me?"

Carole stood and took hold of Fiona's other arm. "You need to cool off, girl."

Fiona pushed Carole up against the wall, dislodging one of the paintings, which crashed to the floor. Carole fell as well, but she shot back up and lunged at Fiona.

From across the table, Billie eyed me, urging me to do something. I dashed over and pulled Fiona away as Joe took hold of Carole, still steaming. She twisted against Joe's hold as she stared at Fiona. "You're gonna pay for this, Fi! You're gonna pay for everything!"

This tussle had come so far out of left field that I couldn't make sense of it. Fiona had been petiteness itself one minute and a lustful tigress the next. I know booze's effect can be unpredictable, but this was something outside my experience.

Charlie was suddenly there beside us. "Didn't you hear what I said earlier?" he said, glaring at Fiona and then at Carole. "I warned you that if there was one more outburst you're off my walk. That was no idle threat. I want you all to pack your bags tomorrow and leave."

"What?" Carole roared. "You've got to be kidding!"

"I'm quite serious," Charlie countered.

Pratt took Fiona's arm. "Nice work, sis," he said.

"But what are we going to do tomorrow?" Jenna asked. "This is ruining all our plans!"

Fiona eyed Jenna. "Looks like y'all will have to make other plans, doesn't it?"

"Our plans are still the same, girl," Brock said. "And you'd better not let us down."

She glared at him and walked off.

Carole reached into her pocket. I thought she was going to take another pill, but it was just her eye drops. She squirted some in her eyes, took Joe's arm, and gave me a triumphant look, as if she had accomplished what she'd intended.

A half hour later, Billie and I were seated in the main room, enjoying the desserts we hadn't gotten around to because of Fiona and Carole's scene. Mine was an apple crumble, and Billie's was a decadent-looking creation called Chocolate Nemesis. Everyone else had either returned to their rooms or gone to the bar.

"What do you think Brock meant with that comment about Fiona not letting them down?" Billie asked.

I slowly finished a forkful of my crumble. "I have an idea, but I'm not sure yet."

"I was hoping we would get through the night without one more explosion from the Uptons. No such luck. What a bunch of loonies."

I took a sip of beer to wash down the rest of my crumble. "The whole thing doesn't seem right," I said.

"Of course, those Uptons aren't right. Is it something genetic, you think? But that wouldn't apply to Carole, I suppose."

"No, I mean there's something not right about this entire situation. Why was Fiona drinking so much?"

"She's an alcoholic?"

"Could be. Brock talked about her 'limit.' But something was on her mind."

Billie took a bite of her dessert and nodded. "You're right. They're all on edge about something. It might have something to do with why they came over here."

I shared Jenna's prediction that "one of us won't be leaving here alive."

Billie's eyes widened. "She really said that?"

"She sure did. But we know she's superstitious, what with the blackbird, the room-number flap, and the astrology stuff."

"Don't bad-mouth astrology," Billie said. "It can be helpful. I always make sure to stay away from Aries people, for example. Too blunt and impulsive."

"What about Leos?" I asked.

Billie eyed me with a smile. "Such as yourself? Confident and smart. And you love life. But Leos can also be outspoken and opinionated. So don't get too full of yourself."

I chuckled.

"Do you think that was fair of Charlie to kick the Uptons out like that?" Billie asked. "I can't say that I blame him for getting fed up, but . . ."

"He was completely within his rights, but in a way, I'm disappointed. I was getting fed up with all the squabbling too, but frankly I'll miss the Uptons."

"They are certainly anything but dull," Billie admitted.

"There's a puzzle there," I said. "With them gone, I may never get the chance to solve it."

Billie finished the last bite of her dessert. "What is the puzzle exactly?"

"As you've said, something doesn't add up. Why was Fiona asking me about statutes of limitations at dinner? She clearly has some offense in mind and wonders whether it is still prosecutable. I got the feeling it has something to do with that car accident her parents died in."

"But that was ages go, wasn't it? And what crime would have been involved?"

I shrugged. "That's what I mean. There are too many questions without answers. And now, with the Uptons out of the picture, we may not get any."

Billie sighed. "To be honest, I'm looking forward to a walk with no puzzles to solve. I've got enough to worry about when I get back home."

I reached out to take her hand. "That's another thing. I can't bear the thought of you not being able to pay your living expenses. I'm not rich, but I have enough saved up to help you out."

She patted my hand. "That's sweet of you, Chase, but I won't hear of it. I'm nothing if not resourceful. And who knows? Marie might suddenly show up, profuse with apologies, and vow to pay me back tenfold."

"Well, if that doesn't happen, my offer still holds."

"No way. You'll need your money for moving expenses. When you come over here to be with Mike."

I smiled. "Let's take that one step at a time. Which reminds me, I need to check in to see how he's doing. I think I'll go back to my room and get ready for bed."

We both stood and headed for the stairs.

I found two text messages from Mike waiting on my phone, one inquiring about the day's walk and the other updating me on the progress he was making in connection with his local health problem (using no complex medical jargon, thank goodness). I wondered whether that had any connection with the sheep virus up in my part of the country.

I texted him a reply, making it a point not to go into any detail regarding the Uptons and their issues. I ended my message with the same affectionate send-off that he gave me, but, as I sat back after sending it, I felt no satisfaction. It was as if I was still back in California, separated by thousands of miles instead of being in the same country. This wasn't how it was supposed to be.

I wanted to hear his voice, but saw by the clock that he would likely be asleep if I called. Instead, I pulled out my journal to log the day's events.

There was a lot to jot down, and my observations of the Uptons took precedence over notes about the scenic countryside. That should tell you about what was commanding my thoughts. Under normal circumstances, this regurgitation of the day's details served to clear my mind for sleep, but that night's entries only made me uneasy. They seemed to be daring me to piece them together and discern what lay beneath.

By the time I drifted off to sleep, my mind hadn't worked out the answer. But I had the distinct feeling that when and if I ever did, it wouldn't be something good.

Chapter 9

Monday Morning
Broadmoor Hall Breakfast Room

Given the shaky status of our walk, I was pleased to find a generous buffet laid out in the breakfast room the next morning: steaming porridge, rashers of thick bacon, scrambled and poached eggs, and a wide assortment of muffins, pastries, and granola. Even if the Uptons weren't going to be doing any more walking, they still needed to eat.

Charlie came in as I was filling my plate. "Good morning," I said. "Billie and I were wondering if the walk is still on, now that there are only three of us."

Looking a bit sheepish, he said, "It will be the full complement, I fear. Parker cornered me after dinner and convinced me to give his family one more chance."

"Parker did that?" I asked. The man was hardly the type I'd expect to craft a rational argument.

"I believe it was him. The awkward one, without the cowboy hat." Charlie sighed. "You can call me a pushover, but he made such a pathetic plea that I gave in. He went on about how important this walk was to his sister, as well as to the rest of his family. He vowed to hold his temper in check and keep watch on the others. It all sounded very earnest, yet I warned him that one more chance means just that . . . one more chance."

As I wondered whether ultimatums would be effective with the Uptons—probably not—they began coming in and lining up at the buffet as if everything was normal. All were dressed for walking (they'd no doubt heard of Parker's successful negotiation with Charlie) and seemed to be in a cheerful mood, except Jenna, who looked hollow-eyed. Medicated perhaps? Fiona was acting calm and not the least bit hung over.

Brock and Jenna sat beside me. He speared a large rasher of English bacon, ate it in two bites, and said, "This is my kind of breakfast!"

When Billie joined us, I told her about the Uptons being given a reprieve. Before she had a chance to respond, Fiona and Parker arrived. A server set down large pots of coffee and hot water for tea, and I began filling my cup.

"I need to apologize for my behavior last night," Fiona said sheepishly. "I—I don't know what came over me. I behaved abominably. I'm so glad they're letting us stay on."

What could I say? I admired that she had the presence of mind to own up to her mistake. Parker reached out and lovingly gave her shoulder a squeeze. She returned his smile and patted his hand with hers. Turning to us, she said, "My suitcase finally showed up, thank the Lord. I was afraid I'd have to keep wearing the same clothes all week."

"Not all of our cases showed up, Fi," Carole said from the next table. "I still don't have my cosmetics case." There was no trace of the previous night's animosity in her voice.

"You can buy cosmetics over here, C.W.," Fiona said. "Although there was more in your case than just makeup."

It sounded like a dig at Carole's fondness for pills, but she didn't look offended. "They don't have the stuff I want over here," she said.

I turned to Parker. "Good job on getting Charlie to change his mind. I'd have been sorry to see you all go."

He nodded. "But we must behave." Turning to Fiona, he said, "Right?"

She smiled at her brother. "Right, Scoot."

Parker stared at his plate. "Forgot my toast." He stood and headed for the bread station.

"Where does that 'Scoot' nickname come from?" Billie asked Fiona.

Fiona laughed. "When I was little, Parker gave me his old scooter from when he was a kid. I loved that darned thing! Still have it somewhere. If I ever have kids, I'll pass it along."

Parker came back and let out a laugh just as Pratt laughed from the next table. I'd heard somewhere that twins often share emotions psychically.

"Pratt's in a good mood this morning," Fiona said. "He thinks that investment he's made is about to pay off."

"I hope he knows what he's doing," Billie said. "Investing hasn't turned out so well for me. What did he put his money into?"

Fiona took a bite of toast and shrugged. "Some high-tech gadget. He explained it to me, but it went right over my head. He borrowed a pile of money to get in on the deal. I don't know what he'll do if it goes bust."

After breakfast, we gathered near the hotel entrance to board the van. I was leafing through the morning paper and stopped to peruse an article when Jenna peered around my shoulder and pulled the paper from my hand. "This doesn't look good, Brock. Your horoscope says, 'Don't go too far afield today. Home will be the safest place.'"

"How am I supposed to do that?" he asked. "We're no-where near home."

She looked again at the paper. "I think it's telling you to stay where you are and not venture out."

"What horse pucky! You know how I feel about anyone telling me what to do."

Carole was again squeezing drops into her eye.

"I saw you doing that yesterday," I said. "Are your eyes giving you trouble?"

She did the same with her other eye. "They get dry. It seems to be worse here for some reason."

Charlie appeared, carrying his small pack, accompanied by Ramses. "Everybody ready?"

We followed him outside. The day promised to be clear and pleasant, the sky pure cerulean blue without a cloud in sight. We quickly put our gear in the back of the van and climbed inside. Joe and Carole nestled together and began speaking in low tones to one another, oblivious of the rest of us.

As the driver pulled us away, Charlie said, "We're heading back to the village of Cleator, not far from where our walk left off yesterday. We'll walk through a small patch of forest before climbing Dent Hill and Raven Crag." That was the most challenging part of the week's walk, I remembered him telling us.

Ten minutes later, the van came to a stop on the shoulder of the road beside a stream. Climbing out, I took a deep breath. The air's moist, crisp bite made me wonder about Carole's claim of dry eyes. The air was damp with mist. Yet everyone's eyes were different, of course.

After collecting our knapsacks and walking sticks, we followed Charlie beside a low stone wall bordering the stream and across a wooden bridge. From there, the path led us away from the road, through a pine-tree farm that soon became a thick, black forest. The canopy of trees blocked out most of the sunlight.

"I feel like we're in a children's storybook," Billie commented as she walked beside me.

"I hope it's one without ogres or evil spirits," I said.

"I prefer to imagine lively wood sprites or faeries."

Everyone was silent, perhaps subdued by the forest's shadowy, cathedral-like solemnity. I found it strangely comforting and womb-like. Too soon, we were back in the sunlight, looking up at an intimidating hill slope.

"This is Dent Hill," Charlie said. "It's a rigorous climb, but the payoff will be worth it. You'll be treated to incredible views of the entire region."

No one spoke as we started our way up. I didn't find the incline particularly challenging, but as we continued, the others, noticeably Brock and Carole, began having difficulty. They paused every few steps to collect their breath.

The ascent grew rockier and steeper. Carole seemed to have gotten a second wind, but Brock was struggling, frequently stopping for breath. Jenna encouraged him to keep going. There was no space for the rest of us to walk around them, and we were forced to pause until they moved forward.

At intervals, Charlie, in the lead, stopped and waited for Brock and Jenna to reach him. "Are you all right, Mr. Upton?" he asked at one point, holding out a bottle of water.

"I'm hot," Brock said. He took the bottle and drank.

Charlie nodded to Brock's walking pants. "Why don't you take off the bottom half of your trousers?" he suggested. "They should zip right off. That should help cool you down."

Brock shucked his backpack, sat on the ground, and began wrestling with his pants. "How in the holy blazes do these work?"

I knelt and helped him unzip the lower part of each pant leg. A woman with a large red Irish setter walked past, going in the opposite direction.

"See?" Pratt said to Brock. "If that dog can do this walk, so can you."

Ramses gave a quick bark to remind Pratt that he was part of the group as well.

Brock stood and put his pack back on. "I'm better now. Let's go."

From there, it only took us minutes to reach the summit, and the view lived up to Charlie's hype. Toward the west, a colorful patchwork of farms and meadows spread out to the sea, while, to the east, we viewed the Lake District's fabled peaks and fells, as well as a glimpse of two lakes. I had seen photos of these vistas in magazines, but they couldn't compare with being there. The vistas were complemented by a hint of breeze, the calls of distant birds, the warmth of sun on my neck, and the invigorating scent of the surrounding heather in the crisp air.

Before us on the summit was a flat area in the middle of which stood a large pile of rocks, festooned with small banners and flags made from scarves and other items of clothing.

"What's with these rocks?" Joe asked.

"It's called a cairn," Charlie explained. "You often see them on hilltops or at key junctions on a trail. Basically, it means we're going the right way. Some walkers celebrate the climb by leaving reminders of their visit."

Pratt hooted, ran to the cairn, and lifted up his arms in a *Rocky*-like pose. "I'm king of the mountain!" he shouted.

"It really is beautiful up here," Fiona said, looking around.

"See over there?" Charlie said, pointing to a peak not far away. "That's Haystacks, Alfred Wainwright's favorite peak. His ashes were scattered there."

"We won't be climbing that, will we?" Carole asked.

Charlie laughed. "Not unless you want to."

"No thanks," Carole said. "I already know where y'all can scatter my ashes. On the second floor of Neiman Marcus."

"In the plus-size section?" Pratt teased.

"Pratt!" Fiona shot back. "What's got into you today? Knock it off."

We resumed walking. The trail continued to another, smaller pile of rocks that Charlie informed us was the true Dent Hill summit. Pratt didn't do another victory yell, however. We headed down to a clearing where our path intersected with two others. Charlie guided us toward the one leading toward the northeast. After a few hundred feet, we came to a tall, ladderlike stile crossing a much shorter wall.

"Why did they make this thing so high?" Carole asked as she struggled over.

"To keep out deer," Charlie said. "Believe it or not, some deer can surmount shorter stiles."

I watched carefully as Brock climbed over the wall. He appeared to have regained his energy. I gave him a congratulatory pat on the back.

"My ticker might be a little off," he said, "but I'm stronger than any of the others, believe me." We continued on the trail, heading uphill again, this time at a sharper angle. "Our daddy would be rollin' around in his grave if he saw how they turned out. Pratt a business failure, Fiona still runnin' around like a horny teenager, and Parker . . . well."

"He seems to be doing all right," I said. "He convinced Charlie to agree to let you back on the walk, didn't he?"

He eyed me with disapproval. "Hey, I've been around Park ever since he was born. I think I know him better than you do."

I held up my hand as a sign of surrender; the last thing I wanted was to insert myself into a years-old family squabble. Something else was commanding my attention, anyway. The path had become narrower and more rocky, and I was relying on my walking pole to maintain my balance. The incline was giving my hamstrings and calf muscles a workout, not too subtly letting me know that maybe I hadn't adequately trained for this.

Looking ahead, I saw Billie, the oldest of our group, climbing the hill like a mountain goat. The others, ahead and behind me, were carefully watching their steps. Although the slopes on either side of us were not steep, any fall or misstep could send someone tumbling head over heels.

Just when I was wondering how much more of a climb I could handle without a break, the trail began to level. Charlie and Pratt were ahead of me, waiting for the rest of us to arrive. My heart was thumping, and my face was damp with sweat, but it felt good. That was part of the reason I was doing this. Soon we were gathered on the small plateau that formed the summit of Raven Crag, at first too winded to speak.

"Congratulations!" Charlie said. "As I said, this was the steepest leg of the trail, and you all handled it marvelously."

Brock was still straining for breath, his hand on his chest and his face constricted. I went to him and asked, "How are you doing?"

"I'm . . . fine. Just need to get my breath back."

"You need one of your pills," Jenna said, holding out one in her palm along with a bottle of water. He scooped it up, popped it in his mouth, grabbed the bottle, and took a swallow. I waited a moment or two while his face regained its normal coloring and went over to Billie.

"If Brock made it up here, he should be okay the rest of the week," she said.

Charlie waited until everyone had recovered and began leading us forward again. We all were grateful, I was certain, that the path was now heading downward at an easy angle. Vegetation again began appearing around us.

"How beautiful!" Jenna said as she stopped to finger a large purple flower.

"Careful with that," Charlie called out. "It's lovely, yes, but deadly poisonous. It's what's known as wolfsbane, or monkhood."

"Goodness!" Jenna said, backing away. "Should I wash my hand?"

"There's no need. It's only lethal if you ingest it."

Carole and Parker came to take a closer look at the plant. "Why do they make it look so pretty?" she asked.

"Let's move away from those and keep walking, all right?" Charlie urged.

After a few minutes, we reached the valley floor and crossed a series of flat rocks spanning a small stream. I tensed as Brock and Parker ventured across, but no scuffle erupted between them this time.

The bucolic tranquility of the walk—and the good behavior of the rest of the group—was at last putting me in the mental space I look forward to on walks; I felt serene and uplifted. I wasn't even obsessing over Mike not being there. A bird soared overhead, and Joe whipped up his camera, snapping two shots before he turned, beaming, toward me.

"A Chilean flicker!" he said. "I only dared hope I would see one of those. And, on the crag, I spotted a rufous-tailed plant-cutter. Incredible!"

Carole was at his side as we resumed walking. "What's with you and birds, anyway?" she asked. "What's the big turn-on?"

He smiled. "I was on a vacation in Aruba a couple of years ago with some college friends. We ran into this big group of British birders, all dressed in green and carrying expensive gear, including a particularly large scope. It was like something out of a movie. I asked one of them why he went to such lengths just to see birds. He told me he investigated war crimes for a living, and birds were his escape. Turns out the others all had high-pressure jobs too, and all said the same thing—there's nothing like birds to get you out of the world of men and into the world of nature."

I'd never heard it put that way. "Walking has the same effect on me," I said. "It transports me into the world of pure spirit."

"Y'all gettin' too woo-woo for me," Carole said. "I just like bein' outdoors and movin' around!"

We approached another clearing, where Charlie encouraged us to seat ourselves on one of the fallen logs or the grassy earth. He pulled a bag of trail mix from his pack and passed it around.

Billie and I spread out under an ancient, twisted oak and took a handful of mix from Charlie's bag. She said, "I shouldn't mention this, but I overheard something interesting on the trail."

"Interesting? In what way?"

"Fiona was walking with Pratt behind me. They were close enough so I could hear what they were saying. He was asking about the man she was seeing before her husband died. He didn't sound happy about that affair."

"Fiona admitted to me that she 'stepped out' on her husband before he died," I said.

"Fiona swore it was all over to Pratt. She said when her husband died, her lover ditched her at the same time. He was the kind who only liked to be the other man. She sounded sad about it. Or was she sad because her husband died? It's hard to tell."

Fiona was dealing with remorse, there was no question. "Interesting. But it has nothing to do with us, you know."

Billie nodded. "You're right. It's easy to get distracted by that."

We were eating more trail mix when Pratt's voice nearby pierced the quiet. "I don't care if he likes it or not!" he shouted, his cell phone pressed to his ear. "Tell Kurt to make up his mind within the next twenty-four hours or I'm pulling out my money!"

He terminated the call. Fiona asked, "Bad news?"

"Those jerks are stalling! I told them I'm out of patience. I don't want to wait anymore."

Parker said, "You don't want to work."

Pratt darted over and grabbed Parker by the collar of his shirt. "What do you mean by that crack?"

"Everyone needs a job," Parker said.

Pratt pulled Parker closer so their faces were inches apart. "I'll show you what you need."

"Uh-oh," I said, rushing over to separate the brothers before another fight erupted. Joe had the same thought. He came over and put his hand on Parker, while I grabbed Pratt.

Fortunately, Charlie was several feet away, playing a game of fetch with Ramses and out of earshot. Pratt apologized for flying off the handle as I led him away.

"Parker's the one you need to watch out for," he said. "You never can tell what he'll do. I don't know if it's because of his condition or the meds he takes for it. He's like a bomb waiting to go off."

Brock, and even Pratt himself, seemed to fit that description more than Parker, but his words struck a chord with me.

A bomb waiting to go off.

I'd heard that phrase before. It was the same thing people who knew him said about the Scorpio killer.

Chapter 10

Tuesday Afternoon
Low Cock How Farm

On the move again, we crossed a cattle grid into another forest. Normally, the iconic sights of an English walk—cattle grids, kissing gates, acorn-marked way markers—lulled me into a blissful reverie, one in which I found that elusive balance between mindful appreciation of nature and mindless escape from the stresses of the world. They weren't working this time. Even though the Uptons were walking without incident, they continued to unnerve me. I again considered abandoning the walk and going down to Devon, where I could be with Mike.

The trail leveled, and the flatter countryside held less allure. Straggly gorse had taken over the surrounding landscape like an invasive rash. That was disheartening enough, but I also had to listen to Pratt and Fiona bickering behind me.

"I don't want to talk about money right now, okay?" she said. "And why do you need it anyway? You keep telling us you're about to strike it rich."

"I am, I am," Pratt replied. "But until then it would help if I were on firmer footing. I'd pay you back with interest, Fi; you know I would."

"Honestly, Pratt, you must think I'm a whole stack of stupid. Besides, I haven't gotten any of Steve's estate yet. The lawyers keep dragging their feet."

Joe shouted, "Over there! A speckled teal! It has to be!"

He aimed his camera in the distance, where something like a small bird appeared to be flying our way.

As it neared, it looked more like a small airplane than a bird: a huge grayish-brown creature about two feet long and three times as wide. We stared up in awe as it swooped down toward us.

"It's an osprey!" Joe said as he photographed it.

It soared close enough over us for me to see the intricate patterns on its wings. It was also close enough for me to view a stream of white dropping from its rear end.

"Aaagghh!!"

I turned to see Pratt frantically trying to brush a healthy dollop of bird poop off his neck and shoulders.

"That bird crapped on Pratt!" Brock said and started laughing uncontrollably.

"It's not funny, Brock!" Fiona said, pulling out tissues from her pack and going over to Pratt, now trying to get the excrement off his arms and hands. Carole joined her, pulling water from her pack. The two began working together to clean him up.

"That damned bird was aiming at me!" Pratt said. "I'm sure of it!"

"They don't do that," Joe assured him.

"It's a sign!" Jenna proclaimed.

"Can it, will you, Jenna?" Fiona said. "Everything has to be a sign with you!" She turned to Charlie. "We can only get so much of this stuff off him. Is there somewhere nearby with a bathroom?"

"We'll be stopping for lunch pretty soon," Charlie said.

"You can wash him off, but he'll still be fouled," Jenna said, sounding like a Southern preacher. She then began sneezing, in rapid bursts, and pulled a bottle of allergy pills from her pack.

"Are you all right?" Billie asked.

Jenna downed a pill. "This whole expedition is cursed!" She scanned her eyes over the rest of us. "All of you should be careful!"

We soon reached a small farm dominated by a large, white-washed house with adjoining riding stables. Charlie announced it as Low Cock Farm, often the first night's accommodation for Coast to Coast walkers. "It isn't technically an inn," he said, "but they always agree to provide light lunch for my groups."

We left our packs and walking sticks at the door and entered a dark, yet inviting room with a small window casting daylight on two large oak tables. Bright flowers in jars offset the dark stone walls. A large, middle-aged woman came in, wiping her hands with a towel. Charlie introduced her as Mrs. Trower.

"Get off your feet and rest a bit," she greeted. "I'll be bringing the food out in a flash. There'll be some ale as well."

Pratt asked where he could find the men's room and walked off.

"Poor guy," Carole said, watching him go. "He's stressed out enough by that investment he made, and then this had to happen!"

Fiona leaned close. "Keep quiet about it, or you'll set off Jenna again."

We found the table that had been reserved for us and took our seats. With Charlie assisting, Mrs. Trower brought out foaming glasses of ale. Once she'd placed them all down, Pratt returned.

"I managed to clean most of it off, but I'm afraid I'll stink for a while," he said as he sat down next to Parker.

"Feel-good freshness!" Parker said. Whether this was a shared joke or one of Parker's non sequiturs I couldn't tell, but Pratt seemed to be comforted and smiled.

The beers were quickly followed by large plates piled with

food: a Lancashire cheese soufflé and slices of Cumbrian lamb with broad beans and mint jelly. We were encouraged to help ourselves.

"Lamb again!" Brock said. "No, thanks. I'll stick to this cheese dish."

Everyone else took some of the lamb, including me and Billie, whose concerns over any possible health hazard had apparently subsided. Like me, she swooned after taking her first bite.

"Unbelievable!" she gushed. "Isn't this delicious?"

I agreed, although the meal seemed a bit heavy for the "light lunch" Charlie had promised. After the heavy breakfast, I feared it might weigh everyone down rather than pep us up for the afternoon's walk.

As if on cue, Charlie began outlining the upcoming stretch of the Coast to Coast. "There won't be any steep climbs this afternoon, just a leisurely walk of about three miles through Hickbarley Forest and a broad valley as we head toward Ennerdale Bridge. We'll stop there for our afternoon tea."

I was expecting questions, but the Uptons were silent, unusually so, focused on their meal. They ate almost in a coordinated rhythm, alternating bites of food with swallows of ale. Mrs. Trower brought out another round of glasses. I watched Fiona carefully, hoping she wouldn't overindulge. When she started in on her second glass, I was going to speak up, but Parker beat me to it.

"Enough," he said, reaching out and placing his hand over hers.

She pulled her hand away. "Just a little more, Scoot."

He put his hand back and held hers fast. "They're out of olives."

Fiona appeared to understand. "All right," she said, pulling back her hand and pushing her beer away. If Brock or Pratt had made that demand, there would definitely have been fireworks.

Charlie told us that it was time to get back on the trail. A few of us felt the urge to visit the loo. I let Pratt go ahead of me and waited in the small vestibule as Fiona, Brock, and Jenna walked past. Despite not finishing her second glass of ale, Fiona was walking unsteadily. She stumbled on a threshold, and Brock reached out and wrapped his arm around her waist.

She jumped back as if she'd received a shock. "Knock it off, Brock!"

He stepped toward her. "Give me a break, Fi. I was just trying to keep you on your feet." She swayed again, and he reached for her.

"Don't touch me!" she commanded. "One more step and you'll pull back a bloody stump."

Jenna took his arm. "Come on, Brock. Let Fi fall on her face if she wants."

When they left, I asked Fiona how she was feeling.

She put her hand to her head. "I'll be okay. It's just that Brock pisses me off."

Keeping my voice low, I asked, "Does your brother have a history of touching you inappropriately?"

My question took a while to register. "What? Oh. Sorry you had to see that. It's nothing you need to get involved in."

"Please call me Chase—that's what my friends do."

She gave me a small smile. "Chase? That must mean you cut to the chase. You call things as you see them, right?"

That was an interesting interpretation of my nickname—and one I hadn't heard before—but it didn't answer my question. Pratt returned and ushered Fiona out the door.

After leaving the farm, we crossed another cattle grid, passed through another grove of trees, and then walked alongside a one-lane road that I could have sworn we had just walked. Longer walks are like that; they often seem to be on a continuous loop, the same sights appearing again and again.

Despite the heavy lunch, everyone was walking briskly. Joe

occasionally raised his field glasses to scan the sky for birds. Carole stayed close by his side. No one spoke. That could have been due to the hearty meal or the splendor of the countryside, but I suspected another reason. Hovering over the Uptons was an unspoken air of anticipation.

"Do you feel there's something brewing?" I asked Billie, walking beside me.

"You mean a storm?"

I looked around. Parker and Pratt were ahead of us, and Brock and Jenna were far behind. "Everyone's on edge," I said. "They're anxious about something."

"Do you think it's that bridge? Could it be the one their parents drove off? It's hard to see how it could be. Fiona said she's never been here before."

"She told us she hadn't. But remember yesterday, at tea? She said she remembered how to prepare a scone with cream and jam. It's possible she'd learned that back in Texas, but it didn't strike me that way."

Small houses appeared on the horizon, and within minutes, we passed a sign announcing our entry into the village of Ennerdale Bridge. It looked self-consciously precious with its whitewashed buildings, but I wasn't paying attention to those. Like the others, my eyes were peeled for the bridge. When it finally appeared, it was so unassuming—a simple, gray-stoned arch spanning a slow-moving, unthreatening river—that we nearly passed it by.

Once the others realized we had, indeed, reached the bridge, they came to a stop and moved to the side of the road to view it in its entirety, the river streaming beneath.

"Would you like to take a break here?" Charlie asked, puzzled as to why everyone had stopped walking.

"Give us a minute, okay?" Carole said.

Was this the bridge where the Uptons' parents met their deaths many years before? It hardly looked like a death trap to me. There was only an eight-foot drop into the water, hardly enough to kill someone. The river might get rougher and more threatening in rough weather, however.

Her siblings' eyes turned toward Fiona, who was studying the bridge as if it were a puzzle she needed to solve. Her brows tightened, and she started walking down the slope toward the river.

"Careful," Charlie called out, and Fiona paused, staring at the bridge. As she looked around—studying the slow-flowing river, the trees trembling slightly in the breeze—the rest of us remained still and silent. The tension was palpable.

After regarding the bridge and the water beneath it for a few more minutes, Fiona turned and walked back up the bank toward us. Her family gathered around.

She looked at them apologetically. "Sorry. I don't remember a thing."

Chapter 11

Tuesday, Late Afternoon
Ennerdale Bridge

Brock marched up to Fiona, his face twisted in anger. "You're lying!"

Fiona took a deep breath. "I'm sorry, Brock. I wish I could tell you that everything all came back to me in a blinding flash, but it just didn't."

"Dammit, Fiona, *think!*" Brock urged.

Pratt approached as well. "Make an effort, Fi. For me?"

Fiona closed her eyes, but I suspected she was trying to block out the exhortations of the others more than anything else. She opened her eyes and said, "Nothing's coming. Sorry."

"Liar!" Jenna said.

"Stop it!" Fiona screamed, backing away. "I'm telling you I don't remember, and I don't! What more do you want from me?"

Pratt went up to her and looked her straight in the eye. "You know what? I don't think you would tell us if you did remember."

"Now why wouldn't I do that? For goodness' sake, Pratt."

"Because it would make you look bad," Brock said.

Fiona held up her head and stepped over to him. "You still

think I caused Daddy to drive off the bridge, don't you? Because God knows he was so perfect that he could never do such a thing."

"He wasn't driving, I'm sure of it," Brock said. "It had to be our mother."

"We know both our folks' bodies were found in the river," Pratt said. "I don't care who was driving. What we don't know is if another vehicle was involved."

"Use your head, Pratt," Carole said. "Look around you. This ain't exactly Interstate 10. We haven't seen a car go by the whole time we've been standing here. And we're here in the daytime, not at night. Or in the rain even."

"Do you think an animal may have run in front of the car?" Joe suggested. "A deer maybe?" Nobody responded.

Brock grabbed Fiona by the shoulder. "You better not be playing games, little girl. We didn't bring you all the way over here for you to make fools of us."

Fiona shoved him away. "What did I tell you about touching me? I've been talking to Chase over there. He says sexual assault crimes can still be prosecuted no matter when they happened."

Brock looked as if she had slapped him. "Sexual assault crimes? You're out of your damn mind!"

Charlie stepped forward. I was fully expecting him to kick them off the walk again. Instead, he asked, in a reasoned tone, "Perhaps I'm being a bit slow, but what has all this been about?"

The Uptons looked at one another accusingly. Not surprisingly, it was Carole who responded. "This is the bridge where Fi's folks bought the farm twenty years ago. It was a rainy night, and Bobby had had a few too many and drove their rental car off the bridge into the river."

"That's not what happened, C.W.!" Brock raged.

She ignored him. "The fact is, the car went into the river,

and both Bobby and Paloma drowned. Thank God, Fi got out alive."

"There's much more to it than that—" Pratt said.

"The police report was done in a hurry—" Brock added.

"They could have been forced off the road—" Pratt continued.

"Enough!" Charlie said. "I believe I understand the matter at hand here. Why hadn't any of you told me of this before?"

His question was met with silence.

"Very well," Charlie said. "I don't want to hear any more about it. You can continue your discussion back at the hotel. In the meantime, we need to move on."

The Uptons, though, weren't ready to abandon their big moment. They glared at Fiona, daring her to dredge up buried memories, and she glared back, resistant. When it became clear they were at an impasse, Carole said, "Listen up, y'all. Do ya think this is a delayed reaction kind of thing? Fi may wake up in the middle of the night and that whole horrible night will come back, clear as a bell. In the meantime, let's finish the walk."

That broke the détente. Fiona even managed a small appreciative smile and nod to Carole. The Uptons began following Charlie and the rest of us on the path as it led out of town, away from the bridge.

Finding myself walking beside Carole, I asked, "So this bridge was the reason for all of you coming over here? I remember you said it was 'to set someone's mind at ease.' Why is it so important that Fiona remembers what happened?"

After looking around to see if others were in earshot, she said, "There's a lot of different reasons. Most of us believe Bobby was driving, but Brock will never believe his papa was the sloppy drunk he really was. He hoped Fiona would remember that her momma, Paloma, was the one behind the wheel. Jenna, too. But there could be a downside to that. If Fi definitely remembers her father was driving, it could invalidate Bobby's will."

"You mean, because it could be considered suicide?"

"Something like that," she said. "It's complicated—the kind of thing lawyers love to fight over because they can charge big bucks. It could also complicate the insurance settlement. Brock got everything, and the others have been mighty upset about it ever since."

"What about Pratt? He seemed so certain another vehicle was involved."

"Well, we don't know, do we? There could have been another drunk driver on the road that night who forced Bobby off the bridge. Anything's possible, right? Although I don't know how you'd find out something like that after all this time. It's been twenty years, for God's sake. But Pratt's after something else."

"What would that be?"

"Bobby always wore this big gold necklace, something he got working on ranches down in Mexico when he was a college kid. Some kind of precious Mayan artifact. I always thought it looked ridiculous, but he wore it everywhere he went. Probably even slept in the damn thing. Pratt loved that necklace, too, and his daddy promised to leave it to him in his will. But when they pulled him from the river, the necklace was gone."

I let this sink in as I walked. In addition to its sentimental value, a valuable gold Mayan artifact would be worth a lot of money. "And what about Parker? Does he have a stake in all of this?"

Carole gave a small chuff of a laugh and shook her head. "Poor Parker just wants everyone to get along. He loved his mama and hated his daddy, though, that's the God's truth. His daddy used to rag on him worse than Brock. I believe he'd love Fi to remember without a doubt it was Bobby behind the wheel."

Questions were swimming in my mind. "What were the three of them doing over here in England, anyway?"

Carole looked at me. "Well, it was because of Fi, of course. She loved those Peter Cottontail books. You couldn't get her to shut up about how she wanted to see where he lived. Never mind that it was just make-believe—I think she knew that deep down—but she was just a kid, in love with fairy stories. Who'd have thought it would end so badly?"

We reached a nearby café, where three small outdoor tables had been prepared for our afternoon break. The episode at the bridge still seemed to be on everyone's mind; we all sat without speaking. Billie and I found ourselves next to Fiona and Parker. A server promptly brought out four pots of tea and an assortment of biscuits.

"Let me see if I understand this," Billie said to Fiona. "Your parents brought you over here to England when you were a little girl? Because of your love for the Peter Cottontail books?"

Fiona nibbled a biscuit and nodded. "It was for my birthday."

"But your brothers didn't come?"

"Why would they want to come to England? Beatrix Potter was my passion, not theirs. Even my father didn't want to come, but Mama talked him into it."

"I wanted to come," Parker said.

Fiona smiled. "Nice of you to say, Scoot, but you really didn't."

"And you came back this time to see if you can recover your memory of that night?" I asked.

Fiona gave a small roll of her eyes. "It was Brock's idea. He's never believed that our daddy could have done such a thing. He read somewhere that memories can be restored if the circumstances are recreated. It's a bunch of hogwash, but he was set on it. I only agreed by getting everyone else to take this walk with me. I'll be damned if I'm going to come halfway around the world just to look at some stupid bridge and make Brock happy."

This should have explained it all. Yet something still didn't sound right. Making this trip was not an inconsiderable effort—it took money and planning.

As I filled our teacups, Billie asked Fiona, "You truly don't remember anything?"

Fiona paused before shaking her head. "Nope. I wouldn't lie about it. I want to be sure of what happened, along with everyone else."

"It's not unusual for people to block out traumatic experiences," I said. "Particularly young children. How old were you at the time, eight?"

"Nine," she said. "And ever since then, I've been torn between wanting to remember and wishing to hell I could forget."

"I can't forget," Parker said. He looked down at a small spider crawling on his knee. He gently placed his finger out, let the spider crawl upon it, lowered it to the ground, and let it crawl off.

Fiona placed her hand on his. "Sometimes I wish I could trade places with you. You deserve to forget."

Chapter 12

Tuesday, Late Afternoon
Borrowdale

The drama at the bridge pervaded the rest of the afternoon's walk, which was leisurely, the trail mostly level as it followed a sleepy, one-lane road. I found myself walking between Carole, who stopped from time to time to squirt drops in her eyes or take a drink of vitamin water, and Joe, who paused occasionally to scan the sky for birds. At one point, he dashed off the trail to pursue a particularly rare one.

"Isn't he cute with that bird stuff?" Carole said, as she watched him run off.

"Bird-watching can be an addicting hobby," I conceded.

"Fortunately, he likes people too," she said with a giggle. "Especially women." Her face clouded. "Gee, I'm sorry. I don't mean to suggest that there's anything wrong with guys who don't like women."

I'm old enough to remember when it was common to disapprove of gay people in everyday conversation. Nowadays folks bend over backward not to appear bigoted. "No offense taken," I said.

"I've got lots of gay friends," Carole said. "Some of 'em swing both ways, but I just can't get into that. I like guys too much. That makes me sound like a little slut, doesn't it? But I'm not! That is, not like other people I could mention." She glared at Fiona, walking ahead of us.

"You seem to resent Fiona. I thought you were her best friend."

Carole was silent for a moment. "We've been friends ever since we were little. But when Steve got sick, she showed her true colors."

"You mean because she was cheating on her husband? Isn't that her business?"

"Steve was a fine man, and Fi didn't give a pig's whistle about him."

"She told me she loved him deeply."

"Well, she'd say that now, wouldn't she? I ended up spending more time with him than she did. Poor guy."

"The doctors couldn't do anything for him?"

She pulled out the eye-drops bottle from her pack. She had mastered the art of positioning it above her eyes and squeezing it while maintaining her stride. "There was always more chemo and stuff like that. But none of that helps if someone is dead set against it."

"You mean he'd given up?" I asked. "He wanted to die?"

Carole looked at me. Her eyes were moist, either with tears or her eye drops. She looked quickly at Joe, a few feet away, field glasses to his eyes, then she moved close to me. In a low tone, she said, "It was Fi who wanted him to die. She'd been stepping out on him for nearly a year. He wouldn't divorce her, and she didn't want to wait for the cancer to do its work. So she hurried it along."

Even coming from Carole, a shameless gossip, this was quite an accusation. "Hurried it along? How would she do that?"

"She used to work for a doctor. Toxicologist. You know, poisons?"

"Are you saying that Fiona poisoned her husband? What evidence is there for that?"

She gave a look that indicated perhaps she'd said too much. "Let's just say I know. I've been Fiona's friend since she was four years old. I know exactly what she's capable of."

Joe bounded back. "A rush tyrant!" he said. "This is a day for the record books. Here, Carole. Take a look." He handed her his field glasses, which she grudgingly accepted—mostly, I suspected, to please him.

"Over there," he directed. After looking for a moment, she said, "Yes, I see it. The little yellow and blue one? How cute!"

She handed Joe his glasses back. He took them reluctantly, perhaps dismayed by her assessment of his rare bird find as "cute."

Carole's comments about Fiona were still on my mind when we passed through a kissing gate and came upon the weir marking the southern edge of Ennerdale Water, the second of the region's lakes on our route, its glassy dark blue surface spread out before us. The van that would take us back to Borrowdale was waiting.

"We'll return to this spot tomorrow morning and pick up where we left off," Charlie advised us as we boarded.

Instead of taking us directly to our hotel, the van driver left us off in the center of Borrowdale village—two blocks of tearooms, guesthouses, and curio shops. Charlie told us we could take as much time as we needed to look around (it wouldn't take much, from what I was seeing) and then return on foot to our hotel, a kilometer or so away.

Carole said she was tired of walking, so she and Joe went to rest on a bench in the small town green. Pratt was anxious to check on the status of his business deal, so he excused himself, pulled out his phone, and began walking back toward the hotel. Parker followed him, which left six of us.

Billie and I separated from the others and headed up a street. Fiona joined us. Charlie, Brock, and Jenna weren't far behind. We passed a quintessentially British post office/general store, the day's newspapers and tourist curios on display. Although the shop struck me as painfully twee, it made me thankful that no Starbucks or McDonald's had yet invaded. The next shop sold antiques and collectibles. A full collection of vintage Beatrix Potter books was on display in the front window.

Fiona laughed. "Those stories made me feel so good when I was little, especially after my folks died. Isn't that strange?"

"Not strange at all," Billie said. "Beatrix Potter created Peter Rabbit to comfort a little boy. He was ill, and Potter felt that a story about a rabbit, complete with pictures, could help him pass the time and cheer him up."

"Really?" Fiona said.

Billie smiled. "Librarians have to know things like that. Potter included important lessons for children in her books, such as the usefulness of camomile tea when you're sick and the importance of listening to one's mother."

Fiona's expression turned sober. "I don't remember much about my mother. And I definitely don't remember her telling me anything helpful."

We didn't enter the antiques shop. Over the door of the next storefront was a blue sign with gold lettering: MADAME ROSE, PSYCHIC AND SEERESS.

"Oh, lordy," Fiona said. "I hope Jenna doesn't see this. She can't resist fortune tellers."

We moved on, but I looked back and saw Jenna pause before Madame Rose's door. She tested the handle, but it didn't open.

It didn't take long to check out the rest of the village. We returned to the green and told Joe and Carole that we were going back to the hotel. They told us they would come along in a few minutes.

Our route out of town followed the main road to the north, affording us views of the hills on either side of the valley, the late-afternoon sun gleaming on the slopes. The road then turned and entered a tunnel passing under another road. A couple of teenage boys, one carrying a soccer ball, were walking toward us at the other end, their voices magnified by the tunnel's acoustics. One was boasting about a goal he'd scored.

As the path left the tunnel, Fiona stopped, looking disoriented.

"Something wrong?" I asked.

"It's weird," she said. "But I think I just remembered something."

"You mean about your parents' accident?" Billie asked.

She rubbed her eyes. "Yes. I remember being in the back seat. I remember the rain and the lightning. And I remember seeing . . . a big blue face."

"A face?" I asked.

"Yes, a man's face. He was smiling and looking right at me from outside the car window."

"And he was blue? You mean the clothes he was wearing?"

Fiona forced her eyes closed. "No, his face was blue." After a moment, she opened her eyes. "Sorry, it's gone. The memory lasted just a second."

Brock and Jenna had caught up with us.

"Fiona remembered something," Billie told them.

"You did?" Brock said.

Fiona held up her hand. "It was nothing. Just a quick flash. Nothing important."

Brock looked as if he'd just won the lottery. "But it means that seeing the bridge did have an effect! Maybe it was just as C.W. said—maybe it takes a while. You need to concentrate, Fiona."

Fiona glared at him. "I'm tired of concentrating, Brock. Trust me, I'm not going to remember anything else." She walked off.

Brock was about to go after her, but Jenna took hold of his sleeve. "Let her go, honey. If she remembers, she remembers. There's no making Fiona do anything she doesn't want. You should know that by now."

He didn't look convinced.

Chapter 13

Tuesday Evening
Broadmoor Hall

Our arrival back at Broadmoor, its grandeur still startling amid the rustic beauty of the Lake District, should have been comforting after a good day's walk, but I was preoccupied with Fiona's revelation. What could explain her vision of a "blue man"? Was it just the product of dim threads of a childhood memory mixing with a storybook fantasy? That, along with Carole's claims about Fiona being a murderess, and the erratic behavior of the others, had me so muddled that I wanted nothing more than to retreat to my room, draw myself a hot bath, and call Mike.

Which is exactly what I did.

After immersing myself in the bathwater and closing my eyes for a few moments to let the warmth and fragrance soothe me, I punched in Mike's number on my cell phone. I set it on the table beside the bath so I wouldn't accidentally drop it in the water.

Mike answered instantly and seemed pleased to hear from me. I asked how he was progressing on the mysterious death he'd been investigating.

"Very nicely. I think we've gotten control of this thing. It appears to be some sort of ovine virus."

My ears perked up.

"Fortunately," he continued, "there's a precedent. A similar incident occurred about thirty years ago, and we've been able to apply many of the remedies that worked then. It's early days, but I think we've gotten a handle on it."

"Does that mean you can come up and join me?"

"Perhaps in the next day or two. I don't want to make any promises. This whole situation has been so vexing."

It was so like Mike to use a word like "vexing."

"But enough about me," he said. "How is your walk going? How many lakes have you seen? Getting along with the folks in your group?"

Oh, brother. Where do I begin? I wasn't up to going over the unfolding Upton drama in a phone conversation. Instead, I said, "It's been wonderful, of course. Lives up to its publicity. Have you ever traveled to this part of the country?"

"Sorry to say I haven't. It's always been one of those bucket-list items. If I don't make it this week, I'll get around to it someday. Would you mind doing an encore?"

"I'd love nothing more," I said, and paused. I'd used the word "love," and I wanted more than anything to use it again—in regard to my feelings about Mike. What was holding me back?

"I would love that, too," Mike said. "I want to be with you more than I can say."

That's what I wanted to hear. "I feel the same way. We need to make this work, Mike. I've been so frustrated only hearing your voice. I so wanted to be able to be with you . . . completely." I paused, then added, "I think I love you, Mr. Tibbets."

"Oh, Chase," Mike said, his voice lower, more earnest. "I love you, too. I thought I'd never find a man like you, and it's a blessing that I have."

Just like that, my world changed. I was no longer Doug's widower, that peculiar guy who takes long-distance walks, rattles off Red Sox statistics, and whistles Hank Williams tunes. I was again a man in love, with someone who cared just as much about me as I did about him.

Mike and I had already spent hours sharing our life stories. I'd told him about my years with Doug, and he told me about his few failed relationships, none lasting nearly as long as mine. He'd come out later in life than I had, yet still had to tread carefully around his homophobic siblings. As we move forward, there'd be those issues to contend with, as well as the big one of geographical distance. Yet love conquers all, isn't that what they say?

We promised to connect the following day. With a much lighter spirit, I dressed and hurried out in search of Billie, finding her at a small corner table in the bar, knitting something mauve, a half-full schooner of beer before her. I ordered my beer from the bar and joined her.

"I can't quite make out that pattern," I said, looking more closely at her knitting. "Not another pair of socks for me, I hope."

She gave me a grudging smile and held up her creation. The design seemed to be interlocking dollar and pound signs. "It's an affirmation that I'll get my investment money back."

"Couldn't hurt, I guess." I raised my glass. "In the meantime, we have something else to celebrate. Join me in a toast."

She raised hers and looked at me questioningly. "Celebrate what?"

"A new chapter in my life: Rick Chasen's Second Chance at Love." We clinked our glasses, and I told her about my conversation with Mike.

"How wonderful!" she said. "It's about time you found happiness again. But how are you going to resolve the problem of living on separate continents?"

"Hey! Don't rain on my parade. We'll work it out. One step at a time."

Brock and Jenna walked in, followed by Carole, Joe, and Pratt in his ten-gallon hat.

"We're going to that tavern in the village for dinner," Carole said. "Care to join us?"

I was on such an emotional high that even the prospect of subjecting myself to the possibility of another Upton outburst didn't faze me. Billie and I agreed to go along. When Joe and Parker arrived, I inquired about Fiona.

"Isn't she here?" Parker asked, looking around. "She'll probably be down any minute."

Sure enough, Fiona appeared, looking gorgeous as always in a modest blouse and slacks. She smiled, but it struck me as forced. She knew she was still under scrutiny to remember more about her parents' accident. I wondered if she'd told anyone else about the blue man.

We set out on the short walk into town. Charlie hadn't joined us; I assumed he'd had enough of the Uptons and was enjoying an evening alone with Ramses. The night was cool, bordering on cold. I wasn't wearing a coat and regretted it, but the walk was a brief one. Beside me, Billie was bundled up in one of her bulky sweaters.

As we walked, Brock started asking Fiona if any further memories had returned. At first, she didn't even dignify his questions with an answer. He persisted, and she swung on him.

"Lay off, Brock, will you? I told you. I'll let you know if I remember anything else."

Pratt stepped forward, took Fiona's arm, and turned to Brock. "Give her a break, will you, old man? What good is pestering her?"

I feared I was again going to have to break up a battle, but fortunately we'd reached the edge of the town, with other people on the street around us, and tempers calmed. In the nascent night, the village's tavern was clearly visible, the only establishment with lights ablaze.

The Royal Oak was one of those pubs trying to figure out its identity as the classic British institution struggled to rebrand itself in an age of gastropubs and takeovers by brewery conglomerates. This tavern's approach seemed to be to include entertainment in the form of a small band. A drum set and guitars were set up at the side of the main dining room, as was a small space for dancing.

No one seemed to be serving as host, so I asked at the bar if we could seat ourselves. The barman nodded his approval distractedly. Fortunately, there were only a few other diners there. I guided our group to a large table and explained we would need to order our drinks and food at the bar and collect our orders when announced; there didn't appear to be a waitstaff to do that. The evening's meal selections were displayed on a wall-mounted chalkboard: spiced lamb shank, mutton shepherd's pie, chestnut and mushroom soufflé, courgette fritters.

"Good gravy, more sheep!" Brock said. "What if I want a big juicy steak?"

"Then fly back to Lubbock," Carole said.

Billie offered to note everyone's meal and drink selections on her phone and relay them to the bar staff. Once they did, she dashed to the bar, and soon the barman brought the ales out.

Brock raised his glass. "Here's to more recovered memories!"

His toast didn't receive the enthusiastic response he was expecting, especially from Fiona. "Give it up, Brock," she said. "There won't be more."

After a pause, she added, "Except one."

He cocked his head. "You remembered something else?"

She gave him an icy stare. "Yep, I remembered. What you used to do to me when I was a little girl. I remember that really, really good."

A hush fell over the table. An attractive young black woman

appeared, tying a serving apron. "Running late tonight, so sorry. Have you ordered? Good. I'll bring out your starters." She disappeared and returned with small plates, mostly the sweet-corn-pancetta salad, and began distributing them.

There was little conversation in the wake of Fiona's remark other than making comments of approval about the food. At least it gave Brock and Fiona something else to do with their mouths than argue. I didn't know how much more of their rancor I could take.

"This isn't the usual bunch you get on these walks, is it?" asked Joe, seated to my right. He kept his voice low.

"Not quite," I said, also in an undertone. "Of course, there's always the odd loose screw, but nothing like this. It's stopped being fun. I'm considering bailing on the whole thing."

"I hear you, buddy. I'd do it myself but . . . there's a little lady over there who is making up for all the bad feelings."

I was glad that Joe and Carole were finding comfort in one another, but to my mind, she was as much a contributor to the "bad feelings" as the others.

The server brought out our main courses, which also received approving murmurs. The sudden crash of a plate on the floor caught everyone's attention. Everyone's eyes turned to Parker, who had sprung to his feet. Shepherd's pie was dripping down the front of his pants.

"Way to go, pea brain," Brock called out. "You're supposed to eat your dinner, not wear it."

"It was just an accident, Brock," Fiona said.

"He doesn't care," Parker snapped. "He's a lost sock."

"You can't even talk normal," Brock said. "What a loser!"

Parker picked up his dinner plate and flung it across the table at Brock, who managed to duck as it whizzed past his head and broke into pieces against the wall.

I went to Parker and placed my hand on his shoulder. "You'd better go outside to cool off," I said.

Parker stood in place, breathing heavily. His jaws were clenched, his face crimson. He shook off my hand, reached for his backpack, and stormed off to the back of the pub.

I had a good idea what he was planning to do.

Jenna rose as if nothing had happened and scooted back her chair. "I need to visit the ladies," she said and left as well.

"I need another beer," Fiona announced and walked to the bar.

The rest of us focused on finishing our meals as a young man came to clean up Parker's plate. Four other young men—two looking just shy of fifteen—took the stage and picked up guitars. After some tuning up, they launched into a rowdy version of Shania Twain's "She's Not Just a Pretty Face."

Fiona returned with her beer, most of which she'd already drank. After another gulp, she said, "This is one of my favorite beers so far! It makes me want to act a little wild!"

She set her glass on the table, grabbed my hand, and pulled me onto the small dance floor. Despite being a bit sloshed, she began to execute a respectable Texas two-step, bringing back old memories of many nights I spent at a gay country-and-western bar in Alameda on the San Francisco Bay. Two other couples joined us on the floor, but as Fiona started to make broader steps, they backed off to give us room. Fiona hooted and laughed, surprised as much as me at my dexterity as I matched her step for step.

Just as we were getting into the groove, Brock came over and tapped me on the shoulder. "Mind if the big brother cuts in?"

Fiona's smile vanished as Brock took my place. I turned to go back to my seat when Pratt stepped up, grabbed my hand, and said, "Keep dancing!" He curled his other arm around my waist, and we began shuffling alongside Brock and Fiona as the crowd in the tavern yelled and clapped.

"You're the first dude I ever danced with," Pratt said over the music. "How do you decide who leads?"

"Whoever wants to," I said.

He spun me around, dipped me, and we executed a showy step-walk across the floor. The band finished the song with a flourish, and Pratt and I gave a bow to a chorus of cheers. When the band began its next number, Pratt was game for more dancing, but I held up my hand. He was a good twenty years younger, and those years make a big difference when it comes to stamina. I thanked him and went to join Billie back at the table.

"Pretty fancy moves, Chase!" she said. "Your hidden talents never cease to amaze me."

"If they play a slow number, what do you say we cut a rug together?"

She laughed. "I hate to break it to you, but nobody's said 'cut a rug' for seventy years. Not even me. But that's beside the point. This band probably doesn't know any slow songs."

Fiona was still allowing Brock to lead her around, but I could tell from her expression that her patience was wearing thin. Finally, she pushed him away, shouting something we couldn't hear over the music. When he went to grasp her again, she flat out slapped him and marched off the floor and toward the bar.

Pratt came over to Billie and me. "Have you seen Parker?"

"Still in the men's room, I think," I said, getting to my feet. "I'll go check on him."

"I'm going with you," he said. We headed to the back, where doors were marked GENTS and LADIES. The GENTS door was locked.

"Park? You in there?" Pratt called. He pounded on the door, but got no response.

Something was wrong. "We need to break in," I said. Pratt nodded grimly. On a count of three, we rammed the door open. Parker was on the floor beside the toilet, his eyes shut, a syringe clutched in his hand. Pratt knelt to lift his head, and

I picked up a small vial at his side labeled BETAMORPH—
morphine.

Pratt lightly slapped his brother's cheeks, and Parker's eye-
lids fluttered open, dazed and large-pupiled.

"Can you stand?" Pratt asked. He managed to pull Parker
to his feet.

I held out the vial to Pratt. "Did you know about this?"

He nodded. "Park needs it to manage his panic attacks. He's
usually good about not going too far with it, but . . ."

"Morphine is too serious a drug to use casually," I said. "I
can't believe there's a doctor who permits him to do this."

Pratt began to slowly lead his brother out of the restroom.
"You don't understand Parker. I'll take him back to the hotel."

As they walked off, I took a deep breath. The dancing had
been fun, and I still had a residual high from my discussion
with Mike, but this latest episode left a bad taste in my mouth.
I might not have understood what Parker went through in
Afghanistan, but I was fairly certain his problems—and those
of his family—stretched back further than that. Increasingly,
the parents (as is often the case) looked to have been a toxic influence on their children. Bridge accident or not, it was probably a good thing they were no longer in the picture.

When I returned to the dining room, most of our group had
dispersed. Fiona was drinking alone at one end of the bar, and
Joe and Carole were nuzzling each other not far away. Brock
sat alone at the table, apparently waiting for Jenna. Billie was at
the other end.

I walked to her. "Let's call it a night."

She smiled and stood. "Another of your great ideas."

We said goodbye to Brock and went out onto the street. The
night air felt icy after the warmth of the tavern. I'd shared
with her the condition Parker was in when Pratt and I encountered him.

"So he has a drug problem," Billie said. "That explains
a lot."

"Yes and no. It might have something to with what happened to him in Afghanistan."

We walked past the fortune teller's shop, a light shining within. "Listen," I continued. "I don't know about you, but putting up with this group isn't what I had envisioned for this week."

"Me neither."

"I'm going to call it quits and head down to Devon tomorrow to be with Mike. Would you be okay with that?"

"Call it quits? I thought you wanted to figure out the puzzle that is the Uptons."

"That was more or less resolved at Ennerdale Bridge. There are a few other unanswered questions, but not enough to keep me here."

Billie thought this over as we walked. "I'm not sure I'm ready to give up quite yet. I paid for a walk in the Lake District, and that's what I plan to get. But let me sleep on it. I might feel different in the morning. You may too, for that matter."

"I doubt it."

Despite the late hour, a big truck was heading up the road toward us. Large block letters on its side proclaimed HENNESSEY'S MEAT & POULTRY PURVEYORS. Above those words was an image of the large smiling face of a grandfatherly man.

It was entirely in blue.

Well, that certainly brought an interesting complication into the equation. Maybe I wouldn't be calling it quits on this walk after all.

When I called Mike later that night, I told him about spotting the truck and how that might have something to do with the "blue man" Fiona saw on the night of her parents' accident. It was an intriguing point to explore. Nevertheless, I confessed being torn about staying on the walk.

He chuckled. "Chase, I know you well enough by now to

understand that you don't give up when you're faced with a puzzle. And as barmy as this Texas family sounds, there's a puzzle there. If you throw in the towel now, you'll never forgive yourself."

I could credit Mike with being perceptive, but Billie had said the same thing. If I gave up now, I would have another unresolved riddle rattling around the back of my mind, and there were enough of those as it was.

So I decided to hold off, at least for another day. The next twenty-four hours promised to be interesting, at least.

Chapter 14

Wednesday Morning
Broadmoor Hall

At breakfast the next morning, I got Brock aside and told him about the blue face on the meat truck. He lit up as if he'd just won the lottery.

"See? I knew my old man didn't drive off that bridge! Some fool of a truck driver forced him off."

"Let's not be too hasty," I cautioned. "Just because Fiona remembered that truck doesn't mean it has anything to do with the accident."

"Why else would she remember it? That truck must have been mighty close to my daddy's car for her to remember it, which means that it was too close."

He did have a point. But convincing as it was, the image on the truck was still circumstantial evidence, and not even that. It was evidence based on a long-distant memory.

"We need to go and speak with that meat outfit," Brock said. "They're hiding something, I know they are."

"It's been what, twenty years? Do you think they still have records from back then?"

Brock stabbed a breakfast sausage with his fork. "It's worth a try."

Billie walked in, clad in a lightly knit sweater of greens and yellows in which I detected a subtle pattern of birds.

"They're finches," she said when she noticed my scrutiny.

"Don't let Joe see you," I said. "He'll start photographing you."

She laughed and crossed over to the buffet. "You still planning on quitting the walk?" she asked as he spooned fruit onto her plate.

"I'm reconsidering," I said. "How about you?"

"Like I said, where am I going to go? This walk is already paid for, and given my financial situation, I might as well enjoy it while I can. Also, I don't have a lover to run off to like you do. No, I'm going to stick it out."

Something in me bristled at hearing Billie refer to Mike as my "lover." That term always sounded demeaning, something more physical than emotional. But what other word could she use? "Boyfriend" sounded even worse. I went to help myself to another serving of eggs when Fiona appeared, slack-faced, her eyes slightly glazed.

"How are you feeling this morning?" I asked.

"Don't ask," she said, looking at the buffet as if it was an array of alien food she'd never seen before. "I'm sorry I ever agreed to come over here."

I took her arm and gently led her aside. "Let me give you some advice. You're in one of the most beautiful places in the world. Forget about your family and all their demands. Focus on the beautiful countryside you're seeing when you're on the trail. Concentrate on your breathing, the rhythm in your arms and legs and hands. Take a deep look at each hill and valley, each lake and stream. You have a once-in-a-lifetime opportunity to learn from the world rather than be defeated by it. Take it from me, it will be worth it."

As I spoke, I realized I could benefit from my advice also.

Fiona's eyes sparked with renewed awareness. "You're right,

Chase. I don't know why I let myself become such an idiot. That's what Brock does to me."

"Families are strange things. One minute you can't live without them, the next you want them a million miles away."

She gave a small laugh. "That's truer than you know. We look like a loving family at times, but it can fool you. Let me tell you something. If the others had a chance, they'd do away with me in a hot minute. Trust me. Each and every one of them wants to see me dead."

That was quite a statement, and not one I was expecting. "That can't possibly be true," I said.

Fiona took a deep breath. "Well, the hell with them all. You're right—I'm going to enjoy myself."

I resisted giving her another piece of advice—lay off the liquor. She clearly had a short fuse with the stuff.

I loaded my plate again and returned to my table, where Jenna and Brock had joined us. Jenna was perusing the local paper, most likely looking for her horoscope, and Brock was buttering his toast as if it was a task beneath him.

"I may bow out of the walk today," Brock said. "I want to speak to that meat company."

Jenna turned toward him. "No, please don't do that. The stars clearly advise . . . what is it they say?" She thumbed through the newspaper. "Here it is. Cancer. They say that you need to 'adhere to your plans, or disappointment will result.' "

"Honey, you know how I feel about that bull pucky."

"Do it for me, please? Domingo texted our charts this morning, and they mostly say the same thing."

The previous day, I'd have bet money that Brock held the upper hand in that relationship, but Jenna knew her power. Brock melted. "All right," he said. "I'll go on the walk, but I still want to visit that meat outfit."

* * *

When we left Broadmoor, the sky was gray, but Charlie said no rain was in the forecast for the rest of the day. On the way to Ennerdale Water, however, the driver turned on the wipers as drops began to fall, softly at first, then harder. Carole and Pratt questioned whether the walk was still on.

Charlie laughed. "Cancel the walk because of rain? If I did that, I'd never lead another walk again. This is England, you know."

Billie said to Carole, "As long as you're wearing the right gear, you'll be fine."

We all affirmed we'd brought waterproof jackets.

When we arrived at the lake's south shore, the rain had lessened, but the lack of sun had turned the lake surface glassy, giving it an ethereal, almost sacred quality. As we donned our jackets, Charlie told us we would be walking along the lake's south shore, passing over Anglers Crag on our way to the Ennerdale youth hostel, where we would have lunch.

Once we were on the trail, my concerns of the night before slowly melted. The rain was steady, but not heavy enough to make walking uncomfortable, nor to make the path muddy (it was mostly stone and gravel anyway). The path undulated, up and down, over small rises. The lake, its serene surface unbroken by boats or birds, was always visible to our left. It was a somber morning, but glorious.

The rain finally stopped, and soon we reached Anglers Crag, a high, steep slope bordering the lake. The trail wound around its base, becoming uneven and precarious, with a sharp drop to our left. Charlie advised us to use caution, noting that a woman had fallen to her death there a few years before. "But you should have no problems if you play it safe," he added.

Even with his warning, a couple of us slipped as we navigated around the crag. We made it through, only to encounter another challenging stretch of rocky ledges known as Robin Hood's Chair. They required strenuous climbing, straining my calf muscles. Most of us had to pause occasionally to recover our strength. Despite the climb, everyone appeared to be doing well, proceeding steadily, if not quickly, forward—until Brock froze and dropped to his knees.

Parker and I went and knelt beside him. Brock's face was flushed, and he was out of breath.

"My heart pills," he managed to mumble.

A few feet away, Jenna said, "Here!" and tossed us a bottle. Parker caught it, opened Brock's palm, and tapped out several pills. I opened Brock's water bottle and gave it to him. He scooped the pills from Parker's hand and was about to swallow them but paused, his eyes wide.

"I can't take all of these!" he said, glaring up at Parker. "What are you trying to do, kill me?"

If those were nitroglycerin pills, Brock was right—taking too many could be fatal. Parker mumbled an apology as Brock pinched up one pill, put it in his mouth, and took a gulp of water. Fortunately, he was too compromised to start another big fight.

Charlie joined us. "You going to be all right?" he asked Brock.

Brock took another sip of water and nodded. Parker helped him get to his feet. Brock's color looked better; the pill (whatever it was) had done quick work. "I'll be fine now," he said.

Charlie eyed him doubtfully. "Fortunately, we're through the rough spots. However, because of this morning's rain, the next stretch might be a bit muddy in places. If you can make it through that and to the hostel, we'll reassess. Sound good?"

Brock nodded. He walked over to Jenna as Charlie again led us forward.

Parker looked at me, distraught. "I didn't want to hurt him. I didn't know I was giving him too many pills."

"Don't worry about it," I said. "It all happened so fast, it was easy to make a mistake."

My intent was to reassure him, but I didn't entirely buy his explanation. From what I'd seen, Parker had every reason to detest Brock. What could be more convenient than slipping him an overdose of heart pills and then claim confused innocence?

The next section of the path was known as The Side, as it ran alongside the lake, with a mossy forest to our right, riven with small streams. Once we made it through, we stopped to rest by a small stone bridge and dipped into Charlie's trail mix.

Billie looked out over the water and back to me. "Is this what you expected from a Lake District walk?"

"The scenery, yes," I said. "The company, no."

"Do you think we'll ever walk with regular folks again?"

I laughed. " 'Regular folks'? Is there really such a thing?"

After our rest, we continued along the path as it traversed a broad meadow and eventually reached a small group of thatch-roofed buildings, one of which was the hostel at which we were to eat lunch. We grabbed our small lunch bags from a table inside and sat on benches in the sheltered courtyard. The food turned out to be a modest offering of an apple, crisps (potato chips to us Yanks), and a bun encasing two strips of ham and a slice of cheese. Scarcely a feast, but it was filling.

Charlie checked in with Brock, who'd recovered from his health scare but still didn't seem in top form.

"Would you like to return to the hotel, Mr. Upton?" he asked. "The van can take you and come back for us when we've finished walking."

Brock looked at Jenna, who nodded. He turned to Charlie and said, "I sure would."

"No worries," Charlie responded. "Not unusual."

I knew from my own experience that senior walkers often couldn't maintain the pace of the younger ones and frequently needed to forego some of the more challenging stretches of trail. It hit me that I could be considered a "senior walker" as well. Of course, I wasn't as energetic or spry as I was when I was twenty, but I prided myself that I could hold my own with the rest of them.

Pratt finished his lunch and pulled out his phone, stepping aside to make a call. He was anxious, I knew, about the status of his questionable "investment." The more I learned of it—an investment stream that required more and more people willing to invest—the more it seemed like a Ponzi scheme intended to bilk its investors. As he spoke, I watched the changes to his expression—concern, astonishment, fury. He flung his phone to the ground and let out an inarticulate scream.

Fiona rushed to him. "Pratt, what's wrong? What is it?"

"Would you believe it?" he said. "Kurt, the guy I'd trusted with all my money, has flown the coop! He's gone! Do you know what this means? I'm dead! I've borrowed a ton of money and can't pay it back!"

Fiona tried to reason. "But he can't do that, can he? Why don't you call the police?"

He gave her a withering look. "I'm not the only one, okay? There are a lot of us, and we've all been swindled. The other guys are scrambling around, calling everyone they can, but Kurt is probably in Paraguay by now. He knew exactly what he was doing."

Billie couldn't help hearing their discussion. She turned to me and said, "Sounds a lot like my situation, doesn't it?"

I turned to her. "You think your investment advisor is in Paraguay with Kurt?"

"Who knows where Marie is? Paraguay is as likely a place as any other."

If I were an investment swindler, my place of refuge would be somewhere like Biarritz or Lake Como—not Paraguay, for God's sake. I pictured banana plantations riddled with goats and pigs, but maybe I was being unfair; I'd never been there.

Fiona wasn't having much success calming down Pratt. She

put her hand on his shoulder, and he shook it off. "First a bird craps on me, then I discover I've lost all my money!" he moaned.

"I'm sure you'll find a way out of this," she said.

"If you're so concerned, why don't you give me some of your money?" Pratt said. "You're rolling in it!"

"I already explained that I haven't seen any of Steve's money yet. It's tied up in paperwork."

His look into her eyes hardened. "You could get it if you wanted to."

"No, I really can't."

"Big load of help then, aren't you? My caring sister! You couldn't even remember what happened to my dad's gold necklace!" He stormed off to get his lunch.

Fiona shook her head slowly, watching him go. She turned to me and said, "I've never seen Pratt like this. Why does money screw everything up?"

I gave her what I hoped was a comforting smile. "It's not so much money. It's how people misuse it."

After a few minutes, Pratt reappeared, looking more composed. Had he indulged in his own secret stash of drugs? He didn't look high, or even happy, but he wasn't wild-eyed with fury anymore either.

Brock boarded the van to go back to Broadmoor Hall. Jenna offered to accompany him, but he insisted that she stay with us. We were eager to resume the day's walk—even Pratt, who needed to burn off his anger. My goal was just as basic: I wanted to get through the afternoon and retreat to my room for another soothing bath to handle the absence of Mike.

We geared up and began a push along a lengthy track through a forest plantation. It was mostly an easy amble. At one point, we encountered a flaming heap of rubbish in a small bin beside the path. Charlie said it would burn itself out eventually, but Parker picked up a discarded can and collected water from the nearby stream to extinguish the flames. I was glad at his quick response (a breeze could easily have spread the fire to nearby trees) but also puzzled by it.

"Good job," I said to Parker as we started forward again.

"Fire is the devil's only friend," he replied. Wasn't that a song lyric? As with many of his comments, it could have meant nothing, or it might connect to something in his past. Was he remembering what he'd seen in Afghanistan?

Charlie stopped us for a midafternoon break. It was hard to believe we'd been walking for more than two and a half hours since lunch. I'd been able to shift into a more contemplative mental zone, and those often played tricks with time. Given that our midday meal had been spartan, we all were ready for a midafternoon snack.

We found a grassy spot and sat to relax as Charlie handed out plastic-wrapped tea cakes, which we accepted gratefully, along with small bottles of purified water. He set a small bowl down for Ramses. Although not in top spirits, the Uptons ate quietly. Pratt looked disconsolate. He stared down at his tea cake as if it was a strange fungus that had somehow crawled onto his hand.

"It'll make you feel better if you eat," Billie said to him.

He grunted. "I don't have an appetite. Being stone broke can do that to you."

"Well, as they say, it's only money. A trusted friend cleaned me out too, so I'm sort of in the same boat as you."

Pratt took a swig from his water bottle. "What are you going to do about it?"

Billie shrugged. "Haven't figured it out yet. But I'm not going to worry myself to death. Money is important, sure, but as Dorothy Parker said, 'If you want to know what God thinks of money, just look at the people he gives it to.'"

This got a laugh out of Pratt. "I don't know who this Dorothy person is, but she isn't half wrong."

After our snack, we geared up and went back on the trail, which remained mostly level as it continued east and, after passing through a few gates, brought us to a river. We walked along the riverside, and after a mile or so, Charlie halted us, pointing to a tree off to his left. "That's an English yew. A beautiful tree, but deadly. At this time of year, it produces its bright red berries. Whatever you do, don't eat them or go anywhere near them. They're fatal."

"Yipes!" Billie said. "There seem to be poisonous plants lurking all around us. I'm surprised we don't find dead bodies strewn out all along the trail."

I wondered why Charlie was taking such care in pointing out dangerous berries and fruits. It wasn't as if our group had been sampling every one that came our way. Perhaps he didn't want to complicate matters further with the Uptons.

After passing through another tree plantation, we came to a fork in the path; one choice led to the east, and the other to the north. Charlie nodded toward that one and said, "This trail leads up to Haystacks, Alfred Wainwright's favorite peak."

"Are we going up there?" Pratt asked.

Charlie chuckled. "I'm afraid not. It's quite demanding. Wainwright himself said the walk is for only 'the very strong and experienced.' It crosses a number of summits—Red Pike, High Stile, and Haystacks. I've tackled it a few times with Ramses, but it's not something to undertake lightly. It's the descents that kill you. They're murder on your knees."

"I'd like to try it," Pratt said.

"Are you nuts, Pratt?" Fiona said. "Why knock yourself out?"

Pratt asked Charlie, "Does the trail connect back with the one you guys will be on?"

Charlie looked at Pratt with concern. "Well, yes. It joins our trail not far ahead, right before Black Sail, near the end of this afternoon's walk. But it's a much longer trail than the one we'll be taking. You seem fit, but that walk will take you a good hour or two longer, and it will be much more challenging. As I mentioned, it's not a trek to be undertaken lightly. And not alone, either."

Pratt eyed the trail, weighing his decision. "Someone just robbed me blind, and I need to get my mind off of it. I'm in good shape. Is there any chance I can get lost?"

"There's always a chance," Charlie said. "But that trail is easy to follow. Still, I caution against it. It might be more difficult than you realize."

Pratt smiled defiantly. "The harder the better, that's what I say."

Parker stepped forward. "I'm coming too."

"No, Park," Pratt said. "You're not used to this kind of hiking. I'm in much better shape than you."

"I'm in shape," Parker said. He was right; the two looked similarly fit to me.

"I said no," Pratt replied firmly. "I don't want to worry about you the whole time. That would take all the fun out of it."

"He's right, Scoot," Fiona said. "It's best you stay with us."

Parker looked disappointed but joined us back in the pack.

Charlie walked up to Pratt. "Here's what I would suggest. Take Ramses with you. He knows the path better than most hikers. He'll make sure you don't go wrong."

Pratt looked down at Ramses, who seemed to be smiling up at him, his long tongue hanging from the side of his mouth. "No offense, Charlie, but I'm not your dog sitter. I want to be on my own."

"I'm afraid I must insist." Charlie crouched down and looked Ramses in the eye. "I want you to go with Mr. Upton, all right? Keep your eye on him and keep him moving forward. We'll meet up with you at Black Sail. Okay, boy?"

I have tremendous respect for dogs, but it was hard for me to believe Ramses understood any of that. However, he gave a small "Woof!" that could be construed, I suppose, as a sign of agreement.

Charlie made sure Pratt had plenty of water and told him to

give some to Ramses now and then. "My strongest advice is don't push yourself. If you feel fatigued, stop and rest."

"I have my phone," Pratt said. "If I feel dizzy or anything, I'll give you a call. You can send in the Mounties or something, can't you?"

"Yes, but phone service often isn't strong on the peaks. If you get into trouble, Ramses will come find us."

Pratt tightened up his pack, looked down at Ramses, then turned and surveyed the path before him. He shouted, "Kowabunga!" and the two headed off.

Chapter 15

Wednesday Afternoon
Black Sail

Once Pratt left, our own path became straight, level . . . and, to be perfectly honest, tedious. It continued through the forest plantation, the river delivering a soothing rush beside us, but as a country trail, it offered little variation. I found myself wondering about Pratt. From what I'd observed, it was in character for him to attempt something gutsy, but perhaps not wise, given his low spirits.

Billie saw I was lost in thought. "Maybe you should take up birding, Chase. You've done nothing but stare at your boots for the past ten minutes."

She was right. Despite the monotony of the path, I looked up to see many one-of-a-kind views. Off to our left rose the imposing summit of Haystacks and the other peaks that Pratt was no doubt scaling at that very moment. I should be looking at them, not my boots.

"Thinking about Mike?" Billie asked.

"I'm ashamed to say that I wasn't. I was wondering about Pratt."

"What's to wonder about? He probably just wanted to get away from his family. Can't say I blame him."

I looked around. We were far enough from the others that there was little chance they'd hear us. "Something about it just doesn't seem right," I said.

"Well, to paraphrase Dr. Seuss, 'He's got brains in his head, he's got feet in his shoes, he can steer himself in any direction he choose . . . es.'"

Billie is an inveterate Seuss fan. "Does the doctor have any pithy saying that applies to me?" I asked.

"Let me think." After a moment, she said, "'You're off to great places! Today is your day! Your mountain is waiting, so . . . get on your way!'"

That made me laugh. "Very wise."

We continued on, and I began whistling a familiar song, timed to the rhythm of my stride.

"I know that one," Parker said from behind me. I hadn't realized he'd gotten close.

"It's 'Move It On Over,'" I said. "Hank Williams."

"Dad liked him. 'Attitude Adjustment.'"

"That's a song by his son, Hank Williams Jr. He was a good singer, but he couldn't hold a candle to his old man, who wrote most of his own songs. Unfortunately, most of them were about heartbreak and despair."

"I'm like that," Parker said. "I can't hold candles."

I wished I had a decoder ring to make sense of Parker's statements.

"Brock thinks I'm not like my dad," he said. "Of course I'm not. He's dead."

Brock's intended meaning, no doubt, was that he thought Parker wasn't as smart as his father. Yet Parker's self-esteem issues weren't exactly the stuff of on-the-trail banter. I was debating how to respond when we started off again.

The trail became so narrow we needed to walk in single file. Soon we began climbing a series of steep stone steps. It was a good thing, I reasoned, that Brock had decided to forego this afternoon's leg. When we reached the crest of the hill (which Charlie informed us was named Boggy Saddle), we encountered another confusing junction. Again, the most logical trail seemed to be one continuing in the direction we were heading, but a way marker directed us to turn right into a more eastward trail. Charlie led us in that direction, and soon a rock cairn appeared, signaling that it was the right choice.

The seven of us proceeded along the top of a ridge, with views of Buttermere Lake to the northwest. The sky had mostly cleared, and the sun was bathing the lake and the surrounding hills and fells in a golden, late-afternoon glow. We passed further junctions that fortunately were clearly waymarked to keep us on the right path. After another short climb, we reached a summit called Grey Knotts and stopped to rest.

"I'd never imagined this area could be so beautiful," Fiona said as she gazed out on the panorama before us. "When I was here as a little girl, we never did any hiking. If we only knew what we were missing!"

Charlie pulled a small, worn paperback book from his rucksack.

"What a perfect lead-in you've provided, my dear. Let me share Alfred Wainwright's own words about what we're all, I trust, experiencing."

Charlie proceeded to read a passage from Wainwright's autobiography, *Fellwanderer*, in which he chronicles the exuberance he felt exploring his beloved Lake District. I was struck by Wainwright's assertion that no man could ever sit alone atop one of the region's hills and contemplate planning terrible things like a murder or a robbery. Looking around at the attentive faces of my fellow walkers as they listened, I could almost believe he was right.

Charlie gently closed the book and let us spend a few moments reflecting on those words. It was very inspiring, yet I wondered why Wainwright had slipped in a mention of murder. Had he encountered such a thing in his travels?

It was with renewed dedication that the group began walking again. Soon we passed an old iron gate, with another trail forking off to the left beyond it.

"That's the trail Pratt took, isn't it?" I asked Charlie. "This is where it comes back to join this one?"

"That it is," he acknowledged. "But don't expect him to be coming along anytime soon. His trail is more than twice as long as ours, plus it traverses three peaks. Depending on how fit he is, he might be on it for another hour or so."

"I'll call him," Fiona said and pulled out her phone. She punched in his number and held the phone to her ear but quickly shut it off. "No coverage. Which means if he's in trouble, he can't call us either."

"Give him time," Charlie said. "Let's wait until we reach Honiston House. We can decide what to do there."

We started off again, and I became instantly befuddled. Charlie was leading us into a thin, almost undetectable path to the east rather than along the much wider, clearer path to the southeast. All logic dictated that we follow that one.

"Trust me, this is the correct path," he called out, as if reading my thoughts. "Most people think they should take the broader one, and they end up completely lost. I keep saying somebody should put up a sign. I'm afraid it will have to be me."

I would have taken that other trail as well, sign or no sign. Chalk up another point for the benefit of having a guide.

"Shouldn't one of us stay here and make sure Pratt takes the correct path?" I asked Charlie.

He paused and gave this consideration. "Ramses will know the way, but you're right, Chase. Pratt might want to override him."

"I'll stay here and wait," Parker offered.

"Are you sure, Scoot?" Fiona asked, looking as concerned as me. I was more nervous about leaving Parker alone than I was about Pratt getting misdirected.

"I want to help," Parker said.

"Very well," Charlie said and faced Parker. "When your brother arrives, just proceed along this path"—he motioned in the direction we were heading—"and you should have no problems reaching Honiston. There will be plenty of way markers, and Ramses knows the way."

Parker nodded. After making sure he had plenty of water and a cell phone, we continued on the trail. Even though it had widened so we could walk two or three abreast, everyone was still under the spell of Wainwright's words and didn't speak. As we headed down, we spotted the open pit of a disused quarry. As we reached a valley floor, the trail swung abruptly at a right angle.

"This is what Wainwright called the 'straightest mile in Lakeland,'" Charlie informed us. "At the end, we'll arrive at the Honister Slate Mine, where our van will be awaiting us."

We walked past the quarry, and I heard the distant, familiar refrain from the day before.

Val-de-ri, val-de-ra, val-de-ri, val-de-ra-ha-ha-ha

"Good grief!" Billie said. "Don't tell me that bunch is back."

Sure enough, the same group of blond-haired youths from the day before came striding enthusiastically toward us, smiling widely in greeting as they sang.

> *Oh, may I go a-wandering*
> *Until the day I die!*
> *Oh, may I always laugh and sing,*
> *Beneath God's clear blue sky!*

We moved to the side of the trail to let them pass. Once they were out of earshot, Fiona asked, "Who the heck are they? They look too old to be scouts."

"They seem to be some type of Alpine walking group," Charlie said as we began walking again. "You meet all sorts on this path. It's world famous, you know."

Fiona laughed. "You're right about that! Who would expect to find a gal from El Paso over here?"

After twenty minutes, we reached Honiston House, the modest youth hostel with the yellow van we'd ridden in earlier in front.

"Are we going to wait here for Parker and Pratt?" Fiona asked.

"I'll ask the van driver to come back and collect them," Charlie said. "You lot might as well relax at the hotel rather than here."

"I'm not sure how much 'relaxing' I'll be doing," Carole said. "I'm worried about Pratt. We should never have let him go off on his own."

"He has the dog with him," Joe said. "And the weather is good. He's got water, and he's a fit guy. He'll be okay."

The rest of us agreed that there wasn't need to worry. We climbed into the van, which promptly delivered us to the hotel, but Charlie instructed the driver to drop us off at the main drive entrance rather than at the front portico. That allowed us an opportunity to view the hotel's famed topiary gardens, which were bathed in the rays of the late-afternoon sun.

We followed a winding path that, after passing through conventional flower gardens, led us to an other-worldly tableau: dozens of figures—peacocks, foxes and hounds, witches and ogres—carefully crafted from hedges, trees, and other foliage. Jenna began sneezing. "My dag-blasted allergy again!" she said as she rummaged in her pack for some pills.

"Check this one out!" Carole said, stopping before a tall shrub that had been cut in the image of a tall, severe-looking man. "Looks just like Brock!"

Jenna was having trouble twisting the lid off her allergy-pill bottle. "I won't tell him you said that, C.W."

We continued through and came upon an older man standing in the middle of the path, dressed in worn work clothes, looking down at two dead birds, black with deep blue necks, on the gravel path.

Noticing our curiosity, he said, "Grackles."

"What happened to them?" Fiona asked.

"I killed 'em, that's what. They feast on my raspberries and blueberries." He nodded toward a plot of the berry plants a few feet away. "Mind that you don't sample any yourselves—I put poison on a few sprigs but didn't mark 'em."

Carole gaped at him. "You mean to tell us that you use poison around here?"

The groundskeeper chuckled. "No need to worry yourself about it, miss. Just don't eat the fruit on the ground and you'll be fine."

"We have problems with birds all the time on our ranch," Jenna said.

"Boy, do you ever!" Carole said. "They're always tearing up your vegetable garden." She turned to the groundskeeper. "Do you use a spray? A powder?"

The man smiled. "Come with me, and I'll show you."

He led us to a weathered, barnlike building and into a large room filled with pots, bags of compost, tools hanging from pegs on the walls, and an array of bottles and cans lining the shelves. It was like a cavernous potting shed, smelling of peat and dirt. The groundskeeper reached to the shelf and picked up a bottle filled with a pale red liquid.

"This is the one I use on the grackles," he said. "I apply it to the berry bush with a damp cloth."

"Does that get rid of them?" Carole asked the grounds-keeper.

"Mostly it just makes the blasted birds sick, but some of them die. Either way, they never bother me again."

"That's awful," Joe said.

"Aye, but it's either them or my berries."

"There must be other ways of discouraging these beautiful creatures besides poisoning them," Joe said.

The groundskeeper put the bottle back on the shelf. "You may think they're beautiful, but to me they're a right nuisance."

"We just spray the birdbath back home," Jenna said, wrestling to open her allergy-pill bottle. "Damn! The bottle top fell on the floor."

She started looking around for it, but Fiona said, "You can come back and search for that later, Jenna. I want to get away from the poisons. Let's get to the hotel and see if Parker and Pratt are there yet."

As we walked outside, my cell phone buzzed. It was Mike. I excused myself from the others and walked off to answer it, my heartbeat speeding up.

"How's everything going?" I asked.

"Good news!" he said with buoyant energy in his voice. "We've finally brought our little crisis to a close. It looks like I'll be able to join you tomorrow."

A warm rush came over me. "That's wonderful! Be sure to bring your walking boots. I'll inform the group that you'll be joining us."

"I'll be driving up," he said. "Expect me sometime in mid-afternoon."

I made sure he had the correct directions and told him not to be discouraged if we hadn't returned from the day's walk by the time he arrived.

It was with a lighter step that I started heading for the hotel.

I spotted Joe ahead in the distance, holding up his field glasses. I paused, not wanting to frighten off any rare bird he might be tracking. After he snapped a couple of photos with his camera, I expected him to walk off toward the hotel as well, but he went in the opposite direction.

I found Billie and the others in the hotel bar and told them that I'd seen Joe out on the lookout for birds.

"He's so cute with that bird stuff," Carole said.

"I wish I had a hobby like that," Fiona said. "It would take my mind off Pratt."

"Don't worry about him," Billie said. "I'm sure he'll show up any minute."

"I wish I had your confidence. Pratt can get so sure of himself, and then everything goes haywire. Just like with that sure-thing investment of his."

"Why don't you call him?" Carole suggested. "His phone may be working now."

"Good idea," Fiona said and stepped away to make the call. A minute later, she returned, looking more discouraged than before. "I couldn't get an answer from either of them, Pratt or Parker. I'm really worried now."

"Maybe we can get a taxi to take us back to where the trails meet," Billie suggested.

"I'll go see if the front desk can get us one," I offered.

"It's too late," Jenna said, in that ominously confident tone she assumed when sharing signs of disaster. "It's too late, I'm sure of it."

"Please, Jenna," Fiona said. "That's not helping."

The man at the front desk called for a taxi, and the four of us—Carole, Fiona, Billie, and I—went to wait for it. Charlie came from around the corner, surprised to see us assembled there.

"We're worried about Pratt," Carole said. "A taxi's coming to take us back to where those two trails come together. Maybe we can find out what's happened to him."

Charlie shook his head. "Ramses will take care of him, don't you worry."

"I love your dog, Charlie, but maybe he's in trouble, too!" Fiona wailed.

"You need to calm down, honey," Carole said.

"Don't you tell me what I need to do!" Fiona yelled.

I was about to tell them both to quiet down when a louder voice rang out. "Why the hell are you all so worked up?"

We turned to see Pratt seated on a small bench beside the hotel's front door, a cocky grin on his face and his long legs crossed in front of him. A few feet away lay Ramses, clearly tired, his eyes looking up at us somberly.

Chapter 16

Wednesday, Late Afternoon
Broadmoor Hall

"Pratt!" Fiona said. "When did you get here?"

"Just now."

"Did you come back with Parker?"

"Parker? I never saw him. I thought you all would be waiting for me at that hostel. When I asked the guy in charge, he said you'd all gone back to the hotel. So I came back here on foot. Thanks a lot for waiting!"

Everyone looked pleased that Pratt was back except Jenna, possibly because her dire predication hadn't come to pass.

"How was the trail?" I asked him. "More difficult than Charlie made it seem?"

Pratt stood and stretched. "A little, yeah. But nothing I couldn't handle. And this little pooch here was the best walking partner I've ever had. Even if he did yap a lot." He reached down and gave Ramses a scratch behind the ears. When the dog let loose a low growl and bared his teeth, Pratt quickly pulled away his hand.

"You worried us half to death!" Fiona said. "We were about to send off a search party. For both you and Parker."

At that moment, our taxi arrived, or at least we thought. Everyone was surprised to see Parker get out.

Fiona ran over to him, gave him a hug, and led him to us.

"Why didn't you wait for Pratt?" Carole asked.

"I did!" he said. "I could tell he was getting near, so I went to meet up with him. But I couldn't find him. That never happens!"

Pratt laughed, came over, and squeezed his brother's shoulder. "Our twin telepathy doesn't always work perfectly. Sometimes there's a lapse. I think that's what must have happened. You went to the place where you sensed I was a few minutes earlier. By that time, I was already a mile away."

Charlie reappeared and was clearly relieved to see Parker, Pratt, and Ramses. He gave Pratt a pat on the back, turned to us, and said, "Dinner will be at seven tonight on the hotel's terrace. For this evening, they've converted it into a sort of beer garden, with music and dancing."

A quiet pub dinner sounded better to me. I'd had enough dancing the previous night to last me a while. Of course, Mike would be joining me the next day . . .

I turned to go back into the hotel and came face-to-face with Brock, coming out. "There you are, Chase. I talked with Mrs. Cooper. That meat company's offices aren't far, and they haven't closed up for the day yet. Want to go over there with me? The van driver said he'll take us."

The bigger question was, how much did I want to get caught up into the Upton drama? Visiting the meat company seemed like a wild goose chase, and I already had had enough of Brock Upton for one day. But . . . dammit, my curiosity was whetted, and we had enough time before dinner to get there and back, so . . . I agreed.

Once we were situated in the van, I said to Brock, "Don't get your hopes up. We're talking about something that happened twenty years ago, remember."

"Hey, I've come five thousand miles to find out the truth. I can't do nothing when we're so close."

Hennessey's Meat & Poultry Purveyors was housed in a large, industrial-looking building just outside the village. Behind it were long buildings that might have been slaughterhouses at one time, but most likely now contained storage freezers. A truck with the company's blue-man logo was parked beside them. We asked the van driver to wait and went in the main building's entrance, where we were faced with hallways running to the left and right. On the wall before us was a framed portrait of the large blue man. I could see how it would make an impression on a nine-year-old girl; even though he was smiling, with his intense eyes, the man looked more menacing than kindly.

A middle-aged woman wearing a casual skirt and blouse came out carrying file folders and saw us regarding the image. "That's my grandfather, Jake Hennessey. Scary old bastard, isn't he? Look, we're about to close up for the night. Unless you're here on an urgent matter . . ."

"This won't take long," I said. "We're here to inquire about something that happened twenty years ago."

She raised an eyebrow. "Twenty years ago? Very well. My office is right down here."

We followed her into a windowless room containing cabinets and bookshelves, a desk piled with papers and coffee cups, and potted plants that looked surprisingly healthy until I realized they were artificial. "Have a seat," she said. She set down her folders and sat behind her desk. "I'm Alice Hennessey. I manage this little freak show."

We introduced ourselves, and Brock quickly related the details of his parents' accident, his family's decision to return to the bridge where it happened, and Fiona's recovered memory. "I wonder if you have any records of that evening . . . anything that might show if one of your drivers was at the scene of the accident," he said.

Alice's eyes widened, and she let out a sigh. "That's quite a tale. Well, let me see." She turned to one of the filing cabinets and pulled out a drawer. "I wasn't working here at that time. My father ran things back then, so none of what you said rings any bells with me. But you may find it interesting to learn that we still have the same delivery driver as we had in those days."

That was surprising indeed. Also surprising was Alice's willingness to indulge us; she must have realized that if we found her driver liable for the accident, there could be trouble. Nevertheless, she officiously riffed through files in the drawer. "We do keep logs on deliveries, so we can verify if and when they were made. It's all done on computers now, of course, but I might still have some of the handwritten logs dating back that far. I'm utterly hopeless when it comes to cleaning out files. My associates are always keeping after me to have all of this . . . what's the word, digitized? Ah—here it is."

She extracted a folder. "These are the log sheets for the time period you mentioned. What was that date again?"

"June 12, 1999," Brock said. I could tell by his voice that he was as surprised as me that this visit might actually pay off. I had been certain we would be laughed out the door.

Alice sat and scanned a couple of pages. "Here it is. What time did this accident occur?"

"Around eight-thirty at night," Brock said.

Another moment passed as Alice studied the log. "Well, this is interesting indeed. Donald did make a delivery that would have taken him through Ennerdale Bridge that evening, and at about that time." She studied the file more closely. "What's more, there's a notation here, which is quite unusual."

"What does it say?" I asked.

" 'Front left wing damaged. Lorry skidded in rain.' "

"What's a wing?" Brock asked.

"That's what the Brits call the fender," I said.

Alice put the sheet on the desk and faced us. "I may be slow to grasp things after a long day's work, but I hope you're not seeking to pin the cause of your parents' accident on one of my drivers. Surely the police investigated it, didn't they?"

"The police report didn't mention any other vehicles," Brock admitted. "But my sister swears she remembers . . ."

Alice gave another sigh and shut the file folder just as a plump, gray-bearded man appeared in the doorway. He looked to be in his seventies. "I'm done for the day, Alice," he said before noticing us. "Oh, sorry, didn't realize you had visitors."

"Well, speak of the devil," Alice said. "Donald, these gentlemen are inquiring about a delivery run you made many years ago. I checked the log sheets and saw that you had made a notation, which you hardly ever do."

The truck driver looked more than surprised—"gobsmacked" would have been the British term for it. "How many years ago?" he asked.

"Twenty. It was a run that took you over Ennerdale Bridge."

"I cross that bridge almost every day."

"Yes, but on this particular evening, it was raining heavily, and a couple were killed when their car drove off the bridge. They were this gentleman's parents."

Donald's astonishment stayed, but I detected a subtle shift from innocent surprise to caution. "Killed, you say?" he asked, his eyes darting to Brock and me.

"That's right," Alice said. "Your note on the log sheet mentions there was damage to the lorry's wing. I know it's been donkey's years, but do you have any recollection of that evening?"

The man looked down at the floor, but not, it seemed to me, as if he were trying to remember. He was clearly shaken. Finally, he looked up and, in a voice of wounded pride, said, "How in bleedin' hell do you expect me to remember something that happened twenty bloody years ago? I can't even bleedin' remember what I did this morning!"

Alice paused and said, "Quite so. Thank you, Donald. I'll see you in the morning."

"Now wait just a minute!" Brock said. "This all sounds fishy to me. How did your truck get damaged, I'd like to know?"

Before Donald could respond, Alice said with exaggerated force, "He said he doesn't remember, gentlemen. I'm afraid that's the best we can do. You know the way out."

Brock said, "I'm not leaving until I—"

"Come on, Brock," I said, getting to my feet. "There's nothing more we can accomplish here." Turning to the driver, I said, "One more question, if you don't mind. Do you go out alone on these deliveries? That is, do you ever have an assistant with you?"

Now on his guard, Donald kept silent. Alice responded instead. "We're a lean operation, but sometimes Donald may take someone with him if the delivery is a large one. That isn't noted on the log sheets, however."

I thanked her and ushered Brock out the door. I would have given anything to hear the conversation Alice was having with Donald now that we'd left. As we walked away, I strained to listen, but she may have been waiting until we were well on our way before saying anything.

Once outside, Brock said, "That driver had something to do with my father's death, I'm sure of it. Didn't you see how guilty he looked?"

"He did look a little spooked," I admitted. "But even if he was partially responsible, how would you prove it? Just a notation about a dented fender isn't going to reopen an investigation into a twenty-year-old incident."

"Maybe," was all Brock said.

As we headed toward the van, Donald emerged from a side door and saw us. He called out, "Why don't you go back where you came from and stop trying to make trouble?"

Of course, this provoked Brock, who marched toward him.

"You'd better tell us what you know, you bastard. It just so happens that my sister was in the car you smashed into. She remembered the face on the side of your truck. Don't be surprised if she remembers you."

Donald let loose a dismissive laugh and began walking away. Brock started to go after him, but I called him back.

"That's not how to solve this," I said. "Miss Hennessey mentioned that there may have been someone else with Donald that night. This is a small town. Maybe we can ask around and find out who that might have been."

Brock watched Donald get into his car. "Good idea. But isn't tonight our last night here? That doesn't leave us much time to ask around, does it?"

With a twinge of disappointment, I realized he was right. My detective instincts had been ignited, and now I would have to back off. "You can always come back here when the walk is over," I said.

"This damn walk!" Brock grumbled. "I don't know why I let Parker talk me into it."

Chapter 17

Wednesday Evening
Broadmoor Hall

The sky was dark when Brock and I arrived back at Broadmoor. As we walked toward the hotel, we heard music coming from around back; a guitarist and flute accompanist were making their way through "All My Loving." Apparently, kitschy takes on old Beatles songs were to be our entertainment for the evening.

Once inside, we could more distinctly hear the buzz of voices from the crowd assembled on the terrace.

Brock paused before heading to his room. "Thanks for going with me, Chase. I'd better go see how Jenna is doing."

"Will you be joining us for dinner?" I asked.

He formed a grim smile. "Do I have a choice?"

"I'll see you there." Brock walked off, but I didn't need to visit my room. The evening was informal, and I just wanted to eat as quickly as possible so I could rest up for Mike's arrival the next day.

Out on the terrace, I spotted most of our group off to the side of the makeshift bar, beer glasses in hand. Carole and Joe were laughing together. Pratt was wearing his Stetson (looking more out of place than ever), while Parker stood beside

him, somewhat lost. Surprisingly, the twins wore dissimilar outfits: Pratt was clad in a blue chambray shirt and deep blue
trousers, while Parker wore a yellow shirt and khaki slacks.

"We'll be getting our own food from a buffet, just like at
breakfast," Billie said as I joined them. "Charlie's reserved us a
table, over there."

I looked out at the crowd. A buffet made sense. Table service would have taken forever with this group, given the hotel's
limited staff.

"It's our last night here, so I'd like it to be a fun one," Charlie said. "Tomorrow night we'll be in Grasmere, and it might
not be so lively."

Mike would be with me the following night, so that would
be lively enough for me. Which reminded me—I hadn't yet informed Charlie that Mike would be arriving. When I told him,
he happily approved, saying the more the merrier. I suspected
he was glad there wouldn't be another Upton family member.

"Is this Mike a friend of yours?" Carole asked.

"More than a friend," Billie said with a sly smile. "Chase met
him on our last walk, and sparks flew. They're definitely an
item."

"Congratulations," Joe said. Smiling at Carole, he added,
"It's great to find romance on a vacation." She beamed back
at him.

"Congratulations aren't in order quite yet," I said. "We need
to work out the challenge of a continent and an ocean separating us."

"You'll figure it out," Carole said. Looking at Joe, she
added, "Things like that don't matter when your heart is involved."

The room hushed. I followed everyone's stares and saw
why. Fiona had appeared, wearing skin-tight jeans and a low-
cut, fringed cowgirl top that amply displayed her curves.

Aware of the attention she was drawing, she smiled and walked over to us.

"You all started without me," she asked. "What are you drinking?"

"They have an amazing black IPA," Joe said, raising his glass. "It's not too strong and even has a slight taste of chocolate."

"It's made by a local brewery, using fresh local spring water," Charlie added.

"I'm sold," Fiona said. "Bring it on!" Brock wasn't there to monitor her alcohol intake, and I suspected it might be up to me if I saw her going over her limit.

"I just want a regular beer, nothing fancy," Pratt said.

"I'll get an assortment," Joe promised. "Why don't I bring a round for everyone and meet you at our table?"

"Thanks," Billie said and pointed to a reserved table in the middle of the room. "We're over there."

As we squeezed through the growing number of revelers, I saw Brock and Jenna come in and waved for them to join us. Soon we were all gathered around the large oak table. Unlike the boisterous crowd around us, our group was unusually quiet. Parker looked his typical disoriented self; Pratt was bravely trying to maintain a placid face despite his bad news; Brock was no doubt thinking about the truck that he was convinced ran his parents off the road; and Jenna looked nervous as always, as if expecting a bomb to go off at any second. Carole and Joe were dreamily lost in one another. Fiona was the exception, ebullient and smiling. Billie seemed to be looking to me for a cue on how to proceed.

"We're not going to be able to chat much tonight," I said to her in a loud voice so I could be heard over the din in the room.

"Fine with me!" she responded.

At that point, the small combo began playing a watered-down version of Led Zeppelin's "Black Dog." The music mattered little to the crowd, who drank and laughed and yapped to the point where the band was scarcely audible.

Joe returned, carrying several tankards of ale on a large platter. He was wobbly under his burden, beer sloshing over the tops of the glasses, so I jumped up to help steady the platter and set it on the table. Everyone started reaching for a beer at once; it was like they'd been dying of thirst. Pratt elbowed Brock as he leaned over the full tankards. Joe intercepted, moving the glasses around as if playing a shell game. Considering they all looked more or less alike, I don't know how he knew which belonged to whom. It scarcely mattered; I doubted if anyone could tell the difference.

Soon everyone had a beer and raised their glass to take a first gulp. Jenna's slipped from her hand, exploded on the table, suds spraying everywhere. Everyone jumped up to escape being drenched. The flood swept one of Carole's eyedrops bottles onto the floor.

"I'm so sorry!" Jenna said. "I'm such a klutz."

"No problem," Joe said, getting to his feet. "I'll get you another."

A server appeared with towels and began cleaning off the table. We stood aside to let him work, but there wasn't much room. I was jostled by others on their way to the bar or the buffet along the side wall. Because all the tables were occupied, many people around us ate standing. Not far off, I spotted some of the blond-haired walkers we'd seen on the trail. In the middle of a group at the back of the room, I thought I saw Donald, the Hennessey truck driver. Nothing else must be going on in town that night; this was where the action was.

Soon our table was clean; the server had managed to wipe up all the spilled beer without upsetting any of the other glasses. Joe returned with a new beer for Jenna, and we made our way to the buffet. The spread was a cornucopia of north

England's best: freshly grilled Cumberland sausage, fish and chips, shepherd's pie. I tried to exercise restraint but ended up putting too much on my plate.

Back at the table, I saw that the rest of the group had been as gluttonous as me; everyone's plate was full to overflowing. Billie was chatting with Joe, and while I couldn't hear them, I hoped she was asking for advice about how to catch the "friend" who'd stolen her money.

Brock was talking with Fiona, probably again inquiring if she remembered anything new about the accident at the bridge. That indeed must have been the case, for she shouted, "Land's sake, Brock, give it a rest," drawing stares from nearby tables. "If I remember anything else, you'll be the first to know!" She reached for her beer and downed it.

"Keep that up, Fi, and you won't remember anything at all," Pratt said.

Fiona reached out, picked up Jenna's beer, downed that as well, and slammed the empty glass on the table. "There! Anyone else want to pick on me?"

"Eat some of your shepherd's pie, Fi," Carole said. "Believe me, it'll really dill your pickle."

"So now you're telling me what to eat?"

Carole looked confused. "What? I did no such thing!"

Fiona was clearly starting to go around the bend again, this time after a couple of beers rather than a strong cocktail. She cut into her shepherd's pie as if she were trying to kill it. After shoving a forkful into her mouth, she smirked at Carole and said with her mouth full, "There. Happy now?"

Carole shook her head. "I don't understand what gets into you, Fi. How can you treat your family and friends like this?"

"She doesn't give a hang about us, C.W.," Pratt said. "She's got all Steve's money now, and none of us will see a penny of it."

Fiona picked up her knife and threw it at Pratt. "*You shut up!*"

The knife hadn't struck him, but Pratt stepped back. "Holy moly, Fi! Are you trying to kill me?"

She stood and slammed her napkin on the table. "Why can't you all lay off? You tell everyone you came over here for my benefit. You all—my 'family' and my 'best friend.' What bull! None of you give a hang about me. Brock won't stop pawing me or nagging me to tell him his dear old daddy was not to blame for killing our momma! Pratt only wants my money. Carole blabs to everyone about what a slut I am—don't look at me that way, C.W., you know you have. Parker hates me because he thinks he wouldn't be messed up if I hadn't encouraged him to join the army. And Jenna has knives in her eyes whenever she looks at me. Well, I've had it with all of you!"

She grabbed the nearest glass of beer—mine—swallowed it, and marched off to applause from other diners. It had been quite a performance, no question. Fiona made a beeline for the blond-haired hikers in the back and started playing up to one of the men, smiling and leaning against him.

"She's shameless," Jenna said, in as cold a voice as I'd ever heard from her.

"She shouldn't drink," I said.

Jenna's icy stare could have frozen my beer. "Wouldn't make a difference. Once a bad seed, always a bad seed."

The band started playing an old Who number, and Fiona began laughing and swaying with two of the blond hikers. Soon she was hidden behind a sea of dancing bodies. I turned my attention back to my meal when a voice called out, "Quick! Somebody help!"

"Fiona!" Billie said.

I pushed my way through the crowd, followed by Pratt and Brock. Fiona was flat out on the floor, face up, eyes shut, arms and legs askew. I knelt and raised her head. Her eyes fluttered open. She formed a smile and looked at me. "Hi there, cutie."

"Are you all right, Fi?" asked Pratt, who was beside me.

She closed her eyes again and groaned. "No, I'm not."

"Let's get her to her room," Pratt said. "She needs to sleep this off."

I hesitated. Did Fiona need medical attention instead? Her color and breathing seemed normal. Pratt was most likely correct. She probably just had too much to drink and would be fine after a good night's sleep. We got her to her feet, but when it became clear that she was in no condition to walk, we held her between us and half-carried her into the main hallway toward the stairway.

On the stairs, her legs dissolved completely, and she became a lifeless lump in our arms. As I leaned to hoist her up again, she whispered to me, in a low, drunken slur. "Chase?"

I leaned in closer. "I'm here."

Her eyes fluttered open slightly, but they were moist, fearful. In a barely audible whisper, she said, "I don't feel so good." She paused and said, "Looks like someone got their wish."

Her eyes closed. Pratt and I lifted her up and continued up the stairs. I wasn't sure if Pratt had heard what she'd said.

If he had, he didn't remark on it. We soon reached her room. "Let's get her inside," he said, as he fished the room key from her jeans.

Pratt opened the door, and we moved Fiona over to the bed, where we positioned her and placed a blanket over her. I looked down at her. She was breathing normally and looked peaceful, but emitted another loud groan. That didn't awaken her, however; she fell back into what seemed to be a calm sleep.

"Let's go," Pratt whispered to me.

"Are you sure we should leave her alone?" I asked. "Shouldn't one of us stay?"

He moved toward the door. "No, she'll be fine. She's done this before. Trust me. She'll be all bright-eyed and bushy-tailed in the morning as if none of this had ever happened."

Still uneasy, I followed him out into the hall after he turned out the light. He told me he was going to go to his room, so we bid each other good night, and I headed back downstairs. My appetite had pretty much vanished, which was just as well, because when I reached the terrace, I saw that our group had vanished too—others were now seated around the table we'd occupied. The only members of our group I could see were Billie, standing off to the side of the room like a sullen wallflower, and Brock and Parker, seated not far away and doing their best not to speak to one another. I went over and gave them a quick report on Fiona.

"It figures she'd get flat-out drunk before this night was through," Brock said.

"Does Fiona have a history of alcoholism?" I asked.

Brock said, "She sure as hell does!" at the same time as Parker said, "No."

"So does she or doesn't she?" I asked.

Parker started to speak, but Brock cut him off. "Fiona likes the bottle and just can't control herself. We've suggested AA until we're blue in the face, but she flat out refuses to admit she needs help."

All through this explanation, Parker was glaring at him. "Not true!" he said.

"Shut up, peanut brain," Brock snapped. "He doesn't want to listen to you."

"I very much want to hear what Parker has to say," I said.

Brock stood and said, "You know he's just going to lie to you," before walking away.

I took Brock's place on his barstool. "You'll tell me the truth, won't you, Parker? About Fiona?"

He watched Brock leave the room. "Fiona likes margaritas. Life is harsh. Your tequila shouldn't be." He seemed to be confirming Brock's assessment of Fiona, but added, "She just drinks one. Don't drink and drive."

Something else was perplexing me besides Parker's non se-quiturs. "At dinner, Fiona said that she talked you into joining the army. Is that true?"

He looked away. "She said the army would fix me. Nope." Looking down, he started drumming his fingers on his knees, and his legs began shaking. "Words fail," he added. I thanked him and went to Billie.

"How's our cowgirl?" she asked.

"She's sleeping it off, or so Pratt thinks. I wonder if there's something else going on, though."

"You mean someone might be spiking her drinks, like you said last night?"

I nodded. "She got drunk awfully fast. Brock just told me she's always had a drinking problem, but Parker seemed to deny it. I also asked him whether Fiona talked him into joining the army. He seemed to confirm that, and said, 'Words fail.'"

Billie nodded. "'War is what happens when language fails.' Margaret Atwood said that. But how would Parker know about Margaret Atwood?"

"I think he knows a lot more than he lets on."

Billie finished the rest of the beer. "You know what? I'm tired of talking about the Uptons. I'm going to bed and read some Emily Dickinson."

Billie stood and gave me a quick hug.

I didn't linger on the terrace and instead returned to my room, where I sent a quick good night text to Mike and began recording the day's events in my journal. I got everything down—Brock's fall on the trail that morning, Pratt learning that his business partner had run off with all his money, every-one fearing Pratt had fallen off a peak until he appeared, my visit to Hennessey's Meats with Brock, Fiona's breakdown at dinner and her subsequent collapse, and Brock and Parker's conflicting explanations of her drinking. Most noteworthy, of course, was Fiona's final comment. "Looks like someone got their wish." Put together with the comment she made to me the day before, was that "wish" that she would die?

Whatever the answer, I wasn't going to arrive at it that night. I crawled into bed and fell asleep. At some point, though, I was awakened by a ruckus outside my room. I could hear people in the hallway, shouting and stomping past. Someone began pounding on my door. I threw on my bathrobe and opened the door to find Billie, also in her robe, wide-eyed and frantic.

"Chase!" she said. "It's Fiona. Something's wrong with her."

We hurried to Fiona's room, where the Uptons were gathered around her; she was writhing and moaning in her bed, her arms alternatively clutched to her chest and then flailing wildly. Her face was covered in sweat. I asked if anyone had called for a doctor.

"Pratt called 911," Carole said.

"It's 999 over here," Billie said.

"Whatever. What's wrong with her? What can we do?"

"Someone get a wet towel," I said.

Brock headed for the bathroom. Pratt came in and said the medics were on their way. Brock returned with a towel, just as Fiona let out another loud moan, plaintive and desperate, followed by silence.

Her body stopped moving and lay still. Deadly still.

I sat beside Fiona and felt her pulse. Nothing. I opened her left eye and saw only the absence of a living soul.

"She's gone," I said. I looked at the bedside clock, which read 2:30.

"*Gone?*" Pratt screamed. "No!" He fell beside the bed, clutched Fiona's hand, and began sobbing. "Wake up, Fi! For God's sake, *wake up!*"

"Get up and act like a man, you fool," Brock said.

Pratt continued crying as he pressed his face against his sister's. The rest of us were rooted to the spot, like exhibits in a wax museum. I did a quick scan of faces, and they all looked genuinely stunned.

"It can't be," Carole said, clutching Joe's arm. "Someone tell me this is all a dream." Joe wrapped his arm around her.

After a moment, Pratt looked up, his face wet with tears. "It's real, all right. This is no dream. Someone killed Fiona. Someone murdered my sister."

Chapter 18

Thursday, Early Morning
Broadmoor Hall

Despite the late hour, the authorities arrived and swung into action. A medical examiner began looking over Fiona's body, accompanied by a scene-of-the-crime crew, while other officers secured the scene and began collecting evidence.

Brock assumed the role of principal family liaison with the authorities. He confirmed Fiona's full name—Fiona Elena Upton Swain—as well as her home address and date of birth. He dispensed this information robotically.

By the time Fiona's body had been photographed and prepared for removal, the news of her death had spread throughout the hotel.

Numb with shock, our group gathered outside the hotel's entrance and watched Fiona's body being wheeled out and into the waiting mortuary van.

"I can't say I'm surprised," Jenna said. "The universe told us this was going to happen."

Pratt swung toward her. "Nobody wants to hear your loony sky-is-falling crap right now, Jenna! My sister is dead, don't you realize that? Keep your mouth shut."

Brock bristled. "Don't talk to my wife that way!"

"Somebody should have shut her up long ago," Pratt shot back.

"Why you—" Brock lunged toward Pratt, but I stepped in to hold him back.

"Show some respect for Fiona, Brock," I told him. "She wouldn't want you fighting at this moment." He paused, gave a reluctant nod, and turned toward the medical examiner's van, where Fiona's body had been loaded and the doors shut.

Even though I had witnessed such a process many times before, I couldn't help thinking how unceremonious it was, almost insulting. A person's life had ended, and they were being treated like a slab of meat. It was at such moments that, despite the fact that I'd never been a churchgoer, my thoughts drifted toward the spiritual. Somewhere, possibly, Fiona's soul was passing through a heavenly portal, maybe accompanied by a choir of angels or at least a good Beatles cover band. That image made me feel better. The passing of a human being deserved respect, regardless of the circumstances.

Nobody had commented on Pratt's assertion that Fiona had been murdered. Perhaps they wrote it off to the grief-stricken raving of someone dealing with the sudden loss of a loved one. I wasn't as convinced. At some point, he would need to explain himself, but it wasn't time for that yet. I suspected he knew more than he let on. Fiona's death had certainly raised my suspicions, and not just because of her comment to me on the stairs.

When the van pulled away, and with a cold wind blowing in from the north, we saw no need to remain outside. I followed the others back into the hotel and debated what to do next. We were all too agitated to go back to sleep. I checked my watch and saw that it was almost five, too early for breakfast. I didn't have much of an appetite anyway.

Beside me, Billie looked numb and just as adrift. "Let's go into the front parlor," I suggested.

"Good idea," she said. "I can't go back to sleep as if nothing has happened."

We seated ourselves on one of the overstuffed divans. I wanted to get Billie's take on what had happened, but I was still trying to process it myself. On the surface, it looked straightforward. Here was a young woman prone to drunkenness, possibly with some underlying medical condition, who finally (although far too prematurely) pushed it too far. Or was something more nefarious going on? Given the number of pills and the discord I'd seen among the Uptons, some chemical interference seemed a more likely explanation, and yet I always caution others against looking for nefarious plots when the more mundane ones usually prove correct.

Lost in thought, I nodded off to sleep and immediately entered a series of vignette-like dreams in which the Uptons wove around me in a macabre dance, passing by one another without touching, their eyes open in zombie-like stares. When Fiona approached and faced me with a look that was not vacant but supplicating, beseeching, I awoke with a start.

It took me a moment to figure out where I was. Then it all came back: the dinner, Fiona passing out, dying in her room. I remembered it with perfect clarity, although it seemed impossible that all that had happened just a few hours ago. The morning sun was glowing through the room's east-facing window. I was still dressed in my bathrobe. Fiona had long since been taken away, but none of the Uptons had yet returned to their rooms. They were seated around me, most of them asleep except Parker, who sat staring out the window. Were they waiting for the paramedics to return with a revived Fiona, claiming it had all been a mistake?

"Chase?" Billie said. She rubbed her eyes and yawned. "You awake?"

"I think so."

"Coffee?"

"You bet." I rose and looked for a carafe or a coffee station. A young man wearing an indigo Broadmoor Hall waistcoat passed by. "Can you bring us some American coffee?" I asked.

"You'll find it in the breakfast room, sir."

Even though we were still wearing our nightclothes, we went to the warmly lit room, as yet unoccupied and with no food laid out. There were, however, wisps of steam emerging from a polished brass coffee carafe, surrounded by a selection of cups and saucers. I poured us each a cup, and we sat in a corner table.

Billie took a bracing sip of her coffee, shuddered, and said, "Did what I remember from last night really happen?"

"I'm afraid so," I said as we sat at a nearby table.

Billie rubbed her eyes and took a gulp of coffee. "I have to tell you about something I saw. That is, I think I saw it. I'm still not quite awake enough to remember clearly."

"Please tell me. Don't worry about how awake you are."

Billie took a breath. "Fiona's cries woke me up. My room is right next to hers, you know. Of course I had to get up and see what was the matter. I put on my robe and peered outside the door. That's when I saw him slip out of her room."

I stiffened. "Him? Who was it?"

"Parker Upton."

"How do you know it was him and not Pratt?"

Billie thought a moment. "Well, he wasn't wearing that cowboy hat, and I noticed he wasn't wearing that gold necklace either. Plus, he was wearing what he wore at dinner. But there's more of a difference to them than that, have you noticed? Yes, they've got the same facial features, but Parker always looks a bit lost. There's none of that bravado that's always there beneath the surface with Pratt."

"Very perceptive of you. But what would Parker be doing in Fiona's room at that hour?"

"What indeed? At any rate, I saw him quietly close her door

and proceed down the hall toward his room. I don't think he knew I saw him."

I considered this information. "Was he carrying anything?"

Billie reacted with surprise. "Funny you should say that. Something was clutched in his hand. Or perhaps not. The hallway isn't terribly well lit, you know."

"Maybe he was just checking in on Fiona. He seemed to really care about her."

Parker hates me. He thinks he wouldn't be messed up if I hadn't encouraged him to join the army.

We stopped our discussion as Carole and Joe entered. They helped themselves to coffee as well and joined us at our table. Carole's eyes were red and her face tear-streaked. Joe looked as if he was in shock.

"It's horrible, absolutely horrible!" Carole said. "Fiona! Dying in a foreign country! Just months after losing her husband! How could such a thing happen?"

She appeared to be genuinely torn up. Perhaps this wasn't the best time to question her, but I couldn't resist. "This was the second time I noticed Fiona getting drunk just after a couple of beers," I said. "Did this happen a lot?"

Carole wrestled with her response. "Well . . . she liked her beer, that's for sure. She also loved vodka shots and stuff like that. But what's really weird is that Fi usually could hold her liquor. Was it different over here? Maybe because we're up higher?"

Charlie entered, his face taut with concern. He approached me.

"This is terrible, Mr. Chasen," he said. "I've never had anyone on one of my walks die, for heaven's sake."

Unfortunately, that had happened to me once before, and I hoped it wouldn't become a habit. I said, "I'm sure the group wants to know what the plan is from here. It doesn't look like we'll be doing any walking today."

Charlie's face tightened and he nodded. "Hardly so. I'll

need to consult with my management about the proper protocol in such circumstances. Of course, they won't be pleased with this turn of events. Have the police been notified?"

I nodded. "Yes, they were here the same time as the medics. I imagine they'll want to investigate this further. It can't be every day that a young American woman dies mysteriously in a local hotel."

"Mysteriously?"

That word must have slipped out. "They need to verify the cause of death, of course," I said.

At that moment, a stout man with dark, graying hair, dressed in a loose overcoat, walked into the room. He had the bearing of authority. "Is there a Charles Cross here?" he asked.

"That's me," Charlie said, crossing over to the newcomer. I stood and joined them.

The man pulled out a sealed card from his pocket and quickly flashed it. "Detective Inspector Lewis Caldwell from the Cumbria CID." Turning to me, he said, "And you are?"

"Rick Chasen. I'm in the same walking group as the deceased woman." By that time Billie, Carole, and Joe had joined us as well.

"Has anyone heard from the doctors?" Carole asked. "Do they know how Fiona died?"

"It was poison, wasn't it?" Joe asked.

"I'm afraid that information will take a bit longer to discover," the inspector said. "Our local coroner is on holiday in Spain, and it isn't yet clear who his backup is."

Their coroner was on holiday? An idea sprang to mind. "Perhaps I can help. I know a good man who happens to be the coroner down in Devon."

"Devon?" the inspector said, and gave a short laugh. "Thank you, Mr. Chasen, but I believe we'll be able to locate someone closer to home than that."

"He'll be up here today," I said. "For a reason that has nothing to do with Mrs. Swain's death, of course. His name is Mike Tibbets. I'm sure he would be glad to assist you." I didn't know any such thing, of course, and hoped Mike wouldn't resent my offering his services.

Caldwell pondered this a moment. "I'll speak with this Tibbets when he gets here. He might be able to help us out at that."

I knew I'd better notify Mike of this as soon as possible. In view of the fact that we probably wouldn't be doing any walking, he might appreciate being able to help the local authorities. Or so I hoped.

"You mentioned the deceased woman was in a walking group," said the inspector. "How many are in this group?"

Charlie explained that, beside us, there were four others in our group, all part of the same family. He added that we were all Americans. Billie said that the Uptons were likely to still be in the parlor and offered to take the inspector there. I told her I would join them shortly.

When they left, Charlie looked at me questioningly. "Mike Tibbets? Isn't he that friend of yours? He's a coroner?"

I confirmed that he was and confessed that I may have been a bit rash in offering his services up to the inspector.

Charlie smiled. "I believe he'll understand. He must be a very good friend to travel all this way."

"Yes, he's a very good friend," I said, wanting to add that Mike was much more than that.

Charlie went off, and I punched in Mike's number on my cell phone. He answered immediately. I expected to have awakened him, but his voice was peppy.

"Sorry to disturb you so early," I said.

"No worries. Is something wrong? Are you okay?"

"I'm fine, but things have taken a nasty turn here. A member of our party died last night."

After a pause, he said, "How on earth did that happen?"

I gave him quick rundown on Fiona's death, and that a complete examination might not be possible because the local coroner was unavailable. "I'm afraid I've volunteered you to stand in for him," I told him.

There was an ominous pause. Oh, crap. Did I just cross the line?

"Yes, of course," Mike said, without much enthusiasm. "Can you tell me any other information?"

I explained why I believed Fiona's death might have been due to poisoning or an overdose of medication. "I'm sorry if I acted inappropriately in mentioning you, Mike. As much as I want to be with you, everyone here wants this matter wrapped up as quickly as possible. I thought you might be able to step in and help out. But please tell me if you'd rather not. I certainly won't hold it against you."

"Nonsense, Chase. Actually, I'm on my way up there as we speak. I want to see you so badly that I got an early start. Now it looks like this will be a busman's holiday, won't it? Well, an initial examination shouldn't take too long. It certainly won't be anything like I just experienced down here."

He said his drive should take four or five hours, which would get him to the hotel sometime in the early afternoon. I thanked him again and went to the parlor, where everyone was assembled with Inspector Caldwell.

Billie looked up. "Did you reach Mike?"

"Yes, he'll be here in a few hours." To the inspector, I said, "Mike will do a fine job. He is very experienced and thorough."

The inspector didn't appear to be pleased about having to work with someone he didn't know. "I suppose I have no choice. Our regular coroner's staff are a capable bunch, but it will be best for a more senior, experienced chap to step in. We don't get many deaths like this up here. In the meantime, I'd like to gather details about what occurred last night before

Mrs."—he checked his notes—"Mrs. Swain, is it? Before she passed. I understand you had all dined together here at the hotel?"

"Out on the terrace," Joe said. "That's where she was poisoned."

Carole said, "We don't know that for sure, Joe."

"Let's put aside any talk of poison for the time being," Caldwell said. "We'll need to wait for the coroner's report for that."

"I don't know what we can tell you," Brock said. "We were having our dinner, Fiona drank too much, and she passed out."

"That wasn't what happened, Brock, and you know it," Pratt said and turned to Caldwell. "Yes, Fi had a couple of beers, just like the rest of us—"

"A couple?" Brock countered. "She was tossing them back like the town drunk!"

"She drank no more than she ever did," Pratt said. "And sure, that might have made her pass out, but it wouldn't kill her. And definitely not with all that screaming and moaning. She was sleeping just fine when Chase and I left her room. Maybe someone came in and poisoned her after that."

I looked toward Parker. He would need to explain why he'd gone into Fiona's room, but at the moment he looked unfazed by Pratt's remark.

Caldwell pulled out a small pen and began scribbling on his notepad. "Were you all together at dinner?" he asked. Billie confirmed we were.

"Is there anyone here who would have wished to do the deceased harm?"

"Oh, don't call her that!" Carole said. " 'The deceased.' Her name was Fiona, Fiona Swain. And, no, there isn't anyone here would 'do her harm.' For Pete's sake, we're all her family, and we all loved her."

"You're not her family, C.W.," Jenna said.

"I'm as much her family as any of you," Carole said. Looking at Brock, she said, "Maybe even more than some of you, given the way you've treated her."

"Now, you watch your mouth, C.W.—"

"I think that will be all for now," Caldwell said. He looked down at his notepad and folded it shut. "There's not much more I can do until I get the toxicology report. Thank you for your assistance." He turned to walk off.

"Is that it?" Carole asked. "Aren't you going to interview us? Take us down to the police station?"

Taking a deep breath, the inspector said, "As I said, madam, we must wait for the coroner's report before going any further. I do ask, however, that you all remain here until that time." To Charlie, he asked, "Will that be any problem?"

"I'll check with Mrs. Cooper," Charlie replied. "We were due to transfer to another hotel today, but I believe there'll be enough rooms for us to remain here tonight."

The inspector thanked him and left. Carole watched him go, wide-eyed. "Well, at least he has manners. He called me 'madam,' which nobody else ever has." She paused. "I just hope that doesn't mean the same thing over here that it does back home."

As Billie and I headed back to the breakfast room, she said, "I'm glad Mike will be here. A little pleasure will take your mind off this nasty business."

I wasn't sure how much "pleasure" there would be until Fiona's death was resolved. "It certainly isn't turning out like I expected, that's for sure," I said.

"I know you don't want to jump to conclusions, but I agree with the others. I can't help but think that Fiona may have been poisoned."

"It's too soon to begin going down that road. Let's wait for more information."

"Well, if she wasn't poisoned, what could have killed her?"

I didn't want to give a snap answer. My instincts told me there was something definitely suspicious about Fiona's death, given that she and the others seemed to have been swimming in a veritable sea of intoxicants, contaminants, and medications for the past three days. I thought of the sheep vaccine, the poison for the grackles, Parker's morphine, Brock's cardiac pills, Carole's eye drops, Fiona's beers and cocktails, Jenna's allergy pills and supplements . . . there were no doubt more I couldn't remember.

"I just don't know," was all I said.

The breakfast buffet hadn't yet been laid out. There was still coffee, however, so Billie and I filled our cups again and went to our usual table.

Billie laughed. "We're still in our night clothes. I'd completely forgotten."

The others began to arrive, in a flurry of conversation.

"It was the sheep disease," Pratt was saying to Brock. "What else could it be? Fi was fit as a fiddle. She was never sick a day in her life."

"That's not true," Jenna said. "Remember when she had the measles?"

"Oh, for God's sake, that was umpteen years ago," Brock said. "How could the measles have killed her now?"

"Killed her!" Carole wailed. "There's that word again. Why would anyone want to kill Fiona?"

"We're all victims," Parker said. "She paid for our sins."

"You shut the hell up," Pratt barked.

"Just because Fi was a bit of a flirt doesn't mean she deserved to die," Carole said. "I bet we'll find out she had some kind of tumor."

Pratt's eyes widened. "The beer! That weird beer that Joe gave everyone. Maybe she had a reaction to it."

"There was nothing 'weird' about the beer," Joe said.

"Everyone was drinking it, and we're all fine. No, it had to have been something else." His voice was a flat monotone.

"You're right," Brock replied. "We all drank some of that beer."

"Not all of us did," Pratt said. "Jenna didn't drink any."

It took a moment for Jenna to realize she was being mentioned. "So I got a little clumsy and spilled my beer. I wasn't in the mood for it anyway. Besides, Fiona drank mine."

"That's right!" Pratt said. "If that glass of beer was poisoned, maybe it was meant for Jenna."

Brock faced Pratt. "Are you saying someone meant to kill my wife?"

"I don't know! Why would any of us want to kill anyone? We're not a family of murderers!"

I'd heard enough. "Would all of you settle down? The fact is we don't have any information. Once we find out what actually happened, we can discuss it and not start jumping to conclusions. Right now we're flying blind."

"We're not flying completely blind," Brock said. "We do know a few things—that there is some sort of sheep virus going on around here, and that the gardener of this place has been using poison to kill birds."

"He's right, Chase," Billie said.

"You're connecting cause with effect based on nothing but hearsay and circumstance," I said.

Carole said, "I agree with Chase. It's bad enough that we lost Fiona. Let's not squabble like a bunch of plucked chickens. Let's eat! Wait a sec . . . where's the food?"

Just then a young lady entered, a sheepish look on her face.

"You're a little late bringing out the food this morning," I said.

Her brow creased. "Um . . . yes. Cook had to discard all of the dairy products and meat because they had been . . . spoiled. She's waiting for a new delivery. It should be here at any minute." She turned to walk off, and I went after her.

"How did the food spoil?" I asked in a low voice, out of earshot of the others. "You have refrigeration, don't you?"

The girl's eyes darted around. Leaning close, as if she was about to divulge a state secret, she said, "Don't tell Cook I told you, but she had to discard all fruits, vegetables, and baked goods, as well as food in packages that had been opened. You see, an empty bottle of poison was found right outside the kitchen door. Bird poison! We learned it had been taken from the storeroom in the greenhouse."

"Found outside the kitchen?"

She nodded. "Of course, it's probably of no concern. The groundskeeper probably dropped it and hadn't noticed. But we can't be too careful, can we? Imagine if some of that poison had found its way into your breakfast!"

Chapter 19

Thursday Morning
Broadmoor Hall

I hate being put in the position of withholding information from others (it makes me feel like a presumptuous jerk), but telling everyone about the poison would only set off another round of speculation, so I wasn't completely forthright with them about the food delay.

"They're having some kind of delivery problem," I said. "It will be here in about an hour."

Nobody seemed bothered by this except Carole. "Thank God I have two packs of Fritos in my bag—the one the airline didn't lose." She headed to her room.

Inspector Caldwell needed to know about the missing bird poison, so I went in search of him. He was easy to locate—seated alone in the parlor, scrolling through his phone messages.

"Sorry to interrupt," I said, "but I just learned of something that might have a bearing on Mrs. Swain's death."

He cocked his head slightly, probably wondering why the hell I was inserting myself in his case.

"The groundskeeper here at the hotel has a supply of poison

that he uses on grackles," I said. "We were wondering why the breakfast buffet hadn't been set out at the usual time. It seems a bottle of that poison was found outside the kitchen door this morning, and all the breakfast food was thrown away as a precaution."

His eyes widened slightly. "Oh, dear," he said. "Did the bottle have any of the poison still in it?"

"I honestly don't know. But it's worth checking on." I told him about our group coming upon the groundskeeper the day before while he was in the process of laying out the poison, and that he'd shown us the storeroom where it was kept. After some hesitation, I also told him about the scramble at the previous night's dinner, which presented an opportunity for someone to slip poison into Fiona's beer unseen.

Caldwell pocketed his phone and stood. "I'll speak with the groundskeeper later. But first I think I'd better begin questioning the members of your group."

As we walked toward the breakfast room, I gave the inspector a quick rundown on the group and how each was connected.

"That is an impressive summary," he said. "I wish most witnesses had your grasp of the situation."

I'm normally reluctant to divulge my background, but it seemed appropriate to tell Caldwell of my years on the force. He accepted this with an approving nod.

All of our group was in the room when we arrived. Without mentioning the news of the poison, Caldwell announced that he planned to speak with everyone separately about the events of the previous evening.

"Does this mean it was murder?" Carole asked. "And we're suspects?"

"We're nowhere close to knowing if Fi's been murdered, C.W.," Brock said.

"She was murdered all right," Pratt said. "I'd bet my bankroll on it."

"Yes, and we all know how much your bankroll is worth," Brock shot back.

I should have told Caldwell about the Uptons' fractious divisions so he could get an idea what kind of boiling cauldron he was diving into. But he'd probably discover that soon enough on his own.

"Who would like to be the first?" the inspector asked.

Brock stepped forward. "Might as well get this over with. Can you interview my wife and me together?"

"I'm afraid not," Caldwell said. "It's our practice to interview family members separately. Let's go into the parlor, where we can have privacy. When we're through, you can come back here and ask your wife to join me."

As the inspector walked off with Brock, I motioned for Billie to join me outside. I told her about the poison bottle.

"Jeepers creepers! If it's the same poison that was in the storeroom, it certainly increases the odds that Fiona's beer was fiddled with. But the question that remains, of course, is why?"

"And who? Any of us could have stolen that poison. We all heard the groundskeeper talk about it. He showed us exactly where he keeps it. And I doubt he locks his storeroom."

Billie raised an eyebrow. "I don't think the killer could have been any of us, Chase. You certainly didn't poison Fiona."

"And I strongly doubt you did either."

"It also couldn't have been one of the brothers. Remember? Pratt was still on the trail when we visited that storeroom, and Parker was in that village waiting for him to show up."

"Brock wasn't in that storeroom with us either. But think about it. Just because they weren't with us doesn't mean someone didn't tell them about it later."

"That's true." She thought a moment. "But let's get real, Chase. If someone poisoned Fiona, it has to have been one of the Uptons. They're the only ones with any connection to her."

I chewed my lip. "It's too early to begin throwing theories around. Let's wait until Mike gets here and does his stuff." I checked my watch. Mike wasn't due to arrive for another couple of hours. We returned to the breakfast room, where the server was setting out the cereals and pastries.

"You sure this stuff is okay?" Carole asked, scanning the buffet with suspicion.

"The baker just delivered them, ma'am. The hot food will be out shortly."

Soon Billie and I were half-heartedly eating muesli and scones. The others were leaving as well and refrained from further speculation. Fiona's death hung thick in the air, and the only sounds to be heard were spoons and knives clicking against bowls and plates. Brock returned from his interview and told Jenna where she could find the inspector.

"What did you find out?" Carole asked Brock once Jenna had left. "It is murder, isn't it?"

Brock sat. "Sure looks like it. All the inspector asked me about was the poison you all saw in that garden building yesterday. I told him I knew about it, but that was about it."

This revelation was met with uncomfortable silence. The inescapable implication was that the poisoner, if there was one, was one of us.

When Jenna returned, Pratt volunteered to take Parker off to meet with the inspector. "Come on, bro," he said to Parker.

"He won't interview the two of you together," Brock said.

"We'll see about that. He's going to have a devil of a time trying to get anything useful out of Parker without my help."

"The DI is nobody's fool, Pratt," I said. "He might be concerned with you trying to put words in Parker's mouth."

"I'm right here, you know," Parker said. "You think I don't know you're talking about me?"

"I don't put words in your mouth, Parker. But sometimes I can help make sense of the words that come out. Come on. Let's go."

The brothers walked off as chafing dishes with bacon and sausage were brought in. As everyone got up for another pass down the breakfast line, Carole asked Jenna about what she told Caldwell.

Jenna looked at Brock, almost as if she wanted his permission to speak. Did he give her a slight nod? She said, "I just told him what happened last night at dinner. He asked me if Fiona's beer was always in sight of the rest of us."

"Yes, he asked me that, too," Brock said. "Well, who knows if it was or wasn't? And don't forget—Jenna's beer may have been monkeyed with also. Fiona drank it before she got the chance."

"Oh, come on, Brock," Carole said. "It's like we all said before. Who would want to kill Jenna?"

"Who would want to kill Fiona?" he countered.

It took about thirty minutes for Caldwell to interview the others. By the time Billie and I had finished our meal, he was ready for us.

"I might as well go last," I said. Billie nodded and went off. The others were still sharing their discussions with the inspector, and it sounded as if all the interviews had followed the same line of questioning: What did they see at the dinner?

Billie soon returned and said that her experience was the same as the others. "He was focused on that poison we'd seen in the gardener's building. He asked if anyone showed a particular interest in it at the time."

"And what did you tell him?" Pratt asked.

Billie paused, probably debating how much to reveal with

the others gathered around us. "I said that Carole wanted to know how secure the poison was."

"Well, what's wrong with that?" Carole said. "I was just thinking about our safety."

"I also said that Joe seemed upset about using such a poison on birds," Billie added.

"Why should that matter?" Carole said. "He's a bird lover, after all."

"How could that make me a suspect?" Joe asked.

Billie looked as if she wished she hadn't said anything. "All I'm telling you is what he asked."

"Let's not read too much into every question," I said, as I stood to leave. "It's my turn now. Wish me luck."

When I entered the parlor, the inspector was entering something on his cell phone. He didn't look up until he finished. He then gave me an acknowledging nod and motioned for me to sit opposite him. He pressed the RECORD button his phone and asked me to confirm my name. After I did, he said, "I understand you have been on walking tours here in England many times. At least, that is what Miss Mondreau divulged to me."

"Yes, that's so," I said.

"I also understand that you two have been involved in a murder before, which took place on a walk down in Devon a year ago."

I confirmed this as well.

"Is it a habit of yours to sign up for walks in which murders occur?"

Was this a serious question or an attempt at humor? "I realize it's a strange coincidence," I said. "It was during that previous murder investigation that I came to know Mike Tibbets."

"Just so," Caldwell said. "And it also happens you were a police detective in your professional life."

I admitted that was the case.

"Then I'm fortunate," he said. "The others I spoke with were helpful, but not, I suspect, entirely forthcoming. It helps that I have a witness like you, with a heightened sense of observation."

"Well, I can't guarantee how 'heightened' it is at this point," I said.

A crack of a smile formed on Caldwell's lips. "Nevertheless, putting your law enforcement hat on, what did you observe last night?"

I took a deep breath and closed my eyes. A mental picture of the previous evening's meal on the terrace formed. This wasn't one of my deep-dive, time-stops-still moments of recall, but I remembered it clearly. "It was a chaotic scene, noisy and with a lot of people scrambling around. The crowd included more than just the guests of the hotel, and there was a small band as well. Our group had a table at the center of the room, so it took a while for all of us to get seated. Joe offered to get beers for everyone. He went off and brought back a large tray with all the glasses filled to overflowing. There was a lot of confusion as the beers were passed around, and we all tried to find our orders. Then Jenna Upton spilled hers all over the table. That created even more confusion as the staff came over to clean up. Most of us got up to give them room to work."

"I see," Caldwell said. "What happened then?"

"We went to get our food from the buffet," I continued. "That took a while, and I can't be sure where everyone in our group was during that time. When I got back to the table, though, we all seemed to be there. Joe had brought back a fresh beer for Jenna."

Caldwell nodded. "Had anyone drank from their beer glasses by that time?"

"I imagine so, but I can't be certain." I told him that Fiona finished her beer and began drinking a second one. "Then she took Jenna's beer and drank that too, and started getting a little wild, overreacting to comments and getting loud. That was when she threw a knife at her brother Pratt."

The inspector's eyes widened. "She threw a knife at him?"

"I don't think she meant to harm him. She was just acting wild. Then she started railing about how everyone in her family hated her. Before anyone could say anything, she downed another beer, walked to the back of the room, and began flirting and dancing with some of the men. That's when I saw her wobble and collapse to the floor."

"My word," Caldwell said.

"Pratt and I then helped Fiona to her room." I paused, then added, "I might as well tell you something she said to me when we were on the stairs. She came to for a moment, looked afraid, and told me that 'someone had got their wish.'"

This produced an expected reaction from Caldwell. "What wish would that have been?"

"To see her dead. That was the phrase she had used earlier."

The inspector pondered this.

"Keep in mind she wasn't exactly in full control of her faculties," I said. "She'd just told off all of her family out on the terrace, so she might have still been angry about that."

The inspector mulled this over. "I see. Very well. What happened next?"

"Pratt and I got Fiona to her room and placed her in bed. She seemed to be sleeping calmly. Even though she'd been moaning and in pain not long before, she was breathing normally."

"Both of you left her room?"

"That's right. Pratt said he was going off to his room, and I went back down to the terrace."

"Pratt is one of the twin brothers, correct?" Caldwell asked. "The normal one?"

"Normal" struck me as a strange term to describe Pratt, but I knew what the inspector was getting at. "That's right. His brother, Parker, has what I guess you would call 'cognitive issues.' It might have something to do with when he served with the army in Afghanistan."

"I see," Caldwell said. "Did anything else unusual happen?"

"Not directly. But did Billie tell you about what she observed later?"

Caldwell paused. "I believe you're referring to her being awakened in the night and seeing Parker Upton leave his sister's room. Yes, she gave me that information. I'll need to have a further conversation with that man. Would you mind finding him and asking him to return here?"

"Are you through with me?" I asked.

"For the time being. But don't be surprised if I rely on your powers of observation again, Mr. Chasen."

When I rejoined the others, I was bombarded with questions.

"What did the inspector ask you?"

"Does he know what happened to Fiona?"

"Does he think any of us are keeping things from him?"

Instead of answering, I went over to Parker, seated by himself by the window, and told him that the inspector wanted to speak with him further.

When he left, Pratt asked, "What's going on? Why does he want to see Parker again?"

Brock said, "It's probably just like you said. He couldn't understand any fool thing that nitwit told him and wanted to have another go at him."

The others seemed to accept this, finding it as plausible an explanation as any. They soon began heading back to their rooms or to other parts of the hotel.

"I actually pity them," Billie said when the Uptons left. "One of their family has been killed, they're stranded in a strange country, and they're at the mercy of a legal and law enforcement system they're not used to."

I was about to respond when my cell phone jingled.

It was a message from Mike. **I'm here**.

Chapter 20

Thursday, Late Morning
Broadmoor Hall

My heartbeat sped as I hurried outside, where Mike was walking toward me from his car, smiling broadly. Sunlight highlighted his crop of light brown hair and framed his face, diffusing it in an angelic glow. He was carrying a small suitcase. It had been almost a year since I had seen him, and there was never a more welcome sight.

We quickly embraced each other. Realizing we were on public view, we pulled apart more quickly than we would have had we been in private.

"It's great to see you," I said.

"It's been way too long," Mike said, placing his hand on my chest. Our gazes locked for several moments, and then I led him inside the hotel.

I hadn't expected our reunion to have such an effect on me; I felt as if I were dreaming. Forcing myself to get reconnected with reality, I asked him how his drive up went.

"Uneventful," he said. "I put some Miles Davis on, and that helped the hours melt away."

Mike's love of cool, late-fifties jazz was something that seemed at odds with his very precise, science-based occupation. In many ways, he was very ordered and procedural; perhaps it was his way of letting go. Of course, he wondered about my passion for classic country music as well.

"Any new developments on the dead woman?" he asked.

"Well, the local sniffer has arrived and started gathering information. He seems to be competent enough."

"Would you doubt the British constabulary?" Mike teased.

"Not if they were all like you," I said with a smile. "I have to warn you, though. Everyone is waiting on pins and needles for your report."

"Nothing like a little pressure, is there? Hold on a moment—"

He guided me into a secluded alcove off the parlor and set down his case so we could fall into another embrace, followed by a long, probing kiss. I became immersed in Mike's intoxicating scent; the fragrance he wore was something very British, strong and citrusy, but mixed with an essence that was distinctly his own.

Eventually, Mike reluctantly pulled away. "Hope you don't mind. I've been wanting to do that ever since I left Exeter."

We kissed again. "I've been so hungry to see you," I said. "Sorry it has to be under these circumstances."

"It won't always be," Mike vowed.

I took Mike up to my room to deposit his suitcase—and indulge in another kiss—before returning downstairs. We found Inspector Caldwell in the parlor, studying his cell phone as always. He stood when he saw us, and I made introductions.

"You made good time," the inspector said to Mike.

He responded with a smile. "I attribute that to the good weather and my expert driving skills." I knew he didn't identify the real reason—that I was the main inducement.

Caldwell and Mike began chatting and seemed to hit it off. They had an easy, professional rapport and quickly discovered they had mutual acquaintances. I'd begun to feel like a third wheel when Caldwell checked his watch and said that they'd better head over to the mortuary in Carlisle.

I bid them goodbye, and as they walked off, I realized I had several unplanned hours ahead of me. After tracking down Mrs. Cooper and informing her that there would be an additional guest in my room for the balance of my stay (she took this information without batting an eye), I went off in search of Billie, whom I found knitting in a small study to the rear of the house's main floor.

"I'm stumped," she said, setting down her needles. "What knitting pattern best represents 'déjà vu'?"

"A mirror?" I suggested as I sat next to her. "A bad dream?"

She held out her yarn. "Go ahead. Knit me something that looks like a bad dream."

"Why are you thinking of déjà vu?"

She tilted her head in mock surprise. "Another murder, on one of our walks . . . what are the odds?"

"Forget your knitting for a while. I need to get outside. What do you say?"

We went out onto the hotel grounds, only a fraction of which we'd seen the previous day. Besides the topiary garden, there were grand lawns bordered by lush gardens and forests of alders and oaks. We passed a stone labyrinth for meditative contemplation and a large fountain and pool with lily pads.

"It doesn't seem right that there could be a killer among all this beauty and tranquility," Billie said as we strolled.

"Unfortunately, it is often in the most beautiful places where you find evil," I said.

"Well, aren't you Mister Negative! I prefer to take a brighter view of human nature."

"I'm afraid you will always be disappointed, Billie."

"Why aren't you in a better mood? I would think that seeing Mike again would have been a big boost."

"It is, believe me. But I feel bad about bringing him into this mess."

"He's a grown man, Chase. Yes, he's besotted with you, so that might cloud his judgment, but at least some of his gray cells must still be working. And death is his business, after all."

I loved Billie for using words like "besotted." I loved her many other qualities also, not the least of which was that I could walk at her side—or ahead or behind her—without feeling compelled to engage in constant conversation. That's how strong our friendship had become. So we walked in silence for a while.

We passed the garden workshop just as Ian MacMillan, the gray-haired groundskeeper, came out.

"I hear someone took your bird poison last night," I said.

He paused. "That's true. How did you find out?"

"An empty bottle was found outside the kitchen door. The cook had to take precautions to toss out any food that might have been tampered with."

"Yes, I know," he said. "She told me about it, so I went to recover it. It's very distressing, I can tell you."

I paused. "Wait a minute. You recovered it? You mean you took it back from the cook?"

"That's right. I put it back on its shelf."

So much for identifying any fingerprints, I thought. Why couldn't he have had more sense? "Was there any poison left in the bottle?" I asked.

"Yes, there's some. But are the police certain the Avitrol is to blame? We've never had a murder here, and I've worked here for nearly thirty-five years." We followed him into the store-room.

He pointed up to the bottle on the shelf. "There it is, right where it always is. I wonder when someone managed to sneak it away."

The bottle, with its skull-and-crossbones warning label, sat in the same spot we had seen it the day before. It looked about half-full. "Do you lock up this room when you're not in it?" I asked.

"There's really no need," he said, and thought about what had happened. "That is, until now. It looks like I'll need to get a lock for the door."

Inside the hotel, we found our group in the bar, looking bored. Half-empty pint glasses sat before everyone, a small pill bottle beside Carole's. For once, she wasn't glued to Joe's side; he was facing away from her, staring out the side window.

"It's this waiting I can't stand," Pratt said, slouched in a chair. His long legs were crossed before him, the toes of his brown leather boots hooked over one another. "Until we find out what happened to Fiona, I don't feel I can even mourn her properly."

"Mourn her?" Brock said, seated nearby with Jenna. "If you hadn't brought her halfway around the world for this stupid walk, Fiona would be alive and kicking."

"You're blaming me for this?" Pratt snapped back. "You were all for coming on this trip! And wasn't it Parker's idea in the first place?"

Like a pet hearing its name, Parker snapped his head up. "Benjamin Bunny lost a friend," he said. "Fiona missed him."

"Sure she did, after you planted the idea in her brain," Brock said. "You always suggested things all innocent-like, knowing that she had a weak spot for you and would never refuse you."

"So what if Fi wanted to please Parker?" Pratt said. "It's good to know there were at least two in this family who gave a damn about one another."

It was time for me to step in. "Easy, guys. Can't you cool off for even one minute? Out of respect for Fiona? It's not uncommon for tensions to run high at a time like this, but my advice to you is to think before you speak."

My advice resulted in nobody speaking at all.

I considered my next move. The last place I wanted to be

was in the bar with the Uptons. I headed outside and was surprised to see that Billie had followed me.

"Hope you don't mind me joining you," she said as we fell in step. "All along you've been telling me you need to solve the puzzle that is the Uptons. What if solving that puzzle suggests that one of them killed Fiona?"

I gave her a knowing smile. "You're not fooling me either, you know," I said. "You love to figure out this kind of puzzle as much as I do."

"Well, I love mysteries. All those years of helping people find books by writers as good as Agatha Christie or Dorothy Sayers left its mark. And I especially love seeing justice being served."

"Okay then," I said. We'd been heading back toward the topiary garden, and I spied a welcoming bench not far away. "Let's have a quick meeting of the minds. Assuming this was murder and Fiona somehow was poisoned, you tell me your favorite suspects, and I'll tell you mine."

"Now? Oh, Chase, I'm not ready. I haven't had time to think it over."

"Don't give me that. You've been tossing this over in that devious little mind of yours since Fiona gave up the ghost this morning."

She gave me a reluctant confirming smile and sat beside me. Taking a deep breath, she said, "Very well, here's my theory so far. There were six of us who saw the bird poison in the garden building, right? Pratt was off on his solo walk, Parker was waiting for him at Honister, and Brock was up in his room."

"Correct."

"Very well, then. Among those of us who saw the poison, who had the strongest motive to want Fiona out of the way? Well, Joe didn't even know Fiona, so I rule him out, and while Jenna didn't seem to care much for Fiona, I can't see that being a motive for murder. That leaves Carole. She's been harboring a lot of resentment because she had been in love with Fiona's husband and felt Fiona treated him badly at the end. She even confessed to you that Fiona's neglectful treatment of her husband was tantamount to murder."

I nodded. "And calling herself and Fiona 'best friends' never did seem credible, given how they often went at each other like cats."

"Be careful not to malign cats, Chase. Some have been dear friends of mine."

"Sorry," I said with a smile. "Okay. Let me add something to your theory. It's true that Pratt and the others weren't there with the rest of us in the garden room, but someone could have told them later what we saw."

Billie gave a firm nod. "That's exactly what I was thinking! So let's look for motives there. Pratt just found out he's lost a fortune, like I have, but he seems to be taking it much harder. Fiona, we have discovered, was due to inherit a bundle from her deceased husband. It sounds like Pratt could be in a position to get some of that money if she died."

She was confirming my suspicions as well. I said, "Parker is the real wild card. He seems gentle and harmless at times, then gets violent. That doesn't connect with poisoning someone, which would have to be planned and thought out. I don't see him doing that."

"Who can say what's going on in that strange mind of his? But I mostly agree with you. Why would Parker want to poison Fiona? He seems to have been devoted to her."

"Except Fiona believed he resented her for encouraging him to join the army."

"That's interesting. But it doesn't change my mind. In my book, it's Brock who's the likeliest killer. Fiona practically accused him of being a child molester and publicly threatened to bring a lawsuit against him."

"True," I said. "Those were strong allegations. But my question is, why act now? Sure, he got touchy-feely with her, but it sounds like those incidents happened ages ago. Why threaten him now? Seems odd."

Billie sighed. "You're right, but again, who knows? Who's your money on?"

I took a deep breath, released it slowly, and stretched out my legs. "What's bothered me all along is that the Uptons have all been trying to cover up the fact that they brought Fiona over to England in hopes that she would remember exactly what happened in the car the night her parents died. That raised a load of questions in my mind. Why couldn't they just be honest about that to begin with? Why try to cover that up?"

"Maybe they didn't want to talk about something so morbid."

"That's likely, I suppose. They sure talk about everything else, though."

"What about their reasons for wanting Fiona to recover her memory? Do you buy all of those?"

"I don't see any reason why they'd lie about that. But you never know."

"Brock was hoping Fiona would exonerate her father," Billie said. "But if the father wasn't responsible for losing control of the car, it must have been either Fiona herself—who may have distracted her father, and probably wouldn't admit it—or her mother."

"There's also that meat delivery truck. Even though it sounds like it wasn't directly responsible for the accident, the possibility that it could have been sure made the owner of the company pretty damn nervous."

"But what if she did remember who caused that accident?" Billie said.

"What?"

"What if Fiona just told everyone she didn't? Except for one person. The one person she felt needed to know the truth.

And that one person didn't like what he—or she—heard, right? And didn't want her to tell anyone else?"

My eyebrows raised. "That's possible. Except there's one thing I haven't told you." I shared with her Fiona's comment about everyone in her family wanting to see her dead, and her comment about someone getting their wish.

"Wow. Did she say anything else?"

"No, that was it. Those were probably her last words."

She sighed. "That sounds pretty incriminating. Still, it could be that the Uptons aren't as complex as all that. They could just be a typical modern family—one minute at each other's throats, the next planning trips together."

"Except someone did get murdered, Billie."

The sound of tires on gravel near the hotel entrance diverted our attention. Caldwell's sleek Peugeot was pulling up. Excusing myself, I went over to greet the inspector and Mike as they got out of the car.

"Good afternoon," the inspector greeted. His face was set in grim resolve. "I might as well let you know. We are now officially investigating a murder."

I looked at Mike, who nodded. "I performed a quick initial examination, and it was as I expected. Mrs. Swain's system contained traces of Avitrol, the bird poison. It's a horrible way to go—similar to an epileptic seizure, but with pain, delirium, and worse. There was no way she could have survived."

"Could the poison have been administered in her beer?" I asked.

"Yes, it's possible. It would have a slightly bitter taste, but the hops in the beer would cover that up."

"Did you find anything else in her system?"

He laughed. "Give me a break, Chase. This was just a preliminary look. I need to go back and conduct a more thorough analysis. That will take some time."

"But we know what we need to know," the inspector said.

"The first thing I want to do is have a chat with the grounds-keeper. Can you locate him?"

I looked at Mike, who said, "Go ahead. I need a beer. As I said, at some point I'll need to go back and complete the toxicology report. But that won't be tonight."

As I led Caldwell around toward the garden workshop, he said, "Mike also determined that the time of death was approximately between 2:00 and 3:00 a.m."

"We already know that," I said. "I noticed the clock in the room when Fiona died, although someone could have set it to the wrong time. The bigger question is, when did she consume the poison?"

"It must have been at dinner. Mike said that particular poison takes longer to work on humans than birds—about four hours or so. It is far more lethal to humans for some reason, and definitely not a pleasant way to die."

I was glad none of Fiona's family were around to hear that.

We found MacMillan transplanting seedlings in his work-room. After introducing himself, Caldwell asked the grounds-keeper how many poisons he keeps handy.

The man slapped his gloved hands together to shake off the dirt and led us around to the shelves where the Avitrol bottle was on display. "I don't think of these solutions as poisons myself, but, of course, that is what they are, I suppose," he said. "Most are used to kill insects and such. Avitrol is the only one that I use on the birds." He gestured up at the bottle.

Caldwell looked at it. "Is that the only bottle you have?"

"Yes. I only have the one. I don't use it all that much."

"But . . . how did that get here? Do you mean to tell me—"

I nodded. "The cook gave it back, and MacMillan put it back on his shelf."

"Good Lord!" the inspector asked, glaring at the grounds-keeper. "We'll still need to have it analyzed for fingerprints, although that might be difficult with so many people handling it."

He placed a quick call to the station and requested an officer to come down to secure the bottle, then turned again to the groundskeeper. "When you showed Chase and the others where you keep the Avitrol, did any of the party strike you as taking more than a passing interest in it?"

MacMillan mulled over the question. "Hard to say, sir. I did think that young black-haired lady, the plumpish one, seemed unusually concerned, as if she believed the poison could find its way into her afternoon tea."

"Carole Whitebanks," I reminded the inspector.

"But the bloke with her was even more wound up. He couldn't understand why I would kill birds. I explained that, most of the time, Avitrol doesn't kill them; it only makes them sick so they'll avoid our gardens. I know that it can be far more deadly to people."

"Did you mention that to him, or anyone?" I asked.

MacMillan thought a moment. "Don't think so."

"Anything else come to mind?" Caldwell asked.

He thought a moment. "No, not that I recall."

When it became clear we had learned all the groundskeeper could tell us, Caldwell thanked him and turned to leave but froze. "What is that up there?" he asked, looking at the wall on the other side of the room.

In the shadows, a hunting rifle hung from a peg. It appeared well-used, not like the antiques on display in the hotel parlor.

"That's me gun," MacMillan said. "Sometimes I use it to scare the birds off. Don't do it too often, though. Scares the guests as well."

Caldwell stood a moment, regarding the weapon, then thanked the groundskeeper again. We started heading toward the main house. "Was your entire group present when the groundskeeper showed them where the poison was kept?" he asked.

"No," I said. "The twins hadn't returned yet, and Brock—he's the oldest of brothers—was still up in his room. He hadn't joined on the afternoon walk. But the others may have told any one of them about it later."

"Just so."

"MacMillan did tell me he intends to start locking the greenhouse storeroom door."

The inspector huffed out a laugh. "Fat lot of good that does us now. By the way, I did ask that other Upton twin—the strange one—if he visited his sister's room last night. He acted quite surprised and strongly denied it."

"Did he? That's weird. Billie was certain it was Parker. He was wearing the same clothes he had on at dinner."

"He's a bit addled most of the time anyway, isn't he? Some sort of battle shock he experienced in the Middle East?"

"That's the story."

We reached the side entrance to the hotel, and Caldwell faced me. "I'll wait for my man and show him where to get the bottle. Then I need to speak with everyone again, as well as that twin brother. I would greatly appreciate it if you would join me for the interviews, Chase."

I couldn't think of anything I wanted more.

Chapter 21

Thursday Afternoon
Broadmoor Hall

Broadmoor had seemed impossibly large when we first arrived, but after days of everyone confined inside, it had grown claustrophobic. The only spaces in which all of us could congregate were the front parlor and the bar. Brock, Jenna, and Pratt were still in the bar when the inspector and I entered. I informed them that Fiona's death was now regarded as murder, and that the inspector wished to speak with everyone again.

"Murder," Pratt said, uttering the word with all the grave finality—and consequences—it implied.

"We just had lunch, so we're ready whenever the inspector is," Brock said with resignation. "Although I don't know what we can tell him that we haven't already. It's just not possible that any of us killed Fiona. That's crazy talk."

I'd forgotten it was lunchtime. I went to the bar and ordered two burgers and two beers for Caldwell and me. As the barman filled the pint glasses, I had a sudden thought. Going into the adjacent kitchen, I found the cook chopping onions. I introduced myself and asked if all of the beer glasses from the previous evening had been cleaned.

"You mean those over there?" she asked. One long counter

was filled with what looked to be a hundred ale glasses—all sparkling clean. In other words, there was zero chance that traces of the bird poison would still be found in any.

I returned to the bar, picked up the food, took it to Caldwell in the parlor. He gave me an appreciative nod as I handed him a burger and a beer. After taking a bite, he sighed with satisfaction and said, "I want to speak with everyone again, but do it differently this time. Let's question them as a group. People often are provoked to let things slip out when others are around. Bring them in here, will you? I doubt I'll learn anything new, but there's always a chance."

I gladly agreed, went back to the bar, and returned with the others in tow. As they found places to sit, they looked complacent, resigned to another questioning.

Brock grudgingly sat opposite the inspector and said, "There was that huge crowd out on the terrace last night! Why aren't you interviewing any of them?"

Caldwell took another bite of his burger and closed his eyes while he ate. After he swallowed, he said, "Mr. Upton, my approach is always to focus initially on those people who knew the murder victim. Otherwise, I would never get anywhere."

"Strangers kill other strangers all the time back home," Brock said. "What about the guy who drove the truck that night?"

"What truck?" Caldwell asked. "What are you talking about?"

Damn. I'd forgot to brief the inspector on that piece of the puzzle. I quickly briefed him on how the Uptons' parents had drowned twenty years before after driving off Ennerdale Bridge, Fiona remembering the big blue face, and the interview Brock and I had with Alice Hennessey. I also mentioned how defensive the driver, Donald, had been.

"There's your answer!" Pratt exploded. "That truck had to have been involved!"

Caldwell took this information calmly. "I'll need to speak with the company owner. In the meantime, no one should be making unfounded accusations."

I mentioned that I'd spotted Donald in the crowd on the terrace the previous night.

This set Pratt off again. "That driver was here last night? Well, there you have it! Go down and lock that dude up right now!"

"Wait a minute, Pratt," I said. "Think this through. Even if the driver was guilty of something, how would he have known to target Fiona? And how would he have known about the bird poison?"

That sobered him. "Oh . . . well . . . you have a point. But I still can't believe the killer was one of us."

Brock's face lit up. "Maybe one of those kraut hikers killed Fi! You never can trust Germans. They started two world wars, you know. And don't get me started on Volkswagens."

I said, "My same argument applies. How would they have learned of the poison in the garden storehouse?"

He shrugged this off. "Maybe they did some snooping around on their own."

Caldwell turned to Parker and Pratt. "One of you was spotted leaving Mrs. Swain's room shortly before she died. Mr. Parker already denied he was there. What about you, Mr. Pratt?"

Frightened, Pratt looked at Parker, who maintained a blank face, and back to the inspector. "Who said that?"

"Just answer my question, please."

"Well . . . no, I wasn't there . . . that is, I was when Chase helped me bring Fiona to her room, but . . . why would I have gone back?"

"Why indeed?" Caldwell said. "So you both deny being there?"

Again Pratt looked at Parker. "Well . . . of course."

Caldwell leaned toward Pratt. "That's quite a striking neckband you're wearing."

Shaken by this change of subject, Pratt paused. "Uh . . . well, thanks. Yeah. It's like one my father used to wear. I got it from the same region of Mexico."

Caldwell leaned close and appeared to study the band—its intricate assemblage of gold squares—for a few moments. "Forgive my interest, but I've never seen one quite like it. Does your brother ever wear one like that as well?"

"Park? Of course not!"

"I wore it once," Parker said.

"You mean that time I let you try it on? Park, that was years ago!"

"That piece of junk is just—what do you call it—compensation?" Brock said with a laugh. "Pratt kept thinking our daddy was going to give him his own precious necklace. Like that would ever happen!"

Pratt's eyes flared. "He gave me his word! He swore I'd get it when he died!"

"So you say."

Pratt leaped up to take a swing at Brock, but I stood and held him back. "When are you going to stop letting Brock provoke you?" I asked. "He only says things like that to get a rise out of you. And it works!"

Pratt's anger slowly diminished, and he sat back down. Looking at Caldwell, he said, "You need to excuse us Uptons. But you must see this over here, too. How many families are functional these days?"

"Fiona was functional," Parker said in that flat-toned, yet eerily profound way of his.

"What do you mean, Mr. Upton?" Caldwell asked.

Parker fixed his eyes on the inspector's. "We are all broken. Not Fiona."

"Don't listen to him," Pratt said. "He'll babble like this all day if you let him. Take it from me, Parker didn't kill Fiona."

"You didn't either," Parker said to his brother. "I'm glad."

Caldwell looked intently at Parker. "But do you know who did, Mr. Upton?"

Parker's eyes wandered around the room and came back to the inspector.

"I miss bananas," he said.

The inspector contemplated this answer for a moment and turned toward Carole. "Miss Whitebanks? I understand both you and the deceased were employed at a chemists' at one point."

Carole sighed. "Can't you just say her name? Fiona would hate being called 'the deceased.' And by 'chemist,' do you mean a drug lab? If that's what you mean, yep, we both worked for a while at the drug dispensary of a local hospital when we were younger. Jenna knew the main guy and got him to hire us. Fiona worked there longer than me. I never could get the hang of it." She pulled out her small eye-drops bottle. "The only good thing that came out of it was finding this stuff. It's been a lifesaver for me ever since." She took the opportunity to put drops in her eyes.

Sitting beside Carole, Joe kept silent, but with that haunted look I had seen earlier.

"The groundskeeper told us you two seemed unusually interested in the bird poison when he showed it to you yesterday," Caldwell said.

Carole bristled. "Hey! Don't you think it's 'unusual' to find a deadly poison being used near a hotel where you're staying? It certainly seemed so to me. And I was right! Look what happened to Fiona."

Caldwell waited a moment before responding. "The poison didn't pick itself up and deposit itself in whatever glass of ale Mrs. Swain drank last night. Someone stole it from the greenhouse and put it in her drink. Did you see anyone do that?"

Carole looked at Joe, who maintained his haunted-eye look. Turning back to Caldwell, she said, "The only ones there besides Joe and me were Jenna, Billie, and Chase here. We all acted normal, or as normal as you would expect being so close to poison."

"I see." After a pause, Caldwell said, "Let me just ask this straight out. As Mrs. Swain's close friend, Miss Whitebanks, who do you think was the likeliest to want her dead?"

I expected Carole to laugh this off, but she immediately said, "That's easy. Her brother, Brock. They've been at each other's throats for years."

"You'd better close that trap of yours right now, C.W.!" Brock blasted out.

The inspector didn't let Brock's outburst faze him. "At each other's throats?" he asked Carole. "For what reason?"

Carole shrugged. "There are thousands of 'em. It's really just a sibling rivalry thing mostly. They've never gotten along." She looked at Brock. "I'm not saying you're a killer, Brock." Turning back to the inspector, she said, "He comes across as tough as a nickel steak, but he's all hat and no cattle, as they say."

"What about Fiona's claims that Brock molested her when she when she was younger?" I asked.

"Bull pucky!" Brock roared.

Carole shifted uncomfortably. "Well, she never told me about that back then, so it seems strange that she'd bring it up now. Sure, he gets a little too close to her at times—he's done that with me as well—but I think Fi was just razzing him to see him sweat."

It's been my experience that victims of sexual assault, particularly minors, are often too frightened to report it at the time it happens, and may wait years to bring it up, if they ever do. Was that the case with Fiona and Brock?

Caldwell looked at Joe. "Can you think back again to when you brought the tray of beers to the table? There was a big fuss in getting them all handed out. It was almost as if someone was trying to mess it all up."

"Who would do that?" Carole asked.

"You tell me," I said.

"It was Jenna who spilled her beer and made a mess. But she wouldn't have done it on purpose. I mean, why would she?"

"I don't remember much of what happened," Joe said. "I was just trying to make sure everyone got a beer."

Caldwell nodded. "I see."

After a few moments of silence, Jenna spoke up. "How much longer will we be here? I need to get back home and set up Fiona's funeral."

Pratt swung toward her. "Good God, Jenna! Fiona's body isn't even cold, and you're engraving funeral invitations? I might almost think you're enjoying this!"

"Enjoying it?" Jenna shot back, showing more spunk than I'd yet seen from her. "Of course I'm not! But face the truth, Pratt. Fiona had to die. The stars ordained it. It was inevitable."

This set off a heated debate over the reliability of astrology, which in turn set off another of Jenna's sneezing fits. Brock dug out her bottle of allergy pills. Caldwell stood and motioned for me to join him as he left the room.

"We didn't learn much there, did we?" asked the inspector as we walked to the front lobby.

"I'm not sure," I said. "Nothing new was revealed, but there was something . . ."

Caldwell studied me with a probing eye. "If it comes to you, let me know."

Billie joined us, looking troubled. The sparkle in her eyes had dimmed into a cautious yet still alert shadow. Of course, she was still dealing with her financial situation. Now that the walk was over, perhaps that was becoming more real to her.

"I wanted to assure you, Inspector, that even though Pratt and Parker denied it, I definitely saw one of them coming out of Fiona's room," she said.

"Thank you for confirming it," Caldwell said. "That neck-band the normal one wears is rather striking. Did you notice if the person you saw was wearing it?"

Billie shook her head slowly. "No, I didn't. I only took a quick look before ducking back in my room."

"You said he was holding something in his hand, didn't you?" I asked.

"I think so, yes."

"Did it look like a bottle? A syringe of some kind?"

"It was hard to tell. It looked like a small box or package."

I thought of Parker's medicine "kit" that he carried with him into restrooms. Fiona didn't die of a morphine overdose, yet there might have been other nasty goodies in his bag of tricks.

"I'm going to lie down for a bit," Billie said. "Lunch has made me a little tired."

She walked off, and Caldwell said, "I confess I'm at a loss, Chase. It stands to reason that Mrs. Swain was administered the poison on the terrace, and any of this lot could have done it. Yet how are we ever to find out who?"

I sympathized with him. I'd been in his place many times before—that frustrating period after a horrible crime when none of the suspects have yet risen to the top. I said, "You're focusing too much on that one event—what happened at dinner. The answer won't lie there. We need to look at the players involved and examine two key factors: their motive for killing Fiona and their opportunity."

"Ah yes, motive and opportunity," the inspector said. "The old standbys. You've spent some time with this bunch. I know you've filled me in on the basics, but what else have you observed?"

There was quite a bit I hadn't shared with Caldwell. I began revealing information that I felt was pertinent: Parker's history of mental illness, the tangled web of drama surrounding Fiona's

relationship with her husband at the time of his death, the ratio-
nale behind the family's visit to Ennerdale Bridge, and Fiona's
inquiry about statutes of limitation—as well as significant incidents (the scuffles between the siblings, Jenna's prognostications
of doom, the visit to the storeroom), supplemented with a few
of my own interpretations. It all became so overwhelming that,
when I finished, I wasn't certain I had told him everything.

Caldwell listened to all of this without writing down a word.
Did he have total recall? I was thankful that I kept good notes
in my journal.

"That all was very clear and helpful," he said. "I want to ask
one more question, however."

"Shoot."

"Who did it?"

I let out a whoosh of frustration. "I don't know."

He accepted my declaration placidly, if with a trace of disappointment. "Too bad," was all he said.

"But . . . I'm working on it."

Chapter 22

Thursday, Late Afternoon
Broadmoor Hall

Inspector Caldwell informed me he had other business to attend to and would check back in a few hours. I went looking for the others but didn't find them in the usual places. Just as I was about to ask Mrs. Cooper if she'd seen any of our group, Charlie came in from the hotel's side entrance.

"There you are, Chase," he said. "I just told the others that, because of these unfortunate circumstances, my manager has agreed to refund all of your registration fees."

"That's good to hear," I said, refraining to mention that not doing so might have resulted in some unpleasant lawsuits. "Unfortunate circumstances" indeed!

"However," he added, "if it turns out that one of your party is the killer, we will pursue all available means of getting reimbursed."

"Of course. Where are the others, by the way? They don't seem to be anywhere around. I wanted to see how they're taking all of this."

"They're out on the back lawn, enjoying what little sun there is," he said, nodding in the direction from which he'd come. I thanked him, went out into the mild, bright day, and found most of the group seated in a large circle of chairs on the lawn fanning away from the terrace. Parker was the only one on his feet, slowly turning with his arms extended, in what looked like a tai-chi exercise. All were silent, lost in their own thoughts. Billie looked up at me from her knitting and smiled, pointing toward a table on which lime coolers had been set out. I grabbed one and took a seat beside her.

"So, how does this work, Chase?" Brock asked. "Do we just stay here forever or do we get to go back home at some point? They're not going to find that any of us killed Fiona, I can tell you that."

I didn't share his confidence. "Until the police discover who killed your sister," I said, "they're certainly not going to let their main suspects go on their way. Don't you want to find out who killed Fiona?"

"I want to go home and kill the creep who stole my money," Pratt grumbled.

Parker said, "Love of money destroys."

"The lack of money does that too," Pratt replied. "And you don't make much of it refinishing kitchen cabinets."

"You expect Parky to understand finances?" Brock said. "He can barely dress himself."

Parker spun toward Brock, holding his arms as if he was about to hammer them down. Brock braced himself, but Parker slowly spun away, his eyes shut.

Brock exhaled and glared at the others. "I should never have let you all talk me into coming here. I'm gonna call my lawyer. He'll know some way to get us home."

I was frustrated as well. Sipping a lime cooler and soaking up the afternoon sun sounds like a nice way to pass the day, but with so much hanging in the balance, it wasn't very productive. Plus all of this had further kept me from Mike. I reviewed my options: I could return to my room and watch quirky British TV game shows, stay in the bar and nurse another beer long enough not to frighten my liver, or stroll the grounds. Mostly I wanted to get each member of the group alone and get them talking, the best way I knew to dig for the truth. But how to do that? The problem was solved when Carole stood, stretched, and said she was going to her room to exfoliate. I fell into step beside her.

"How are you holding up?" I asked.

"This is all like a bad dream, isn't it? Losing Fiona is bad enough, and now I'm losing Joe too."

"Losing Joe? How is that possible? You two seem inseparable."

She stopped to face me, her eyes troubled. "We were! I really thought at last that I'd found Mr. Right. Then something happened. He changed, almost overnight. I keep asking, is it me? Did I do something wrong? And he says no, it has nothing to do with me, but then he turns away like I've caught the plague or something."

The others were acting strange also, but one of their family had been murdered, after all. Joe had no connection with Fiona. Yet this shift in his disposition seemed to have happened since she was killed. Was he spooked by the thought of a killer at large? And if so, why couldn't he be up front about that with Carole?

"I've learned something about looking for Mr. Right," I said. "Don't base your future happiness on it. When you realize that you'll be fine regardless, that's when you may find him. And if that happens, give it time. If Joe says he loves you, believe him. And until his actions betray his words, trust him."

Carole gave this some thought. "You're smart, Chase, but I don't like to be played for a fool. If Joe thinks he can toy with my affections, he'll be sorry."

As I watched her walk away, I thought of how I'd feel if Mike suddenly turned cold toward me. In one of those moments of serendipity, my cell phone chimed. It was him.

"Just wanted to give you an update," Mike said. "The final lab reports will be ready in a couple of hours, which means I should be back at the hotel around five."

"And then you're on your own time, right?"

"Yours and mine. Nobody else's."

"That's what I want to hear," I said with a smile.

I pocketed my phone and decided to rejoin the group. I headed back and began whistling "Move It On Over" before realizing that, like most of Hank Williams's songs, its bouncy cadence belied the fact that it was about heartbreak and loss. Did that guy ever write a happy tune? I gave it some thought. Only one came to mind—"Baby, We're Really in Love." I began singing "If you're lovin' me like I'm lovin' you" to myself as I walked.

When I reached the lawn, I spotted Joe, sitting by himself, cradling his lime cooler in his lap and staring out into the distance.

I took a seat beside him. "You seem to be taking this hard," I said.

He took a sip of his drink. "Life isn't fair, is it? One minute, you think you've struck it rich, and then something comes along to screw it all up."

"Fiona's death is a tragedy, but it doesn't have to sour the relationship between you and Carole."

He laughed bitterly. "Don't bet on that, pal."

I couldn't think of a decent rejoinder. Maybe he simply didn't want to get involved with someone in the midst of a murder investigation.

I spotted Inspector Crandall coming toward us, walking purposefully but not hurriedly. I wondered if he had news to report.

When he reached us, Brock said, "Hey, Sheriff! I need to make an announcement."

This stopped Caldwell in his tracks. "What sort of announcement would that be, Mr. Upton?"

Brock stood and looked at the others. "I'm prepared to offer a reward to the person who can find out who killed my sister."

Pratt gave a loud hoot. "How big a reward, Brock?"

"A million dollars, hotshot. Is that big enough for you?"

"Brock!" Jenna exclaimed.

"A million big ones?" Pratt said. "Hot dog! I'd better go get my magnifying glass and fingerprint kit."

"Make fun if you want, but I'm dead serious," Brock said.

Caldwell said, "That's very generous, Mr. Upton, but I don't believe a reward will be necessary. Scotland Yard will find out the culprit in due course." He came over to me and said in a lower tone, so as not to be heard by the others, "I was going to visit that meat-packing company in a few minutes. Care to join me?"

I nodded and followed him to his car. I asked, "You can afford a Peugeot on an inspector's salary?"

He gave a laugh as he opened the driver's door. "No, but I can on my wife's."

Within minutes, we pulled up outside the Hennessey building. Donald's delivery truck was again parked at the loading dock, so I suggested to Caldwell that we enter through there rather than through the front entrance. We found Donald seated on the edge of the dock, eating a sandwich. His face clouded when he saw us approach.

"Oh, crikey," he said. "Not you again. What now?"

Caldwell introduced himself, and Donald, realizing he was dealing with the law, sat up straight. He nodded toward me. "I told this bloke the other day that I couldn't possibly remember what may or may not have happened so many years ago."

"Right," Caldwell said. "But let's just go over it again, shall we? When he was here the other day, Mr. Chasen informed you that a woman in his walking group claimed to have seen your truck near the scene of the accident on Ennerdale Bridge involving her parents."

"So he did, but that, blimey, that was twenty years back! My being there was no surprise. I'm often out and about in that area on deliveries."

"Did you know that Mr. Chasen and his group are staying at Broadmoor Hall?"

"Seems likely. Not many other lodges around here."

"Mr. Chasen says he spotted you at Broadmoor last night, at the buffet dinner on the terrace."

Donald eyes narrowed. "Yeah, and what of it? I like to go there on Wednesdays to see my mates. There a law against that?"

"Of course not. But Mr. Chasen also saw you looking intently at the woman in question, the one who remembered your truck."

"Bleeding hell!" Donald said in disgust. "That's utter tosh, innit? How would I know what this lass looks like?"

Caldwell gave him a prolonged stared and said, "Very true." After a pause, he added, "But would it be safe to say that you are familiar with Broadmoor Hall?"

Donald was now cautious, not seeing where this was leading. "Of course I am. Been delivering there for years."

"You're familiar with the grounds? The staff?"

"Anything odd about that? This is a small village."

"How about the groundskeeper, Mr. MacMillan. Do you know him?"

"Ian? Course I do. Known him for ages."

"Have you ever visited him in his garden house? Where he keeps his tools and such?"

Somewhere within Donald, a light turned on. "Hey, wait on a second. What are you getting at?"

"Just answer my question, please."

The driver shifted uncomfortably. "I may have done. Don't remember. What does it matter?"

The inspector didn't respond. Donald's comments had been

interesting, but not exactly incriminating. I didn't see what more we were going to get from him.

"Thank you very much, Mr. Wells," Caldwell said, gave me a slight nod, and turned to leave. Donald sat staring at us as we walked off and got into the car.

"Do you want to speak with Mrs. Hennessey?" I asked.

Caldwell looked up at the building, weighing that option. After a moment, he sighed and said, "Not right now, I don't think. It was this driver I most wanted to meet with. Unless you feel there's more to be gained by speaking with Mrs. Hennessey."

I couldn't think of any reason. We got in the inspector's car, and on the way back to the hotel, we passed Madame Rose's fortune-telling operation. "Stop here a minute," I said. Caldwell pulled his car over to the roadside. "What is it?" he asked.

I explained I wanted to follow up on a hunch. As he accompanied me to the fortune teller's shop, I told him what I wanted to find out. We entered, the bell above the door tinkling, and found ourselves in a small waiting area draped with gauzy curtains and furnished with three worn stuffed chairs and a small table with a lone lamp.

The curtains parted, and a large woman emerged, dressed in a dark blue kaftan that contrasted alarmingly with her overly applied red lipstick and orangish hair. She appeared to be in her seventies. A small oxygen device was slung over one arm, with tubes leading to her nose. This was Madame Rose, I assumed.

"Gentlemen!" she greeted, with exaggerated enthusiasm and a forced smile. "Are you here for a reading?"

"I'm afraid not," the inspector said and proceeded to show his badge.

"Police?" she replied in a much different tone. She straightened herself. "You'll find everything in order here. This is a respectable business. There's nothing shady going on."

"Let me come right to the point. We're here to inquire

about a customer you may have had two nights back. A middle-aged American woman, on the thin side, grayish-blond hair." He pulled up a photo of Jenna he had on his phone.

The woman's mouth opened. "Don't tell me something has happened to her? I knew it, I did. And I warned her!"

"No, nothing's happened to her," Caldwell said. "Do you mind if we ask what she wanted of you? What the two of you discussed?"

Madame Rose looked from the inspector to me and back. "Very well. I normally keep my consultations confidential, but since you are the police . . . come into my reading chamber."

She led us into an adjoining room with a small round table at its center, a chair on either side. She sat, and as there was only one other chair, I nodded to Caldwell to take the other. He sat, and I remained standing.

Madame Rose reached below the table and brought up an ornate gold box. She reached down again and brought up a pack of cigarettes, from which she tapped one out and lit it up. Then she removed the lid of the gold box and extracted a deck of tarot cards. She held them up and said, with a hint of pride, "I only use the Sola Busca tarot. It's the best deck for empaths."

She took a drag from her cigarette and spread out the deck before her, cards face up. "The American woman was extremely concerned about the near future, so I did a seven-card reading. As is my practice, I asked her to fold her hands over the cards for several moments so they could absorb her energy. Then I closed my eyes and followed the divine signals I was receiving to select seven cards, which I laid on the table face down. The first card I turn over is the most significant, as it tells me the direction in which the reading will go. I was somewhat surprised to see that it was the Justice card."

Caldwell and I exchanged looks.

Madame Rose continued. "Unlike many of the other cards,

that one—in its straight-up position—means what it says: justice, as in equity, rightness. It's the following card that gives me more information to work with. In that reading, it was the Queen of Coins—Elena—and it was reversed, upside down. When the American lady saw that, she gasped. She turned to her husband in astonishment. In my readings, that card, in that position, usually signifies a woman, often a close relation or friend, who is duplicitous or overly flirtatious. What was surprising were the next two cards: the Fool and the Queen of Wands. Well, I can tell you, I almost fell out of my chair. The meaning was horribly clear."

"And that meaning was?" I asked.

Madame Rosa looked up at me, cold-eyed. "Death, pure and simple."

"Yes, but whose death?" the inspector asked.

Madame Rose nodded to the image of Jenna on Caldwell's phone. "Why hers, of course!"

Chapter 23

Thursday, Late Afternoon
Madame Rose's Fortune-telling
Parlor

This revelation made Caldwell and I trade looks.

"Jenna's murder?" I asked. "Did you tell her that?"

Madame Rose hesitated. "Well . . . no, I didn't feel it wise to state the situation so . . . bluntly. I tempered my interpretation slightly. I said that the cards implied some imminent danger, and that she should be very cautious."

I nodded slowly. If I had felt there was any credibility to tarot cards, I would have accused Madame Rose of being scandalously remiss in her responsibility. But because I felt it was all a bunch of hooey, I said nothing. The inspector and I excused ourselves and left.

On the way back to the hotel, Caldwell pronounced our expedition a complete failure. "We didn't learn anything at all useful from that truck driver or that Madame Rose," he said. "You can call out the men in the white coats the minute I start believing in fortune telling."

"Oh, we definitely learned a few things," I countered. "We

learned Donald was, in fact, at Broadmoor on the night Fiona was killed, that he was familiar with the garden house and where the poisons were kept, and that he knew exactly who Fiona was."

"He didn't say so."

"Fiona stood out like a Christmas tree in the desert that night. He'd have to be blind not to know she was one of our group. And I saw him looking directly at her."

"Very well. But what about that god-awful Madame Rose? What a load of twaddle. It was Fiona who got killed, not Jenna."

"That's true, but even though Madame Rose didn't tell Jenna the card's true meaning, she may have suspected it," I said. "And though my faith in fortune telling is the same as yours, that might very well still happen. We haven't caught the murderer, after all. At breakfast this morning, Jenna told me that 'it's not over yet.'"

"You believe there'll be another murder?"

"My experience is that when a killer feels threatened, they'll kill again. After all, what have they got to lose?"

"Yes, I have seen that as well," Caldwell said as he pulled up the drive to the hotel. I scanned the cars parked around us and was disappointed not to see Mike's.

Caldwell stopped his car, and when I began to open the door to get out, he held up his hand. "Can I be honest with you, Chase? I'm at something of a standstill. Perhaps it's because I've never had a case that involved only Americans before. I can't truly figure them out. All I know is we have a woman who was killed whilst on holiday with other members of her family. It seems that each had reason to do her in. By all accounts, it appears that she ingested poison in her beer whilst dining in this hotel. All the others were nearby, and any could have slipped the poison into her drink."

I sat back down. "That sums it up, all right. I would add that the decedent also drank her sister-in-law's beer. So if that was the glass that was poisoned, the poison could just as well have been intended for Jenna. Which would align with Madame Rose's prediction."

"That makes it even more muddled."

I hesitated to muddle it even more, but I had to continue. "And then there is that mysterious visit that Billie saw Parker make to Fiona's room right before she died. The mysterious visit that he claims he didn't make."

"True, but the bloke is barmy, isn't he?"

"Yes, but how 'barmy' is he really? He does have moments of surprising lucidity."

"So you think he is our man?"

It was easy to suspect Parker, and not just because of that sighting. He was an unpredictable, drug-addicted, shell-shocked ex-soldier. But I said, "No, somehow I don't think it's him."

Caldwell sighed. "There you have it, then. If there was just one piece of evidence tipping the scale toward any of the suspects more than another, I would go to sleep tonight a happy man. But I have nothing. So I'm asking—are you any closer to a solution than me? Is there anything you haven't told me?"

I paused a moment. I was confident I'd shared everything of material importance with Caldwell, but I hadn't shared all my speculations and hunches. "Rather than share my thoughts now," I said, "give me a night to sleep on it. Otherwise, anything I say will come out all jumbled."

"Fair enough, but if what you say is true about another murder looming, we may not have much time."

He was correct: the pressure was on. As I stepped out of the car, Caldwell rolled down the window to tell me he'd return in the morning, but if I saw anything troubling in the meantime—anything at all—I should give him a call and he'd come running.

* * *

I checked my watch as I walked into the hotel. It was 6:12. Why hadn't Mike returned? I decided to wait in the parlor, where Pratt, Carole, and Parker were gathered on chairs in the corner.

Pratt looked up as I entered. "There's our man. Any news, Sherlock?"

"I'm afraid not," I said as I took a seat. I didn't want to get into a debate about whether Donald, the lorry driver, could be responsible for his father's death, and I certainly wasn't going to relate Brock and Jenna's visit to the fortune teller.

Pratt leaned forward. "If you do figure this all out, could you do me a favor? Tell me, and let me be the one who says he's solved the mystery."

"In other words, Pratt wants the reward money," Carole said.

"Well, Chase doesn't need it," Pratt said. "He's not going to have loan sharks breathing down his neck when he gets home."

I could certainly make use of a million bucks, but basically he was correct. I didn't need the money.

"Wait for the treasure chest," Parker said.

"Translation, please?" Carole asked Pratt.

"I think he means that I'll be getting some of Fiona's estate . . . eventually," Pratt said.

"In the meantime, what do we do?" Carole said, standing up. "I don't know if I can stand being cooped up in this place much more. Can't we go into town for a pizza? Anything would be better than wolfing down another meat pie in the dining room here."

"You forget there's a killer loose," Pratt said. "And seeing as how we're the main suspects, the townsfolk might not want us out mingling among them."

"You're not under arrest," I reminded. "You can't go home yet, but you can certainly go out for dinner."

"Great!" Carole said. "What do you say? Pizza? Mexican? Chinese?"

Pratt laughed. "Where do you think you are, Dallas? This village has one pub and a fish-and-chip shop."

"Let's do the pub then," she said. "It's only a ten-minute walk."

"What about Joe?"

Her face clouded. "I'll send him a text. But don't count on him joining us. He might not want to be with me tonight."

"What's going on with you two?" Pratt asked. "I thought you were about to track down a preacher. Did he find out about your wicked past?"

She threw her arms up. "I don't know what's going on! He just turned off on me, and I don't know why! It's like I committed some huge sin, but he won't tell me what it is. Joe keeps saying he's crazy about me, but if he doesn't start acting like it, I'm gonna have to wash my hands of him." She paused. "And yes, I did tell him about my wicked past." She smiled. "He liked that part."

Carole and Joe's "relationship" couldn't be much more than infatuation, could it? Greased along by being in the beautiful countryside of a foreign land? I thought of when I first met Mike, in a hotel bar in Devon. We only talked briefly, but it was enough. I was hooked, like a love-struck teenager. Yes, I had to admit, love at first sight is possible.

"What about you, Chase?" Pratt asked. "Care to join us?"

I declined, saying that a friend would be joining me.

"Parker's going to stay here, watch TV, and have room service," Pratt said to Carole. "I'll check with Brock and Jenna."

"I need to freshen up," Carole said. "Meet you down here at seven?"

Once Carole left, Pratt got to his feet and stretched. "I wasn't kidding about the reward," he said. "I really need it. Would you consider my proposal?"

It wasn't much of a proposal; he wanted me to give him a million dollars. "What makes you so sure I can find out who killed Fiona?" I asked.

"Because you're ten times sharper than that stuffy inspector. I think he's more comfortable investigating parking violations than murders."

"Don't sell Caldwell short," I said. "He's going by the book, as police must do. That takes time. But honestly, Pratt, any of us could solve the crime if we put our minds to it. Who do you think killed your sister?"

It took Pratt a moment to realize I was asking a serious question. "I know it looks like I did it so I could inherit some of Fiona's bundle. Yeah, getting that money will save my bacon, but seriously? Do I look like someone who would kill his own flesh and blood?"

I wanted to believe him. Pratt had an inherent likability and exuded an earnestness that seemed genuine. Yet I knew how the love of money—or the need of it—can make people do crazy things. I said, "Killers, unfortunately, come in all shapes and sizes. A smiling face frequently disguises ugliness within."

"I'm sure of that," he said. "Just look at the rest of my family."

"What do you mean?"

"I could never kill anyone, but I can't say that about the others. We know Parker was trained to kill in Afghanistan. But Brock? Or Jenna? Even Carole? Trust me. Any one of them is capable of it."

He walked off. I was digesting what he'd told me—which creepily aligned with what Fiona had told me right before she died—when I noticed Pratt had left behind his walking jacket on the settee. I picked it up and was about to call out to him when a few small seeds fell from one of its pockets.

I stooped and gathered them up off the floor. Taking a closer look, I saw that they weren't seeds.

They were yew berries.

Pratt's coat in hand, I went off in search of Billie when my phone chimed. It was Mike, apologizing that his analysis had taken so long to wrap up, but he was finally finished and heading my way. I broke out into a smile as I continued my search.

Not finding Billie in the bar, I figured she was in her room, so I went to mine, took a shower, and changed into fresh clothes. It gave me time to think about what I'd found in Pratt's pocket. Fiona hadn't been poisoned with yew berries, but was he planning to use them with someone else?

Someone knocked on the door. I tossed Pratt's jacket on the bed and opened the door to reveal Mike, smiling sheepishly. I pulled him inside, kicked the door shut, and held him close as we kissed.

"Wow," he said when I released him. "If I'd known that would be my welcome, I would have said the hell with it and left early. But the staff wasn't used to working under a new boss, and many of the tests took longer than expected."

"Did you discover anything else?"

Mike sat on the bed. "No. There were no signs of a struggle, forced intercourse, or any serious health conditions. The Avitrol was the only cause of death."

That was good news. This case already had too many complications.

"So your job here is finished?" I asked as I sat next to him.

He reached over and ran his fingers through my beard. "I can't get over how this is always softer than it looks."

"I soak it every night in goat urine," I said.

His face clouded. I laughed to let him know I was joking, and he gave my shoulder a small punch.

"Back to your question, the answer is 'almost,'" he said.

"I'm finished except for completing the dreaded paperwork, which won't take long. I can do all that tomorrow morning. But let's not talk shop for the rest of this evening."

"Sounds good," I said, stroking his face.

"The question is," he said, "will you be able to get your mind off this case? I remember how committed you were to finding the killer down in Devon."

I moved my mouth close to his. "What case? I don't know what you're talking about."

We went back to kissing, and things started to get more heated. I certainly was ready for that, but I reluctantly pulled away and suggested we hold off until we had some dinner. "What can I tell you? At my age, I need extra nourishment."

He smiled and squeezed my hand. "Enough of that 'my age' nonsense, all right? Nothing wrong with loading up on carbs before the big event. Even teenage athletes do that."

"Thankfully, most of the others are going into the village. So we can eat in the hotel dining room without interruptions."

I gave Mike a quick kiss and picked up Pratt's jacket as we left the room. Downstairs, we found Billie waiting near the entrance, dressed for dinner. She greeted Mike with a broad smile and a hug. "Pratt caught up with me and asked if I wanted to join him and the others at the Royal Oak. I agreed only on the condition that there would be no oompah bands or mob scenes."

"Or murders," I added.

Mike eyed me. "You see? You can't get your mind off of it."

"That was the last time. I promise." To Billie I said, "Speaking of promises, you need to promise me to be careful tonight."

"Don't worry," she said. "I'll keep a close watch over my beer. I won't let anyone near it."

"I don't mean only that. This time period—right after a

murder—is a crucial one. Murders get desperate. They make mistakes."

"What kind of mistakes?"

"Saying too much. Saying too little. Acting differently."

"Trust me. I'll keep my eyes and ears open at all times."

I gave her a nod. "Thanks. And stay with the others at all times."

The Uptons suddenly were upon us. I was surprised to see Joe with Carole, although he still had that hollow, haunted look. I introduced Mike as a close friend, but from the knowing grins I got from Carole and Pratt, I could tell they knew he was more than that. I handed Pratt his jacket. He wasn't wearing his ten-gallon hat.

"I was wondering what I'd done with that," he said, taking the jacket with no apparent concern. "Are you guys coming with us?"

I said that we hadn't seen one another in a while and wanted to catch up.

Once they'd left, Mike and I went into the dining room and selected a table in a small nook, lit by a slim candle.

"This is almost too-too," he said, as eyed me from across the table. "I feel like we're meeting illicitly."

I reached out and held his hand. "It's good to finally be with you in the flesh," I said. After a pause, I added, "Um. That sounded more prurient than I intended."

"Not prurient enough, I would say."

I'd forgotten how strongly Mike attracted me, physically and in every other way. Yes, we'd grown close over the previous year through phone and Skype calls, but sitting across from him, looking at his rumpled salt-and-pepper hair, lopsided grin, bushy eyebrows, and gleaming emerald eyes, I became overwhelmed by a combination of love and lust. Had I ever felt that way about Doug? Most likely, although the lust part faded over time. Physical attraction is mostly a chemical reaction anyway, scientists tell us.

As much as I treasured my years with Doug, there was something enticingly different about Mike. Not necessarily better, I had to remind myself, but different. Was it merely the novelty of a new love? I hoped it was much more than that.

We ordered cocktails and our meals, and spent the next two hours catching up. Mike spoke about his work, how it always threatened to consume his life, and how he constantly had to force himself to carve out time for his passions, which included reading classic novels and playing his clarinet (besides cool jazz, he loved music from the swing era, particularly Benny Goodman). Trying not to sound too maudlin, I talked about having the opposite problem. Doug's death had left a huge void in my life—not just in my soul, but also in my daily routine. He and I had spent most of our days together, so I had to learn all over again the art of being alone. I didn't much like it. Mike and I were perhaps different that way. He'd never had a serious, long-term relationship with another man and hadn't fully come out until he was in his late forties. He'd been married for six years to his ex-wife Joanne (with whom he'd maintained an amiable friendship), and they had two children, Celia and Joshua (who still resented him for leaving their mother). Coming out when he did made him feel old, he told me, and overly cautious, as most of the gay scene was tailored for the young. Then he met me.

We were each dealing with being single in a different way, yet we had far more in common beneath the surface. If there was such a thing as kindred souls, I was convinced that was us. After the server cleared away our plates, I decided that it was time to address the key issue.

"So," I began a bit hesitantly, "how do we work this out, Mike? I want to be with you more than I can say. But there's too much between us."

"I didn't notice anything between us up in your room."

"I'm speaking of the American continent and the Atlantic Ocean."

He gave a small smile. "Is that all? I thought it was something serious."

"You know what I'm talking about. We can't go on just having occasional phone calls. I want to be with you too much."

He paused, lifted his wineglass, and took a pensive sip. "I feel the same about you, Chase, and to be honest, it frightens me. I'm too accustomed to being a solo act. As deeply as I feel about you, I'm not sure I'm ready to make such a big transition."

I reached out and held his hand. "I don't want to own you, Mike. That's not what this is about. It's simply about two people finding companionship and love, which can be beautiful . . . and scary." For a moment, our eyes locked over the candle's flickering flame.

"Don't misunderstand me," Mike said. "I want to be with you too. More than anything I've ever wanted in my whole life. But this is new to me. I never really believed I would find love again. So be patient, all right? It might take me longer to get my head around what's happening."

I gave him a smile to show I understood and squeezed his hand. Yet I wasn't certain I did understand. Did Mike really feel as strongly about me as I did about him? Or was I simply afraid to trust in him and the winds of destiny?

Later that night, after Mike drifted off to sleep, I lay awake, contending with many emotions and feelings that I wanted to sort out. I thought about which feelings were new and which were reminders of the past. Trying to be as quiet as possible, I went to the room's small desk, picked up my journal, and began to write. My notes about Mike, although lengthy, did not bring any flash of enlightenment about our living arrangements. Yet I strongly believed we would find some kind of solution moving forward.

My notes about the rest of the day—had Fiona died only that morning?—were briefer. They were simple observations, not matters of the heart. Once I finished, I looked down at the pages and tried to see what they might be telling me.

Again there was no blinding revelation, but I got the nagging feeling that I had missed something. I read my notes again and couldn't see it. What I was certain of, though, was that an evil presence was still among us, and it hadn't been fully satisfied.

Chapter 24

Friday Morning
Broadmoor Hall

I awoke with Mike's arm around my waist. It felt strange—Doug rarely held me in my sleep, nor I him—but it was comforting. It was also sensual, invigorating, and . . . redemptive. Once again, I felt I'd been given another chance at happiness, and yet I also felt I had to tread carefully or it might disappear.

Mike continued sleeping as I wriggled free and prepared to go out in search of coffee. After I'd finished dressing, I tried to be quiet leaving the room, but heard him stir.

"Chase?" he murmured.

I knelt beside him. "I'm going for coffee. Want some?"

He groaned through a smile and mumbled "later" before shifting and falling back asleep.

I closed the door quietly and headed downstairs. It made sense that Mike didn't want to get up this early; we were in his time zone, after all, and he was far more entrenched in his rhythms than I was in mine. When I entered the breakfast room, I found Billie seated near the window, her hand wrapped around her coffee mug. It struck me as odd that she wasn't knitting.

"Good morning," I said with a smile. "What's the matter? Don't tell me you've run out of yarn."

She managed a half-hearted smile. "Well, look who's all bouncy and cheerful first thing in the morning for a change. No, I've got plenty of yarn. But I'm worried. Get your coffee and let's talk."

I poured a cup and returned to the table. "More bad news about your finances?" I asked.

"No, nothing like that," she said. "It's about something that happened last night."

"Okay. Give it to me. And don't leave out a thing."

Billie gulped down some coffee and took a deep breath. "We were all together at the Royal Oak, the six of us, as you know. The Uptons were on good behavior—no outbursts or bickering. But it became clear to me that something was off between Carole and Joe. He was acting distant, and she kept getting more and more annoyed. Finally, she got up and stormed off. Joe went after her, and we could hear them arguing in the front room. Carole shouted, 'I'll never forgive you for this!' and the next thing I saw through the window was her storming away down the street."

"Do you have any idea what they were arguing about?"

"I didn't hear anything specific. But there was something troubling him that he didn't want to talk about, and Carole thought their relationship had gotten to the point where he shouldn't be holding anything back."

I pondered this information as I took a sip of coffee. "Under normal circumstances, it isn't unusual for couples to bicker a bit as things start out. But these aren't normal circumstances. Someone has just been murdered. The poor guy came over here to drink some beer, look for birds. He falls in love as well, and then, bam! He's in the middle of a murder investigation."

"There's more," Billie said. She took a sip of coffee and continued. "The rest of us didn't linger much longer at the restaurant and began heading back. I walked beside Joe, hoping I could coax some information out of him."

"In that inimitable way of yours," I said. "How successful were you?"

"I could tell he wasn't in a talkative mood, but he wasn't impolite. Just responding to my small talk with simple comments. I was just about to flat out ask him what was bothering him when he stopped, looked me square in the eye, and said, 'I was there. I saw who did it.'"

"What exactly did he see?"

"He wouldn't say! I was just about to tell him that he needed to inform the police at once, but he bolted. Ran away like his life depended on it. I would have told you this last night, but I didn't want to interrupt you and Mike."

"I appreciate that, but next time don't be so polite." I took a swallow of coffee and stood. "We need to find Joe and get to the bottom of this."

She followed me out of the room. "Chase, what Joe said must explain his argument with Carole. Maybe he saw her put the poison in Fiona's beer."

I kept walking. "He could have seen a lot of things. He has a photographer's eye, you know."

We reached the hotel entrance when something sounded outside. I froze.

"Did you hear that?" I asked.

"It sounded like a gunshot," Billie said.

"I'm going to see what happened. You need to stay here."

"No dice. I'm coming with you."

I put my hands on her shoulders. "Like hell you are. If there's someone with a gun out there, I'm not going to let you risk your life."

"What about you? You're risking yours!"

"I'm trained for these situations." Once I was sure Billie wasn't going to follow, I ran outside and headed toward the garden, in the direction of where I'd heard the shot. On the way, I kept my eyes alert, scanning right and left. When I reached the topiary garden, I saw that my search was at an end.

Joe Scarbun's prone body lay beside the large topiary peacock, its leafy plumage spread above him, the morning dew still wet on its fronds. Blood was spreading from a hole in his chest and pooling on the earth around him. He was dressed in a T-shirt and yoga pants, which suggested he'd come straight there from his room without changing his bedclothes. I bent to check for a pulse, but the vacant look in his eyes told me all I needed to know.

I looked around for the weapon, and when I saw nothing, I stood and began a slow reconnoiter of the perimeter of the garden. That's when I spotted a rifle in a path about a hundred feet away, toward the main house, but on a different path than the one I'd taken. This was not just any rifle: it was the one I'd seen on the wall of the groundskeeper's garden shed.

I looked around and saw no one. Of course, Joe's killer would have been long gone. I dashed back inside to Billie.

"It's Joe," I said. "He's been killed. Shot by a rifle."

"Who's been shot?" It was Pratt, coming from the direction of the front parlor.

"What's going on?" asked Jenna, walking toward us from direction of the breakfast room. She was holding a small plate in one hand and a half-eaten Danish roll in the other.

"Jenna?" Brock said, coming in from the terrace. "I've been looking for you! Where have you been?"

"What does it look like? I was hungry and didn't want to wake you up."

The front door swung open, and Carole entered, wearing a light coat and a scarf around her hair. "What's everyone in such a stir about?"

Parker was the last to arrive, coming down the stairs, dressed in the same blue shirt-and-denim outfit as Pratt. "My television is broken," he said.

"I'm afraid I have bad news," I said. "Joe's been killed. We need to notify the police."

"Joe?" Carole screamed. "*No!*"

Everyone began speaking at once, circling me, firing questions. My priority, though, was to notify the authorities. I pulled out my cell phone and texted Inspector Caldwell.

JOE SCARBUN SHOT AND KILLED. SEND SOMEONE IMMEDIATELY.

I pushed SEND and shouted for everyone to be quiet. "Billie, will you come with me, please?" I asked, and she followed me up the stairs.

"Where are we going?" she asked.

"Joe's room."

"Joe's room? What good is that going to do? Won't it be locked?"

I didn't stop to reply. We reached the door to Joe's room, and I tugged my sleeve over my hand as I turned the doorknob. The door opened. We entered, and I did a quick lookaround. The bed was unmade, the blankets thrown to one side as if he had just gotten out.

"Look at this, Chase," Billie said. She handed me a small slip of paper. "It was on the table by the door."

The note said MEET ME AT THE LILY POND, written in block letters. It was signed C.W.

"Put that down," I said. "Your fingerprints might obscure others."

She gently set it back on the table. "This looks pretty cut-

and-dried, doesn't it?" she said. "Carole asked Joe to go the lily pond, and she killed him."

"Use your head, Billie. If that was her intent, why sign the note? Or, for that matter, why write a note at all? Why didn't she just phone Joe or text him? Or why didn't she just shoot him here? Why be so dramatic about killing him beside that topiary bush?"

"You should have heard how angry Carole was last night, Chase. There was definitely murder in her voice."

"Now, there's a talent I never knew you had. You need to write a monograph on how to recognize murderous intent in vocal patterns. It will be a landmark in the history of criminology."

"Don't get cute, Chase. I'm only telling you what I heard. And you know as well as I do that people act irrationally when they decide to kill. That could excuse the note."

We heard a siren outside, growing louder. "Let's get back downstairs," I said.

Everyone was gathered outside when the police van pulled up. Two policemen and two others in coveralls stepped out, one carrying a stretcher. I went over to them and explained where to find Joe. I also said that they should find the murder weapon not far away.

The commotion had drawn others. The hotel's night manager, a young Jamaican woman, had emerged from the hotel's side door, as had the breakfast cook. After I filled them in on what was happening, I spotted MacMillan, the groundskeeper, not far off.

"More trouble?" he asked, eyeing the police van.

"Another murder," I said.

"Good heavens. Not another of your walking group, is it?"

"I'm afraid so. And he appears to have been killed by the rifle that was hanging in your garden workroom. Didn't you tell me you were going to start locking the door?"

A clear look of guilt washed over his face. "Was going to. But who was to think this would happen again so soon?"

I saw Caldwell's Peugeot come up the drive and park beside the police van. Excusing myself, I went and greeted the inspector as he stepped out.

"Bad business, eh, Chase?" he said.

"Bad business indeed," I replied and related more about what had happened. I told him about Joe's comment to Billie the night before. *I saw who did it.*

"Joe didn't say who it was that he saw?"

I shook my head. "He ran off before Billie could question him further."

The two men from the medical examiner's team were returning, carrying Joe's covered body on their stretcher. Caldwell said, "I'm going to go speak with the crime-scene manager and then round everyone up again. Can you help me out with that?"

"The usual suspects?"

"Yes, unless new ones have popped up. I'll be back shortly."

As he walked off, I went to join the rest of the group, watching Joe's body being loaded into the van. They all wore the same shocked faces as when they discovered that Fiona had been killed. Carole stood with her arms folded, her face a frozen, stunned mask. I couldn't help but wonder: Was that the face of a bereaving lover or of a killer realizing the enormity of her act?

Pratt came over to me. "Why would any of us have killed Joe, of all people, Chase? None of us knew the guy before he came on this walk."

"Unfortunately, there's no minimum time requirement for a murderer to know his victim," I said.

Parker came up and said, "They'll never be the same."

"Who won't?" I asked.

"Whoever killed Joe. Whoever killed Fiona."

That weird feeling returned that Parker was telling me something vital in his own special code. Yet I had no idea how to decipher it. I went over to Billie. "Let's go inside."

I led her into the alcove off the main hallway that provided just enough space for us to speak without being seen, or heard, by the others.

"Where were you last night when Joe told you he had seen the murderer?" I asked.

"In that walkway tunnel. You know, the one that runs beneath the main road."

"Was there anyone else in the tunnel at the time?"

She thought a moment. "Brock and Jenna may have been. Maybe Pratt and Parker. But they were nowhere near Joe and me. There's isn't any chance they could have heard what he said. Why?"

Mike walked in. "There you are," he said, and said hello to Billie. "I saw the police outside, and they told me what had happened. Talk about rotten luck! Two murders in two days."

Rotten luck was putting it mildly. Just when it looked like Mike and I were going to get time alone, this had to happen. I immediately reproached myself, though. I wasn't the victim here. Mike said he had already spoken with the medical examiner's team outside.

"A shooting victim calls for a forensics analysis, which is not my specialty," Mike said. "But I agreed to accompany them as they take the body and help in whatever way I can."

"Have you had any breakfast?" I asked.

"I'll grab something on the other end. I'm sorry, Chase. I'll hurry back as soon as possible." With a rueful smile, he turned and walked away.

"That's a good man you have there, Chase," Billie said as we headed back to the breakfast room.

"He certainly is. But I may never get to find out quite how good if people keep getting killed."

"Oh, people will still get killed," she said. "But I've got a feeling you'll soon put a stop to that happening around here."

"I appreciate your faith in me."

As we walked toward the buffet, Billie added, "You've never let me down yet." After a pause, she added, "And you'd better not this time."

Chapter 25

Friday, Midmorning
Broadmoor Hall

Some might wonder how Billie and I still had an appetite after just learning that another member of our group had been brutally murdered. If so, they don't understand what triggers the human desire to eat. It isn't just the need to replenish the body's capacity to sustain itself; it also helps counter grief, frustration, bewilderment, and a million other negative emotions. Food is one of the ultimate compensators (besides sex and drugs), which, I guess, explains the number of overweight people in the world.

That morning, the buffet looked especially inviting: hot rashers of bacon, freshly cut fruit, steaming porridge, and fluffy whipped eggs. Billie and I took more than our share to our table.

After we sat, she unfolded her napkin and said, "I heard from my attorney this morning." This was a surprise; I didn't know she'd engaged an attorney. "He said there are steps I can take to recover what Marie stole from me, but it will take years. My only hope is that the authorities will find her. But since she's probably fled to some South Seas island, I'm not holding my breath for that to happen."

"I'm so sorry," I said. "I'll remind you that I have a little extra in my savings account. I can always help you if you're in a bind."

"Of course I'm in a bind!" Billie said. "Those investment accounts were all that I had besides what I get from Social Security and my pension. But honestly, Chase, I'm not going to take any of your money. I'll find some way to get by. My sister can always put me up if I have to sell my house."

"I won't let you do that," I said with finality. I hated to hear of Billie in such dire straits. At the moment, however, there were more pressing concerns. Inspector Caldwell was relying on me to find Fiona's murderer—and now Joe's as well. The good news (if you could call it that) is the murderer in both cases was most likely the same person, as the odds of two murderers at work within the same group were astronomically high. The pressure was on me not to let the inspector down.

"Not to change the subject—which we need to revisit—but let's talk about who killed Joe," I said. "He said he'd seen who did it. So why didn't he go to the authorities?"

Billie didn't have to think this one over. "I believe I know, and so do you. The one he saw was Carole, with whom he'd just developed an attraction."

I hesitated. "Perhaps. But think of the alternatives. He might have seen another member of the Upton clan do the deed. If he revealed that to Carole, she wouldn't hesitate to call in the police. But Joe might not have been so forthcoming. He would have known the tailspin it would set off within the Uptons. And he was a very conscientious guy."

Billie huffed out a laugh. "Conscientious enough not to bring a killer to justice?"

"You're right. It's another puzzle." I took a bite of my breakfast bun. "My mind feels like one of those bins in which the balls in a lottery tumble around. The winning ball is in there somewhere, but it's always in motion, one minute in view and hidden the next. So here are some things to consider: A bottle of eye drops. Parker's medication kit. Tarot cards. Sound waves."

"Sound waves? Um, you bet, Chase. I'll consider those. Definitely."

Mike was also on my mind, but in a different way. After this second murder, I feared he'd begin to associate me with death and see me as a Jonah of some kind. Death couldn't sound very romantic, even to a coroner.

But then, being the Devon county coroner, he was associated with death as well, wasn't he?

These issues weighed on my mind as Billie and I finished our breakfast mostly in silence before joining our group in the parlor. I was surprised to see Charlie there as well, Ramses at his feet. Caldwell hadn't yet returned from the crime scene.

I seated myself on the only available chair, Brock beside me. "Do you know what kind of gun was used to shoot Joe?" he asked. Nodding to the wall-mounted rifle case across the room, he added, "These are the only firearms I've seen around here. And none of us brought any with us."

I knew the gun was the groundskeeper's, but I chose to play dumb and just shrugged.

"If they wouldn't have been confiscated by airport security, Brock, you probably would have brought your guns," said Pratt, stretched out on a settee.

"If I'd known we'd be rubbing elbows with a killer, you bet your butt I would have."

Carole was curled up in a chair, still looking shell-shocked. Parker sat beside her, tapping his foot on the floor. Jenna stood looking out the window at the lawn and gardens. "My chart said this would be a day in which the darkness of the past continues to take its toll," she said.

Pratt said, "For crying out loud, Jenna, does your damn chart ever predict anything happy?"

Her face remained calm as she faced him. "The stars owe no one happiness."

"You're really a cold old bird, aren't you?" Pratt said. "I can totally see you pumping a couple of rounds into Joe just to make sure your precious 'chart' won't be proven wrong."

"Pratt!" Brock said. "I demand that you apologize."

Pratt shot to his feet. "Apologize? Like hell I will! She practically accused me of killing Fiona."

Brock stood as well. "And how do we know you didn't, hotshot?"

"The sky is out of date!" Parker wailed.

"Stop it, all of you!" I said, drawing everyone's attention. "Being at each other's throats isn't going to help anyone."

Caldwell chose that moment to walk in, pausing to take in the tension in the air. "Is anything wrong?" he asked.

"Of course there's something wrong," Pratt said. "Another one of us has been killed!"

The inspector waited before responding. Pratt and Brock backed away from each other.

"Very well then," Caldwell continued. "Everyone, please take a seat. Because of this new incident, I need to find out each of your movements this morning."

Brock joined Jenna on a love seat, while Pratt returned to his settee. Caldwell pulled a chair to the center of the room, and pulled out a notepad and pen.

"Let's begin with Mr. Chasen and Miss Mondreau," he said. "You were prompted to go and search for Mr. Scarbun when you heard the firing of a rifle, were you not?"

"That's right," I said. "Billie and I had just left the breakfast room when we heard the shot. I knew it was 6:45 or so, because the breakfast items hadn't been put out yet."

"Is that what you remember, Miss Mondreau?" the inspector asked Billie.

"That sounds about right," she said.

Jenna said, "I heard the shot too."

"Where were you?" Caldwell asked her. "In your room?"

"No, I was in the breakfast room. I heard a little boom and just thought it was a truck backfiring."

I told the inspector that I'd asked Billie to remain where she was while I checked out the gunshot. "That's when I found Joe's body and the shotgun not far off."

"And you saw no one else on the grounds?" the inspector asked.

"I did my best to look around while still hurrying back here to report Joe's death," I said. "No, I saw no one."

Caldwell turned to Brock. "Mr. Upton. Your wife claims she was in the breakfast room when the gun went off. Where were you at the time?"

"What do you mean, she 'claims'?" Brock shot back. "Are you accusing my wife of lying?"

"I'm not accusing anyone of anything. But in a murder investigation I need to take what people tell me with a grain of salt. Until their statement is verified, it is just hearsay."

Brock didn't seem placated by Caldwell's explanation, but he relaxed. "I was just waking up when it happened, I guess. Jenna always gets up before me."

"That's true," Jenna said. "Brock was still sleeping when I left our room."

"Just so," Caldwell said. He turned to Pratt. "And what about you, Mr. Upton?"

Taking a breath, Pratt said, "If Joe was shot around 6:45, I was probably either shaving or getting dressed. I didn't hear anything that sounded like a gunshot."

To Parker, he asked. "How about you, Mr. Upton?"

Parker thought for a moment. "The first successful kidney transplant was performed on identical twins in 1954," he said. Turning to Pratt, he said, "Would you give me a kidney?"

Caldwell was used to Parker's mental quirks by that point. "I'm sure your brother would, Mr. Upton. But what about this morning? Where were you around 6:45?"

"I wake up at 6:30."

"So you were still in your room?"

"I like snakes. They predict earthquakes."

The inspector took a deep breath. "We're not talking about snakes right now. I need to know where you were at 6:45 this morning."

"Don't badger him!" Carole said. "He just told you he wakes up at 6:30. How in hell could he go out and kill Joe in fifteen minutes? Get real."

"I want to hear it from him," Caldwell said.

Barely audibly, Parker mumbled, "She's right."

Caldwell sighed. "Very well, then. Miss Whitebanks? Where were you this morning while this was going on?"

Carole said, "I hadn't slept much all night. As soon as the sun started coming out, I got dressed and went for a walk. Mostly to clear my head."

"Why weren't you able to sleep?"

"Because I was upset, okay? My boyfriend told me he didn't trust me!"

"And your boyfriend was . . . the deceased?"

Carole snorted. "Yeah, the 'deceased.' That's a good name for him."

"Not to pry too deeply into your relationship, but why did Mr. Scarbun say he didn't he trust you?"

Carole cast her eyes around the room, studying the way others were looking at her. "Well, he didn't exactly put it that way. He told me he knew who the murderer was. But when I asked him the person's name, he wouldn't tell me."

"Did he say why?"

"He only said that he needed to be absolutely sure before he started tossing around accusations."

"That's commendable," the inspector said. "Did he tell you how he knew the identity of the killer?"

"No," she said. "I think he wanted to tell me—it was eating him up inside, I could sense it—but he couldn't bring himself to do it. I tried not to take it personally, but I was hurt, I have to say."

Her news fed directly into what Billie had heard. Was Joe afraid to divulge what he saw because it incriminated either someone he loved or someone close to someone he loved?

"I see," Caldwell said. After a pause, he turned to the others. "I will ask you again what I asked you before, after the first murder. Did any of you notice anything unusual this morning, either before or after this incident occurred?"

There were a lot of shaking heads, but Parker said, "I saw something."

Caldwell hesitated. What kind of nonsense was Parker going to spout? "Yes, Mr. Upton? What did you see?"

"Flowers. They drop their petals in the morning."

The inspector sighed. "Yes, I see. Thank you. That is very helpful."

"I saw it from my window."

"Quite so. Again, thank you. Anyone else have something to add?"

No one did. Getting to his feet, Caldwell left us with his usual advisory for us not to leave town, but he gave no indication of how much longer that edict would remain in effect. I followed him into the main hallway, where he told me he was going to interview the breakfast cook, night manager, and housekeeper, the only staff present that morning. I told him I needed to get some air, a subtle way of communicating that I trusted him to handle those discussions on his own.

The first thing that struck me as I went outside was the air: bitingly crisp yet not icy, tinged with an electrical undercurrent that perhaps signaled a coming storm. The sky was clear, but that could change in an instant. The breeze was coming in erratic bursts, as if it couldn't decide which way to blow. The effect was unsettling, even if two murders hadn't been committed within the previous three days.

I inhaled deeply, stretched my arms, and twisted a few times. Walking is the keystone of my fitness routine, but it isn't a full-body workout; I supplement it with weight training to maintain muscle tone and more active cardio to get my heart pumping. So I did several toe-touches and ran in place, hoping nobody was watching.

My little workout wasn't much, but it got the job done. Feeling more alert, I began walking briskly up a path I hadn't yet explored, between the herb garden and a group of ash and hazel trees. A bird sang from above. There was a scent of lavender in the air.

The path brought me to the south end of the garden house, near the entrance to the groundskeeper's workroom. I was dismayed to see that the door was once again wide open. Apparently two murders were not sufficient incentive to get MacMillan to lock it.

I recalled the day when we first visited the storeroom. It looked pretty much the same—except for the bottle of poison, which had been removed by the police. When we left the room, I hadn't immediately returned to the hotel with the others, and I'd seen that Joe hadn't either; he was still bird-watching. He had his camera in hand, photographing a bird right on the spot on which I was standing.

Yet how could he have been? Looking straight ahead, all I could see was the groundskeeper's workroom, through the open door. There were no birds in there.

I began walking back to the hotel. A few feet from the back

entrance, I noticed a small trash receptacle, and a small, light red synthetic glove on the ground beside it. I removed a tissue from my side pants pocket and gently picked up the glove, wrapped it in the tissue, and inserted it in my back pocket. In the hotel, I found Mrs. Cooper talking to the housekeeper near a linen closet in a side hallway.

"Hello, Mr. Chasen," she greeted, without her usual effluent bubbliness. "We were just interviewed by Inspector Caldwell. Such a horrible business, isn't it? I hope he catches the killer soon. Having a murderer on the loose isn't exactly good for business."

"I don't think we'll be in the dark much longer," I assured her, which prompted her to form a small, hopeful smile. "Tell me, though, has Mr. Scarbun's room been cleaned?"

The housekeeper, a dowdy woman with stringy gray hair, said, "Yes sir. The police examined it, and I brought all his belongings downstairs to the cloakroom."

"Do you mind if take a quick look?" I said. "I've been helping the inspector in this matter."

Mrs. Cooper smiled. "Why yes, we know you have, Mr. Chasen. Right this way." She led me to the small room, the size of a closet, not far from the main entrance. Joe's belongings—his suitcase with some clothes piled on it—sat in a corner. On top was his camera.

His camera. Joe not only spotted birds using his field glasses; he also photographed them.

"I need to check something," I told Mrs. Cooper, and picked up the camera. She didn't have any objections. I took it into the parlor, thankfully unoccupied. I sat, removed the camera (an elaborate Canon SLR) from its case and turned it over to view the photos he had recently taken.

It didn't take me long to find the photo I was looking for. It was one of the last he'd taken. And it was very revealing.

Chapter 26

Friday Afternoon
Broadmoor Hall

I was just about to go in search of Caldwell when he came into view, walking toward me, finished with his last interview. His necktie was askew, and his collar was loosened. He was looking down at his cell phone, but when he looked up and spotted me, he came to sit beside me on the sofa.

"Learn anything important from our group?" I asked.

He gave a long sigh. "No, but I didn't really expect to. The housekeeper confirms she saw Carole go out for her walk at the time in question. She even bid her good morning. But other than that, nothing. What are you doing with a camera, for heaven's sake?"

I held it up. "This is Joe's. He always carried it with him so he could photograph birds he spotted." I held the viewing screen so Caldwell could see it. "It turns out birds weren't the only thing he photographed."

It took a moment for the inspector to realize what he was looking at. "Good lord. Isn't that—?"

"It certainly is. And it explains his comment to Billie. *I was there. I saw who did it.*"

Caldwell continued to stare at the image, as if he couldn't believe it.

I said, "This may not be as incriminating as it looks, however. It's suspicious all right, but it could still be explained away."

"Yes, you may be right."

I hesitated, then said, "And here's something else." I reached in my pocket, pulled out the small envelope, and handed it to Caldwell. He peered inside.

"These look like berries," he said.

"Yew berries. They're poisonous. I found them in Pratt Upton's jacket. He must have picked them up on the trail."

Caldwell cocked his head. "Except . . . Mrs. Swain wasn't poisoned with yew berries."

I took back the envelope and nodded. "That's true. But it doesn't explain why he collected them. He may have considered using them, but changed his mind."

Caldwell shook his head slowly. "That's another complication that is simply muddying the waters. That image on the camera is far more incriminating."

An idea began forming. Caldwell and I could follow standard procedure and pursue what Joe's photograph strongly implied, but I saw potential pitfalls. There was another tack, however, that I'd always wanted to try. It had its own risks as well, but fewer, I hoped.

I proposed my plan to Caldwell. I was expecting him to either laugh it off as being too theatrical, or approve it with a counterproposal that he be the one to take the lead. To my surprise, he smiled, raised his eyebrows, and said, "Very good, Chase. Please have a go at it. I've always wanted to see someone do that in real life!"

Billie played a role in my plan, so I went in search of her and found her knitting at the small corner table in the bar that had become one of her favorite spots.

"It's such a pretty day, I would prefer being outside," she said. "But not with a murderer running around. It's like *And*

Then There Were None, where everyone is on that island with a killer and getting bumped off one by one. To protect themselves, they always tried to make sure they stayed with someone else." She nodded to the barman, not far away.

"A wise decision," I said. Unless the barman is the killer, I thought.

"I saw you conferring with the inspector. Did you learn anything?"

Instead of answering her question, I asked, "Do you know where the others are?"

Billie thought. "Pratt was in here a few minutes ago. I think he and Parker went to the study or whatever they call it to play a game of pool. Carole disappeared up to her room, poor thing. I imagine the others are outside or in their rooms as well."

I nodded. "Could you do me a favor? I'd like you to find everyone and tell them that the inspector wants to speak to us out on the terrace right after lunch, at one."

Billie raised her eyebrows. "What's he planning now?"

"If I tell you, it'll ruin the surprise. Can you do what I ask?"

She stood and began stuffing her knitting in her bag. "Sure thing. But what about Charlie? I saw him earlier—he'd come by to check up on everyone and make sure Mrs. Cooper could still put us up tonight."

"Yes, ask him to join us as well."

She checked her watch. "It's eleven-thirty. That should give me enough time."

"When you've told them, come back here, and I'll ask you for one more favor."

"Cut the suspense, Chase! What's going on?"

I smiled and patted her hand. "Patience, my dear Miss Mondreau. All will be revealed."

While Billie was off on her errand, I went to the bar and ordered a ham sandwich and a pint of bitter—Teaberry's Tipple, a local brew. By the time the sandwich was ready, Billie had returned.

"I found everyone but Parker and Pratt. The others said they'll look for them. Mmm, look at that sandwich!" She reached over and tore off a chunk of it. "Murder investigations give me the munchies!"

I took a bite as well, and when I was able to speak, I said, "Go order one for yourself and come back here. I need to finish my instructions."

She quickly returned and sat opposite. "I'm all ears," she said.

"I want you to be the last one to join us on the terrace. When you do, announce that Inspector Caldwell has been momentarily detained and should be coming along soon. There'll probably be bitching and speculating about that. Then I'd like you to ask for my thoughts on the investigation. Make it seem natural and casual. Can you do that?"

Billie grinned. "You forget I played Blanche DuBois in college. Compared to that, this will be a piece of cake. But what's up?"

I reached out to give her shoulder a slight squeeze. "As I said, all will be revealed." I went back to my sandwich but couldn't shake the jarring mental image of Billie as Blanche DuBois.

I had one more order of business to attend to. I called Mike, who told me his work at the morgue was just about finished and he'd be able to join me soon. I outlined my plan for the afternoon.

"And the inspector agreed to that?" he said with a laugh.

"It surprised me as well," I admitted, "but he's not the strict by-the-rules guy he seems." I told Mike the role I wanted him to play.

"I'll be happy to do that," he said. "But are you sure things won't get out of hand?"

"It depends on what you mean by 'out of hand.' Actually, I'm hoping things do get a little heated. I want to shake everyone up."

I went to the terrace and took a seat, and a little before 1:00 p.m., the Uptons began to appear. They were curious, but mostly looked drained. Carole's eyes were red and swollen from crying. The others were dry-eyed but with zombie-like expressions. Two deaths within as many days will do that to you.

Brock asked if I knew what Caldwell wanted us for, and I played dumb, saying I was as much in the dark as they were. Soon they were all assembled: Jenna and Brock sat at a small table, Parker and Carole side by side on a love seat, and Pratt by himself at a café table. I felt like a baseball coach about to address his team after a major defeat, knowing each player's hot buttons and weaknesses, preparing to deliver an analysis that was honest without being too brutal.

Charlie was situated away from the group on a bench, as if prepared to get up and leave at any moment. Ramses sat at his feet, as always. The dog seemed the most attentive of all: his eyes gleamed and his ears were perked, as if he knew something was coming.

The tense mood was contrasted by the radiance of the gardens not far away, multicolored and dappled in the waning rays of daylight, reminding us that there was still beauty in the world. I also spotted Mike not far away, seated in one of the alcoves, close enough for him to hear what was about to transpire but out of sight from our group.

Billie was the last to arrive. Pratt looked up at her and asked, "So what happens now? Where's the inspector?"

She sat beside me. "He told me to tell you he's been detained. He should be here soon."

"He must be onto something," Carole said. "Is he going to arrest us?"

"Don't talk nonsense, C.W.," Parker said. "What evidence does he have?"

Brock turned toward me. "You used to be a cop, Chase. Did you ever find yourself in a situation like this after a murder, where there seems to be no solution in sight?"

I eyed Billie and gave a slight (and, I hoped, imperceptible to the others) nod. It was time for her to play her part.

"Brock raises a good question, Chase," she said. "Your detective mind is still in good working order. Would you mind sharing your thoughts with us?"

Billie had done well. Her question sounded spontaneous, and from the expressions on the faces around me, the others bought it. All looked at me in rapt attention.

"Are you sure?" I asked. "If I do this, it might make some of you uncomfortable."

"Go on, man," Brock encouraged. "We can take it."

"Very well." After a pause, I stood (not too dramatically, I hoped) and said, "Yes, I do have some thoughts. First of all"— I paused for effect—"it is my belief that both Fiona and Joe were killed by the same individual, and that person is here with us now."

Chapter 27

Friday Afternoon
Broadmoor Hall Terrace

As I expected, everyone began speaking at once. I held up my hand. "Quiet, please! I can't do this if I'm interrupted. Are we agreed?"

There were nods, some reluctant, all around.

"Okay then. I made that assumption because, whatever you may think, it is the most likely one. Yes, it's possible these murders were committed by some local maniac. However, no other murders have been reported recently, and the likelihood that some killer has popped up and targeted two members of our group is even more unlikely."

Pratt raised his hand. "Can I say something? I see what you're getting at, Chase, but the trails we were on often went through private property. What if there was some local who didn't want a bunch of strangers tromping through their land and decided to take action?"

"We're not the only walking group here this week," Brock said. "What about those Germans?"

Charlie spoke up. "People walk the Coast to Coast all the time. It's absurd to think some crazed local should decide to start going on a killing spree, especially targeting members of one particular group."

Pratt realized the futility of his argument. "Okay, okay," he growled.

I cleared my throat. "In any investigation, the first step I took as a police detective was to rank all suspects from least likely to most likely—even if the differences separating them were razor thin. In looking at our group, that's been an even more challenging task. We have four family members—three brothers and a sister-in-law—as well as a close family friend. Then there are three others who are unrelated to them."

A tense silence fell over the group.

"Since the murder victim was related, more or less, to five other members of this group," I continued, "the logical conclusion is that one of the other members of her family—or extended family—would be a more likely killer than someone who had just met Fiona. So immediately I put Charlie, Billie, and Joe in the category of least likely suspects."

"What about you?" Carole asked.

"Gimme a break, C.W.," Pratt said. "If Chase is the killer, why is he trying to find out who did it?"

"No, Carole's correct," I said. "I could be the killer, as could Charlie or Billie. You don't know much about us. We could be homicidal sociopaths for all you know. But since you asked for my thoughts, I think that I'm innocent. And because I've known Billie for years, I don't believe she is capable of murder either. Of course, the police may not agree. They want to find the guilty party, whoever it is."

"Go on," Brock said, with a trace of impatience.

"Charlie also is a stranger to you. If something provoked him to kill two members of the group for which he was responsible, it has completely escaped my notice."

Charlie gave me a thankful nod. I knew he'd been upset at the Uptons for their occasional brawls, but that didn't seem to warrant a sentence of murder, and it wouldn't explain Joe's death.

I paused to collect my thoughts. "The Uptons and Miss

Whitebanks, therefore, are the likeliest suspects, in my estimation. The next step for me was to rank them according to the likelihood of each being the culprit. As you're aware, I have only known all of you for a short time, so my judgment is bound to have flaws. I had to base it on my limited exposure to you, as well as my experience with and general knowledge of murder."

I debated mentioning that the main thing clouding my analysis was the dislike—or perhaps contempt—that most of the Uptons had for one another. But that would only set off denials, followed by arguments that would only illustrate my point.

I turned to Carole. "Miss Whitebanks seemed to me the least likely killer in this group. She's a woman—which doesn't rule her out, of course, because there certainly have been many female killers, but most are male. The first murder appears to have been through poison, which is a classic female method, but the second involved a rifle, which is not. Carole is a member of the family, but through close friendship rather than through blood. Most family murders are committed by direct family members."

Carole managed a grateful smile.

"Carole also was a long-time friend of Fiona. They became so close that, through the years, she was accepted by the family as one of their own."

Everyone appeared comfortable with this assessment.

"However," I said, turning to the others, "the two friends had not been close lately, despite Carole's presence on this holiday. They quarreled, one time very violently. Carole accused Fiona of having hastened her husband's death through neglect. I'd been told by more than one of you that Fiona had been cheating on her husband, even during the final days of his illness. In fact, Fiona told me that herself. I'd also been told that Carole had been secretly in love with Fiona's husband Steve and deeply resented how Fiona had treated him. The true reason for Fiona's remorse, I was told, was not that her husband had died, but that her lover had left her."

A few of the Uptons shifted uncomfortably in their seats, but nobody questioned my assertions. Carole's lips trembled, and she sniffed back tears. "It's true. We all know it is."

I looked around. "So right there I found a motive. Deception and resentment and jealousy are time-honored motives for murder."

"Wait a minute!" Carole said. "Sure, I thought what Fi did was lousy, but I wouldn't have killed her for it."

"Let him have his say, C.W.," Pratt said. "It's just his opinion, after all. It doesn't mean anything."

I couldn't have programmed his comment better myself. It settled Carole down. "The next least likely suspect on my list was Jenna Upton," I said, turning toward her. She regarded me placidly, revealing no emotion. "She, too, is not an Upton by blood, but by marriage. Like Carole, she seemed an unlikely murderer . . . docile, quiet, a faithful wife."

There was no change in Jenna's expression. It remained calm and neutral.

I pressed on. "Still, it didn't take long for me to discover Jenna's dislike of Fiona. There seemed to be an . . . shall we say unusual? . . . relationship between Fiona and her older brother Brock, Jenna's husband."

"That's enough!" Brock bellowed. He shot to his feet and stared me down. "I was willing to give you free rein, but now you've gone too far."

"How have I gone too far?" I countered.

"You know what I mean. All that stuff about an 'unusual relationship'!"

"Cut the crap, Brock," Pratt said. "You know damn well what he's getting at. You think we've turned a blind eye to your flirting with Fiona all these years? Grabbing her butt and rubbing up against her whenever you got the chance? You don't think we've seen how that's creeped her out?"

"You shut up, too!" Brock roared. "I never behaved inappropriately toward my sister. How dare you suggest that?"

Pratt stood, ready for a face-off. "How dare I?"

"Listen, you two," Jenna said, raising her voice to a level that I had not yet heard. "Stop it, please. Let me just say this. Any 'unusual relationship' between my husband and his sister was entirely Fiona's doing. I hope you'll pardon me, Mr. Chasen, but my sister-in-law was nothing but a common tramp."

"Time out!" Pratt declared. "Can we hear an objection from the other side?"

"Other side?" Brock said. "What in the hell are you saying, Pratt?"

"I'm saying that Fiona was nothing like Jenna just said. A common tramp? Fiona? She was one of the finest girls I've ever known! You aren't worthy to shine her boots, Jenna. What you think is 'scandalous' was her love for life. She liked to laugh and have a good time. She never led Brock on. Never."

All at once everyone began voicing their opinions.

"Stop!" I said. Everyone stopped speaking. "I know you're all on edge. There's a murderer at large, and you're all suspects. But you agreed to let me share my thoughts, so quiet down, and let me do it."

Somewhat to my surprise, my outburst had the desired effect. A silence fell. "Don't worry, Chase," said Pratt, eyeing his family. "We'll behave. Please go on."

I took a breath. "As I was saying, whether it was warranted or not, there was a general belief that inappropriate actions may have taken place between Brock and Fiona. Who was at fault I cannot say. But Jenna may have believed that Fiona was the instigator, and she might have wanted to put an end to that once and for all."

"Bull pucky," Brock spat out.

I couldn't resist a small grin. "About as much bull pucky as tarot card readings? We learned that you and Jenna visited Madame Rose, the fortune teller in the village. She told Jenna that she was going to be a murder victim."

"That was a bunch of crap," Brock said. "I only put up with it because Jenna was so doggone set on getting her fortune told."

Jenna glared at him. "That woman has a gift. What she said made a lot of sense. She told me I was in danger."

I faced Jenna. "And yet Fiona and Joe were the ones actually in danger. Were the tarot cards wrong? Or did someone decide to take fate into their own hands?"

"That's crazy," she said.

I turned to the others. "The next likeliest suspect on my list is Parker," I continued, purposely not looking at him. "Of all the Uptons, he's the most enigmatic. Intelligent, sensitive, caring. Yet he is also troubled and suffers from some sort of emotional or physiological problem that causes him to act violently at times, and for which he needs to be medicated."

"I'm past my sell-by date," Parker said.

"Knock off the self-pity, Parky," Brock said. "It makes you look even more pathetic than you are."

I turned to Parker and said, "You were the closest to Fiona. Yet you didn't like it when she got flirty with others."

" 'She who surrenders her virtue surrenders herself,' " he said.

"And you also were resentful—according to Fiona—because you entered the army based on her encouragement."

He remained silent.

I turned to the others. "Parker is a walking enigma. He's addicted to morphine and God knows what other drugs. He is a smart guy but talks in disconnected aphorisms. He had a traumatic experience in Afghanistan of some sort." I turned back to Parker. "What happened? Were you discharged because you killed someone and couldn't handle it?"

Parker moaned low and ran his hand through his hair. "Animal crackers," he said. "Animal crackers."

I walked close and bent to face him directly. "Is that what it was? Did you get hooked on killing over there? Were you waiting until you got a chance to do it again?"

Parker looked up at me with the pain of the world in his eyes. "A cow can't crow like a rooster," he said.

I leaned even closer. "Is that what you are, Parker? A rooster?"

Pratt stood and cried, "Enough already! Stop tormenting the poor guy. Don't you get it? Park wasn't discharged because he was killing too much. He was discharged because he couldn't kill at all. He fired one shot and went to pieces. They had to institutionalize him. So how could he kill Fiona, or Joe? He is incapable of it!"

I suspected something of this sort when I saw Parker carefully brush a spider off his leg rather than squash it. He was a gentle soul in a cruel world. I backed off, and he lowered his head, rocking back and forth. Jenna went over to soothe him.

"So that seems to rule out Parker as our killer," I said. "But what about the much different twin brother? Pratt is Parker's mirror image, at least in appearance. How far does that similarity extend? As is the case with many twins, they often feel emotions simultaneously. They also communicate in a subverbal way. Yet Pratt's personality is markedly different than his twin brother's—he's clear and well-spoken, but spirited, impetuous, even brash. He also has a classic motive to kill." I paused. "Money."

I expected another outburst, but Pratt regarded me with a bemused smile. "You're absolutely right. I desperately need money, and Fiona had some. Why deny it?"

I nodded. "The only flaw with that as a motive is that you, like your brother, seemed to absolutely adore Fiona." I turned to the group. "Pratt was the first to defend her if someone spoke ill of her, as you saw just a moment ago. He was the one who came up with the idea of bringing her over to the setting of her favorite childhood stories. He was the first to tend to her when she wasn't feeling well."

I reached into my shirt pocket and extracted the small envelope. "Yet Fiona's money was a powerful temptation. If she died, he knew he'd be getting some of her husband's fortune. Brutally murdering his sister, however, was a step beyond for Pratt. But what if she were to die quietly, in her sleep? Maybe if she were helped along by"—I tapped the contents of the envelope into my palm—"some of these?"

Out of the corner of my eye, I saw Ramses, lying beside Charlie, pick up his head. He began to emit a low growl.

"What in the hell are those?" Carole asked.

I spread open my hand to show the group. "Yew berries. Deadly lethal, as Charlie told us. I found them in Pratt's walking jacket."

Pratt stopped smiling.

"I thought Pratt had taken quite a long time walking the Haystacks trail the other day, especially as he is a very fit man. Our walk leader agreed. We all grew concerned when he didn't appear, and when he finally showed up, he didn't seem to have a good reason for the delay. Was the reason he took so long because he went back to the yew tree that Charlie had pointed out earlier and collected some of its berries?"

Ramses gave a bark. Pratt glared at him, then looked at me, but didn't deny it.

"The question was, how to get Fiona to ingest them? At first, I thought he might have considered doing it at our dinner table, with all the commotion going on over the beers. It would have been possible, I thought, to store some berries in those gold blocks in the unique neckband Pratt wears. I saw him leaning over the beers that night, perhaps trying to identify the one belonging to Fiona."

Pratt gave a bitter laugh. "Nice try, but my neckband doesn't work that way. You can check it for yourself."

"No, I believe you. It was too chaotic at the table anyway. You had a better opportunity when Fiona collapsed at the dinner and you and I took her to her room. With her in a weakened state, you could return to her room, slip a few berries in her mouth, or grind them into a drink of some sort and get her to ingest it without much resistance. Let's say that was your plan. You returned to your room and changed into the same outfit Parker wore that night—you have clothes that match. You figured the outfit might protect you in case someone saw you enter or leave Fiona's room. Which someone did. Billie."

Pratt, mouth open, turned to look at her.

"She was certain it was Parker," I continued. "But when Inspector Caldwell asked Parker if he'd been in Fiona's room that night, he vehemently denied it. Of course, a killer would make such a denial. But how about you, Pratt? Do you deny it was you?"

The room fell silent as we awaited Pratt's response. He shifted in his seat, looked down for so long I thought he might be intentionally stonewalling.

Then his head shot up, his face twisted with remorse. "No, I was there. You worked it out exactly right, Chase. When Charlie told us about the yew berries, I saw my opportunity. I knew that once I was on my own, I could head back to that tree he'd told us about and collect those berries with nobody suspecting." He gave a brief, huffing laugh as he looked at Ramses. "Except that damned mutt almost screwed everything up. The minute I started heading back to that tree, he began yapping and wouldn't shut up. I was afraid y'all would hear him and come running."

"You were going in the wrong direction," Charlie said. "Ramses knows these trails as well as I do."

Pratt's expression became more anguished. He closed his

eyes and reopened them. "I can't believe I ever considered killing Fi. It's like you said, Chase. The need for money turned me into someone I didn't know. Money was all I could think about. I hadn't known that somebody else had already poisoned Fi that night. So when I got into her room, I thought she was just sleeping off the beer. I used my pocket knife to crush some of the berries into a glass of tap water. But when it came time to get her to drink it . . . all at once I came to my senses. I became just like Parker—I couldn't bring myself to do it. I ran into the bathroom, threw the glass into the sink, and went back to my room." He choked back a sob and wiped tears from his eyes. "Now I would give anything to bring Fiona back."

I paused to let Pratt recover, but before I could continue, Brock said, "So that leaves me, right? The most likely suspect? Oh sure, I know what you're thinking. What is it they call it these days, 'sexual harassment'? 'Domestic abuse'? Just because all I ever did was joke around with Fiona? Play along when she went into her little tease routine?"

"Would you can it, Brock?" Carole said. "You talk too much. Letting the cat out of the bag is a hell of a lot easier than putting it back in. Quit while you're ahead."

I faced Brock. "Whether or not Fiona considered your behavior a joke, you did assume the role of a father figure. That gave you power over her. There could have been times when you took advantage of that power."

"Bull pucky!" Brock roared.

"Fiona herself made a comment about 'statute of limitations' regarding sexual abuse, for which there is none in Texas. I got the distinct impression she was holding that over you as a threat."

"Of course she was!" Brock said. "But she only just started in on that stuff recently. I think that guy she was cheating on Steve with put all these foolish ideas into her head. He was some kind of lawyer. Those kind of allegations would never stand up in court, especially with no evidence. Do you think I would kill my own sister because of that? Are you nuts?"

I stood back, took a deep breath, and let Brock's denial settle in the air. I could have brought up his obsession with Fiona recovering her memory at the bridge, and his frustration when she claimed she didn't remember and couldn't counter Brock's fear that his father was indeed drunk that fateful night and drove his wife and daughter into the water. I could have mentioned how Brock felt that Fiona—along with her brothers— was a continual "embarrassment" and a stain on the stellar Upton name.

But I said nothing. I walked to the rear of the room and put my hands in my pockets, a classic gesture of withdrawal.

"Is that it?" Pratt asked me. "Is that all you're going to say?"

"We thought you were going to tell us who the killer is," Carole said.

I eyed the half-full beer glass in front of Billie. A taste of that seemed mighty tempting, because I knew that I hadn't finished. The toughest part of my experiment was coming up.

Chapter 28

Friday Afternoon
Broadmoor Hall Terrace

I surveyed the faces before me, waiting for me to continue. Some might be viewing me as their savior, the nice guy whom they'd gotten to know briefly and who now was going to exonerate them. Perhaps even the murderer might be looking at me with trust, confident that I would divert the blame onto someone else. It was one of the reasons I didn't want Inspector Caldwell with us; his presence would have threatened that trust.

I cleared my throat. "So far, I've given you my thoughts about how I assessed each of you according to your likelihood of being Fiona's murderer. But there are other ways of looking at a murder. To the police and the justice system, the opportunity to kill Fiona might take priority over motive."

"But we all had the opportunity," Pratt said. "Her beer was poisoned, right? Any of us could have done that out on the terrace."

"Let's wind the clock back a bit," I suggested. "Somehow our killer learned that the groundskeeper kept a bottle of lethal bird poison in his workroom. Most of us know that because he showed us. But three of us weren't there."

"I didn't know about any bird poison," Pratt said. "Did you, Park?"

Parker shook his head.

"And yet it was on the minds of those of us who were in the garden workroom," I pointed out. "One of us may have mentioned it at dinner that evening, or earlier. All I'm saying is that our killer didn't necessarily have to be in the storage room that afternoon to learn of the bird poison. We can't rule anyone out."

Everyone seemed to accept this reasoning, although furtive looks and shifting bodies indicated heightened discomfort.

Up to that point, I had stood in the center of the room, speaking as if I were in a theater in the round. But I felt the need to be in motion, so I began walking around the group. That also made me look more contemplative, as if my mind was in action as well.

"It's reasonable to assume that Fiona ingested the poison by drinking her beer," I said. "Of course, there's a chance she may have consumed it some other way. But there's no evidence of that. On the other hand, we do know that she became compromised after drinking her beer and Jenna's."

This met with acceptance from the group.

"Therefore, how did the poison get into the beer? Joe brought the beer glasses to the table. It's important to note that we all were seated at or standing near the table at the time, but there were many others around, and all of us were distracted. Any of us, as Pratt notes, could have slipped the poison into Fiona's beer without being noticed."

Jenna tentatively raised her hand. "Excuse me. But . . . what if Joe had put the poison in Fiona's beer before he brought it to the table?"

"Good question," I said. "He certainly could have done that. It's possible that he disliked the way Fiona had treated Carole, to whom he'd grown close, and he was exacting revenge. Yet Joe didn't really know any of us, and for that matter, we didn't know him either. We don't know what kind of man he really was."

"He wasn't a murderer," Carole said. "No way."

"As I said, all of this is supposition based on probability. And the probability is that the poison was put into Fiona's beer at the table. Now, think back to that scene here on the terrace, just two nights ago. There was quite a lot of activity—music, singing, noise, dancing. Everyone in our group was up and down, getting drinks, changing places. Were any of us paying attention to the beer glasses and everyone's movements? I know I wasn't."

Everyone murmured in agreement.

"So how did the poison get in Fiona's beer? Think of what we know. Someone stole the bottle from the workroom. Whoever it was removed poison from the bottle. They returned the bottle to the storeroom shelf the following morning."

"They did?" Pratt asked.

"That's right. They didn't bring the bottle of poison out at the dinner table. So . . . where did the killer put the poison he or she extracted from the bottle?"

Silence.

I stopped my pacing before Carole and faced her. "For the past few days, you've been carrying around a small bottle of eye drops."

Surprised, she said, "That's right. My eyes are sensitive. There's something about the air over here that drives them nuts."

"Where is your eye-drops bottle right now?"

She looked in her purse. "Um . . . I don't know. Probably in my room. To tell the truth, my eyes haven't been bothering me ever since we . . . heard about Fiona. Maybe it's because I've been crying so much."

I began moving around again. "A small eye-drops bottle was

a perfect means of transporting the poison to the dinner table. Carole always had it with her. Nobody would notice it."

"Now hold on just a doggone minute!" Carole exclaimed. "You're saying that I carried around my eye drops so I could put poison in it? And kill Fiona?"

I turned toward her. "I recall that you didn't begin using your eye drops until the second day, right after you found that the airline didn't return your cosmetics case. Given the number of pharmaceuticals you take, I suspect your case contained more of those than it did any cosmetics."

Carole reacted as I suspected she would—with not very convincing shock.

"Did you put other substances in your case that would have knocked out Fiona?" I asked. "We'll never know. As it was, though, any of the joy pills you brought over with you could have done Fiona damage."

Carole was simmering but remained silent.

"You used to work at a toxicology clinic, didn't you? That probably taught you a lot about how to administer poisons."

She was boiling now . . . about to erupt . . .

"And you openly threatened Fiona," I said. "May I quote? 'You're gonna pay for this, Fi! You're gonna pay for everything.'"

That did it. Carole shot to her feet. "I didn't kill Fiona, and I certainly didn't kill Joe! Are you insane? I loved both of them!"

I let her declaration of love settle over everyone. Then I said, "Yes, let's talk about Joe. I've been focusing on everyone's motive for murdering Fiona, but there have been two murder victims, not just one. None of us had met Joe before coming on this trip. Only one of us grew close to him since then. It was you."

"I loved him, I tell you. Loved him!"

I disliked playing the bad cop, but I had to press on. "Right.

You two were lovey-dovey, but then something happened. It was right after Fiona was killed. Joe suddenly turned cold, and you were furious. What happened? What made him change?"

Carole sat down and glared at me, breathing heavily.

"You blew up at Joe at dinner last night," I said. "You threatened him just as you did Fiona and ran back here, to the hotel, alone. Joe ended up walking back with Billie. On the way, he mentioned something very significant to her. He told her, 'I was there. I saw who did it.'"

This had the effect I expected. Everyone's eyes widened.

"Who did he see?" Brock asked.

I turned toward him. "That's the question, isn't it? Who was it that Joe had seen?" I swung back toward Carole. "Did he witness you putting poison into Fiona's beer?"

She shot to her feet again. "He couldn't have! Because I didn't!"

"If he had seen you do that, why hadn't he told Inspector Caldwell? Was it because he was conflicted? Because he was falling in love with you?"

Carole broke down, overcome by sobs, and collapsed into her chair. This was the part of my presentation I had feared the most—where I had to force Carole into a state of extreme despair. But it was necessary to get to the truth.

She suddenly jerked erect and began digging into her purse. She extracted another eye-drops bottle.

"Here it is!" she said. "I always carry several with me. So tell me, Mr. Smarty-pants Detective. Why would I need more than one bottle if I was just going to use it to poison Fiona?"

I took the bottle from her and held it up for all to see.

"An innocent-looking container, isn't it? The perfect means of concealing a deadly poison. And yet, how does one get the poison inside?"

I made a show of attempting to twist off the top of the bottle. "I examined one of these bottles and quickly found that the top doesn't come off easily. In fact, it doesn't come off at all. It is sealed in place."

Still in motion, I walked past Pratt and Parker, both looking at me intently, and then approached Brock and Jenna.

"The only way to get poison into this small bottle would be to inject it inside," I went on. "Using some device such as a . . . syringe."

I stopped and turned toward the others. "Now, who among this group uses a such a needle? Well, there's Parker, of course, who regularly shoots himself up with morphine and God knows what else."

Pratt reached out and took Parker's hand to calm him, but it was unnecessary. Whether or not he understood where I was going, Parker didn't look alarmed.

"But there is someone else who is expert at using syringes, isn't there? In fact, I've seen her do it, administering to Parker during one of his spells." I paused and said, "Jenna Upton."

Brock stood. "Okay, stop this kangaroo court right now. I'm not going to sit here and let some ex-cop toss around reckless accusations. I mean, Jenna? You think my wife is a killer?"

I didn't respond to Brock. "Joe revealed to Billie that he had seen the person do it. Jenna and Brock were walking in the pedestrian tunnel at the time Joe made that confession. They weren't far from the other end, but sound travels easily in that tunnel. I noticed it the first time we walked back from town and heard local boys carousing there. They were on the other side of the tunnel, but the acoustics amplified their voices."

I let this observation settle on the group before looking at Brock and asking, in a soft voice, "Did you hear anything in the tunnel that night?"

He leaned toward me. "What? What did you say?"

In my regular voice, I turned to the group and said, "I doubt that Brock heard Joe in the tunnel. We know his hearing isn't the best. Sometimes he can't hear what someone is saying right next to him."

I took a breath and began to slowly pace again.

"I needed to process all of this, so I went out on the grounds this morning to center my mind. I came to the garden house and remembered seeing Joe there shortly after the grounds-keeper had shown us the poison on Tuesday. I thought he'd been looking at a bird through his field glasses. But when I stood on that spot, looking where he'd been looking, I saw that he had been directly facing the storeroom where the poison was kept. He wasn't looking at any bird. Could he have been watching someone? Someone taking the poison? The person he'd told Billie about?"

Jenna could see where I was leading, yet she maintained a look of smug innocence. "It must have been Carole he was talking about," she said. "Why would I be interested in poison? As you said, Carole's the one with the toxicology experience."

"You filthy cow!" Carole shot back. Turning to me, she said, "Jenna worked for Doc Spender, too! She was the one who recommended me for a job there."

Jenna's smugness disappeared. "And I'm sorry I ever did! All you did was flirt—"

I held up my hand. "Please let me continue. Joe saw some-one do something, confessed that to Carole, and two days later he was killed—shot in the chest with a hunting rifle. Now, I asked which of us has experience with syringes. But who among us has experience shooting rifles? Brock has boasted about his gun collection, but I've already ruled him out as a suspect. Yet he also boasted of his wife's marksmanship—'she's a crack shot,' he told me."

"Okay, I've had enough," Brock said. He rose and stood directly before me. His face was red, and he was breathing heavily. "You're trying to frame my wife, and I won't put up with it."

Pratt stood. "Back off, Brock. Let Chase have his say. When he's done, you can have yours."

Brock was fired up, and I feared another cardiac incident. But he backed off and went to sit beside Jenna, who also looked fit to be tied.

I continued my circuit around the group. "Where was I? Oh yes, talking about who in our group is adept with guns."

"We were all raised with guns," Brock said. "Jenna can shoot, sure, but all of us can. Even Parker, who's crazy enough to use a gun in the wrong way."

I walked back to Brock. "But Parker couldn't even fire his gun in an armed conflict, right? Yet I'm glad you brought him up. His experience in Afghanistan left him a damaged man, and many of his remarks, frankly, don't make much sense. Every once in a while, though, he says something that hits home. This morning, for example, he spoke of looking out the window and seeing flowers dropping their petals."

"Don't try to make sense of anything that pea brain says," Brock growled.

I reached into my pocket. "Could the petals he saw have looked something like this?" I extracted the green latex glove I'd found and held it up "This was on the ground outside the hotel this morning, right after Joe was killed. Its mate was in the trash bin nearby. They look very much like the gloves Jenna wears when she's administering Parker's injections. Did she 'shed' the gloves that day before going around to the front of the manor and walking in to greet us as if she'd just taken an innocent stroll?"

Now Jenna leapt to her feet. "You slimy prairie dog. You don't know anything! What proof have you got, huh? None. All you got is talk, talk, talk. Nothing but damn lies!"

"She's right," Brock said. "This is slander, pure and simple, and you're going to pay for it!"

I paused, took another breath, and surveyed those around me. Except for Brock and Jenna—their faces red with rage—

everyone else was tense but still, waiting to see how I would respond.

"Joe, as we know, was an avid birder," I said. "But he not only looked at birds, he photographed them as well. I'd seen him look into the garden storeroom through his field glasses that afternoon after we'd all visited it, but didn't think much of it, so I walked away. But what if he'd photographed what he'd seen?"

I paused to stop and look at each of the Uptons before continuing.

"There was only one way to find out. I obtained Joe's camera from the cloak closet. I viewed the photos he'd taken. I didn't have to look very far. The very last photo Joe had taken showed what he'd seen in the storeroom."

I paused and looked at the faces around me, expectantly waiting my next statement. All, that is, except for one person, whose face was angry and fearful.

"Joe told Carole that he saw the person do it. At first, I thought he meant he saw who poisoned Fiona's beer. What he meant, though, was he saw who had taken the Avitrol off the shelf in the storeroom."

I turned to Jenna, wild-eyed, mouth open, her hands gripping her knees.

"The image on his camera showed it was Jenna Upton," I said. "Who just asked us, 'Why would I be interested in poison?'"

In steady, measured paces, I moved slowly toward her. "We know that Carole isn't the only one who's familiar with poisons. For many years, Jenna also worked for a doctor whose practice involved toxic substances. We also know that Jenna was no admirer of Fiona. She thought she was a woman with loose morals who provoked her husband intentionally. Jenna knew that Fiona was threatening to sue Brock over something that had occurred when she was a minor. A lawsuit could put him behind bars and, possibly, cost a fortune in legal fees."

I was standing in front of Jenna. She glared at me, as tightly wound as a vicious cat about to attack.

I spoke to her directly. "What made it even worse was that you were certain Fiona would be taken care of without you ever needing to lift a finger, weren't you? Every morning, your horoscope predicted an impending tragedy. Signs of doom and disaster were everywhere—crows and room numbers and broken clocks. Even the tarot card reading you received from the fortune teller foretold death."

"The death it foretold was mine!" Jenna countered.

"Yes, let's talk about that tarot reading. I don't place much credence in that kind of thing, but one of the cards that led to Madame Rose's interpretation was the Queen of Coins, whose name is Elena."

I turned to the group. "Where had I heard that name before? It didn't take long to remember. Pratt gave the authorities Fiona's full name when they came to pick up her body. Elena was her middle name."

Swinging back to Jenna, I said, "So, not only was Fiona still alive, despite all of the signs you saw, but now you imagined she was going to kill you."

She glared at me. "I wouldn't have put it past her." Her lips tightened.

I stared right back at her. "You created the perfect excuse to return to the storeroom and get the poison. You'd dropped the top of your bottle of allergy pills. Just a few minutes ago, Brock handed that bottle to you—and its lid was back on. You returned to the storeroom, found the lid to your bottle . . . and took the poison bottle."

Jenna fixed her eyes on me, as if trying to drill them into my skull. "The stars weren't wrong about Fiona," she said, in a much colder voice. "They're never wrong. I realized that I was to be their instrument. It was up to me to carry out what had already been ordained by the universe. Or else she was going to put an end to me."

Brock turned to her, incredulous. "No, sweetheart . . ."

I looked at the others. "Parker said something else that gave me pause this morning. In fact, he said it a couple of times. 'The sky is out of date.' Most of us thought he was talking his usual nonsense."

Turning back to Jenna, I said, "But it wasn't nonsense, is it? He knew what he was saying. The stars that you rely on to dictate your life and influence your decisions? They don't even exist! By the time the light from those stars appears in the sky so it is discernable to us on Earth, the stars themselves have long burned out. How can a celestial body that died thousands, if not millions, of years ago possibly have any bearing on our lives right now?"

If looks could kill, I would be dead from the one Jenna was giving me. "But they do," she said with icy conviction. "They told me to do it!"

I stood in front of her and looked directly into her eyes, on fire with rage. "Did they also tell you to kill Joe?"

She managed a smile. "You were right, you know. I heard him in the tunnel. I heard him tell Carole that he'd seen me. So, of course, I had to shut him up." Her mouth curled up further. "It made complete sense, you see? The signs all told of disaster and death. Not just Fiona's, but someone else's too. It was perfect."

Brock's mouth was agape as he looked at his wife, shocked. "Honey . . . you don't know what you're saying . . ."

She turned to him. "Don't 'honey' me. You never trusted the stars! You made fun of it all the time, laughing at me. Everyone did! Well, nobody will laugh anymore. I showed them, didn't I? I showed them. I had to carry out the stars' mission!"

She was clearly mad.

Inspector Caldwell, who had been listening to all of this in one of the side alcoves, stepped into view and approached Jenna.

"You'll need to come with me, Mrs. Upton," he said, holding out his hand.

She looked at him as if she didn't know who he was. But she took his hand and let him lead her away.

Chapter 29

Friday, Late Afternoon
Broadmoor Hall

A hush fell over the group after Caldwell escorted Jenna away. They were already numb from shock and grief after the two murders, and the revelation that one of them committed the crimes had sent them into paralysis. I was surprised when Brock slowly got to his feet, walked over to me, and said, in a hollow, drained voice, "I meant what I said. The million bucks? It's all yours."

That he would even think of the reward at this moment, when his wife had just confessed to two murders, struck me as surreal. So did the amount. A million dollars. What on earth would I do with that? Did I even want it?

"You don't need to make good on that offer," I said to Brock.

"The hell I don't. I always make good on my promises. Give me your bank information, and I'll transfer the money as soon as I can."

A bit reluctantly, I pulled a blank check from my wallet and gave it to him. He nodded grimly and walked off to join his wife and Caldwell.

Pratt stood up and came over. "Poor Brock. He never saw

Jenna for the nutcase that she was. Too bad it took something like this to make him see the light."

Carole approached as well. "Really, Pratt? I'm pretty sure Brock knew deep down that Jenna was loonier than a bullbat. But he could never quite believe that like we did."

"We all get loony, Carole," he said. "I almost went in that direction myself."

"You were right up there near the top of my list of suspects," I admitted to Pratt. "But I changed my assessment. You can thank your brother for that."

"Parker?" He looked at his brother, who was mystified as well.

"When I spoke with Parker the morning after Fiona died, he told me his brother hadn't killed Fiona, and that he was glad he hadn't." I turned to Parker. "You said it with conviction, as if you were certain of it. Because you were, weren't you?"

"What do you mean?" Carole asked.

"I've seen the same emotions register on each brother's face simultaneously. Identical twins often experience that, even when they're far apart. Parker knew that Pratt was thinking of killing Fiona. He felt it. And he knew Pratt was in Fiona's room. So he had to act quickly. He rushed over to Fiona's room to save her."

Pratt nodded in numb acknowledgment. "I was . . . I was just about to make Fiona drink the concoction I made with the yew berries when Parker burst in. He grabbed the glass from my hands and threw it in the bathroom sink."

He went over to his brother and gave him a hug.

"So, wait a minute," Billie said. "Who was that I saw coming out of Fiona's room? Parker or Pratt?"

"It could have been either of us," Pratt said. "Parker left first, because it took me a little longer to pull myself together."

I looked at Parker. "So . . . you denied you'd been in Fiona's room when Inspector Caldwell questioned you about it later, because you didn't want to get Pratt into trouble?"

Parker nodded.

All Carole could say was, "Wow."

"What neither of you knew was that Fiona had already been poisoned," Billie said. "It was just taking time to work."

"I wish I had known," Pratt said. "I could have called someone to come and pump her stomach or something."

I placed my hand on his shoulder. "It was probably too late for that. Don't beat yourself up over it."

"I want fried chicken," Parker said. "When's dinner?"

As there didn't seem to be any additional information to collect, or unanswered questions to settle, I thanked them for their cooperation . . . and indulgence. As I began to walk away, Carole approached me.

"You really had me going, Chase. I knew I was innocent, but you made me think my number was up. I was sweatin' like a whore in church."

I let out a loud guffaw. "I really did think at one point you were the likeliest candidate—before Joe was killed—so you had a right to be nervous."

"Know what? This is something I can tell my kids about someday to put the fear of God into 'em. I was the lead suspect in a murder investigation!" She gave me a sly wink as she walked out with the others, leaving Billie and me alone.

"You did good, Chase," Billie said. "But with all that evidence against Jenna, why didn't Caldwell just arrest her to begin with? Why go through that whole rigamarole of laying it all out for everyone?"

Leave it to Billie to use a word like *rigamarole*. Wasn't that from one of the *Wizard of Oz* books? "I suggested that we not confront Jenna straight out because she would have gone instantly into denial mode. Sure, we have that photo of her lifting the poison bottle, but she could have argued how that didn't prove anything. And she would have been right. No, I suspected that gradually zeroing in on her was the way to go. What made her snap was when everyone started questioning her unshakable trust in prophecies and omens. She's got a deep-seated faith in them, and like many deep-seated faiths, they need to be constantly fed and justified. She knew the only way to maintain her faith was to take matters into her own hands. Of course, her hatred for Fiona tipped the scales as well."

Billie shook her head. "Well, she sure fooled me. I was convinced Brock was the killer. In a weird way, I kind of feel sorry for Jenna. She genuinely thought she was doing the right thing."

"A lot of murderers do."

I looked at the corner of the terrace where Mike was standing, smiling. I excused myself from Billie and went to join him.

"That was quite a performance, Chase," he said, grasping my shoulders. "I kept wondering where you were headed. You had me gripping the side of my chair quite a few times."

"It's hard to believe it's over," I said. "Looking back on it now, I was taking a big risk. My strategy could easily have fizzled out."

He squeezed my shoulder. "Give yourself some credit, big guy. You're smarter than you know."

"Thanks. I may need to remind you of those words from time to time. In the meantime, I need a tall glass of beer."

"Food sounds better. I ate just a couple of stale biscuits at the clinic. I'm as hungry as a hound."

"Then let's go have a bite and some ale in the bar. We can celebrate all this nastiness being behind us." I dashed back to Billie and explained I needed time alone with Mike, which she graciously understood.

As Mike and I walked to the hotel bar, I asked him how the examination of Joe's body went.

"No surprises. The forensic pathologist was able to determine approximately how far Joe was standing from the shotgun when it was fired, although I'm not sure how valuable that information might be now that you have the killer."

Soon Mike and I were settled at a small table in the corner of the bar, the late-afternoon sunshine on display through the window beside us, our plates piled with fish and chips and our glasses brimming with Cumberland Corby ale.

I wanted to put the case behind me and focus again on Mike, but he was fascinated about how I zeroed in on Jenna as the culprit.

"You certainly took a chance with that approach, Chase," Mike said. "She could easily have not taken the bait and acted innocent throughout the whole thing."

"You're right," I said, my hand curled around my glass of beer. "I'm only now beginning to realize that. You can blame it on my impetuousness."

"I know you well enough by now to blame it on the fact that you are an excellent judge of character. I know you found that incriminating photograph, but did you strongly suspect Jenna before then?"

"Her husband was still my favorite suspect, but Jenna was the wild card. It wasn't just because of her crazy superstitions, although that clearly singled her out. Mostly it was because she ticked all the boxes."

"What boxes?"

I held up a finger. "Did she have a motive? Yes, she had a feverish dislike for Fiona." I held up a second finger. "Did she have the means? Yes. She knew how best to administer that poison, and she was very adept with a rifle." I held up a third finger. "Did she have the opportunity? Yes. She was with us when we saw the bird poisons, and unlike the other Uptons, she was a forgettable figure, not an outsized personality. She was able to sneak away from Brock and the others to get the poison without anyone noticing she was gone."

I paused before raising a fourth finger. "There was also what I call the fourth box. Did Jenna have a killer instinct? That's the hardest question when it comes to reviewing suspects. I need to think where I've seen that person act heartless or even . . . cruel."

"My word. Had you seen Mrs. Upton behave that way?"

I looked down and nodded. "Yes, on two occasions. One was something others would miss. It was when she saw that Charlie's dog Ramses was coming with us into the pub. She thought the animal was unsanitary, but it was more than that. She gave the dog a cold, icy look that sent a chill down my spine."

"Good Lord," Mike said.

"That was a small thing, but the other wasn't. It was when she administered the naloxone, or whatever it's called, to bring Parker out of his morphine overdose. Time is of the essence when that happens. But Jenna took it all very slowly. It was almost as if she was intentionally dragging it out, keeping Parker on the edge of death. I felt she was enjoying having that power of life or death."

"How terrible!"

"I asked myself which boxes the other suspects checked. Jenna was the only one who ticked all four."

"That's amazing," Mike said as he gave me an appreciative smile. "I work with a lot of blokes in the CID, Chase, and none have that kind of eye."

I chuckled and took a sip of beer. "I doubt that very much. But thanks for the compliment. At the present, however, you're the only one my eye wants to look at."

We gazed at one another as Mike took a slow sip from his beer. Our looks communicated so much more than any of our words. Finally, however, Mike spoke. "So, what's our plan now?" he asked.

Did he mean the plan for our relationship or the rest of the week? I chose the least complex option. "Well, we could check with Charlie and see if he wants to continue the walk with the three of us, but I don't think that would be a great idea."

"Too disrespectful of the dead?"

"Something like that. Plus the schedule is all mucked up anyway."

"Why don't you and I just head back south, to my place? We were going to do that when the walk was finished anyway. There are many beautiful trails down there, as you know."

I reached out and took his hand. "We can do a lot more than walk, you know."

"Well, I certainly hope so!" he said with that crooked smile that made my heart melt. After a pause, he asked, "But what about after that? Will you go back to California and leave me alone for another year?"

Now we were getting to the crux of things. "I don't want that, Mike. Not anymore. It's different between us now. I fell for you last year, but it wasn't until I saw you again yesterday that I realized how much you truly mean to me. I can't lose you."

He reached over to grasp my hand. "I don't want to lose you either, Chase. But please understand that I need more time than you. All of this is a big step I never thought I'd take. I'm not quite ready to leave my job and move to the States and completely upend my life."

"Yes, I understand that."

"What about you? Would you consider relocating over here?"

We both knew my retirement gave me more freedom. Still, uprooting myself from my home country was a tall order, even though the move would be to another country I loved. The good old USA, even with its flaws, always had a claim on me.

"How about this?" I said. "A half-and-half arrangement.

You come to the US for half the year—maybe in three-month chunks—and I do the same over here."

"I can't leave my job for six months," he said.

An idea came to mind. "Why not quit your job?" I asked. "Believe it or not, it looks like I'm going to get a million-dollar reward from Brock Upton for solving this case. If it's money you're worried about, you can have that money."

Mike's mouth dropped open. "That chap is giving you a million dollars for proving his wife is a murderer?"

"I know it sounds weird, but he was as shocked as any of us that she was guilty. What do you say?"

Mike looked down for a moment and reached out to stroke my hand. "It's not about the money, Chase. I could afford to retire now if I wanted. But I've made a commitment to work three more years, which means finding a proper replacement and finishing up some of the changes I'm making to the department. If there's one thing you need to know about me, I'm a man of my word."

I was more pleased than disappointed to hear this. I reminded myself that Mike and I hadn't spent much time together. It might be too soon to test whether we were ready for a full-time commitment. And yet there had to be a better way to handle this than the way we'd been going at it.

"I'll tell you what I can do," Mike said. "I'm not ready to leave my job, but I do have quite a bit of compensatory time banked up. What if I come over to California for two or three months, spread out over the year?"

"And I can do the same thing here," I said. "That's a great suggestion." Even as I agreed, though, I wondered if it was really wise for a man of my age to waste precious time by delaying what I'd hoped would be the inevitable result. Trying out a cohabitated relationship in small chunks was certainly preferable to continuing doing it long-distance, however—and that's how I would have to see it.

Vowing to iron out the details later, and agreeing not to talk about murder or dead bodies, we switched to general chat, which amounted to Mike bringing me up to speed on the members of his family. He told me about his last visit with his eighty-eight-year-old mother (still sharp, agile, and gardening) and his brother, Freddie, who was in the process of divorcing his second wife. "Mum points out that her gay son is the most stable and level-headed of the two," he said. "She's thrilled to learn I've met someone and can't wait to meet you."

The flies in the ointment were Celia and Joshua, his two children. The daughter had cut off communication with Mike completely once he'd come out to her, which particularly hurt because it cut off contact with his granddaughter, Josie, as well. His son, Joshua, hadn't been thrilled to learn of his father's true sexuality either, but grudgingly stayed in touch, if only (as Mike suspects) so he could hit his dad up for an occasional loan. Mike's ex-wife, Joanne, was certain the kids would come around, although both were in their forties and hardly "kids" anymore.

"What with your kids and the squabbles I've seen with the Uptons, maybe I'm better off without much family," I said.

Mike gave a reluctant smile. "It's good to have family, Chase. And the best part is, sometimes the best family is the one you're not related to."

I smiled in agreement. Doug and I had had a big group of friends, and Billie had always seemed like a sister to me. Both of my parents were gone, and other than my sister, Allison—with whom I had a tentative relationship, at best—my closest blood relation is my quirky Aunt Winifred, a dear old bird who lives in Las Vegas with her "roommate" Leila, a slightly younger woman who works as a croupier at the Bellagio. "Of course they're lesbians," I said to Mike, "but Winnie is of the generation that is still uncomfortable with that word."

As we neared the bottom of our beer glasses, we talked

about our other passions. I was pleased that we were both music lovers. Mike loved jazz and had always wanted to visit the sites of the big US jazz clubs of the thirties and forties, even though most are long gone. When he's not practicing his clarinet, his non-work hours are devoted to maintaining his precious garden ("When I say I spend a lot of time on my knees, that's not what people first think of," he joked). I knew I'd probably drive Mike nuts playing my Hank Williams records, and even in our phone conversations, I couldn't resist bringing him up to date on the Red Sox and my favorite TV shows—British police dramas to which, it turned out, he was addicted as well.

Before we realized it, the day was dimming, and the outside lights were coming on. It wasn't late, but I was worn out. That wasn't hard to understand, actually, given that I'd helped solve a murder and begun to plan my future.

Billie came into the bar with Carole and Pratt. They sat across the room at another table. I told Mike I'd be right back and went over to Billie. I took her aside and briefly outlined my plans to stay with Mike and asked if she was planning on heading home the following day.

Shrugging resignedly, she said, "Normally I'd like to stay on, but as you know, I'm stone broke. I need to get back home and see what can be done about my financial situation."

I smiled. "Would a million dollars be of any help?"

She tilted her head and raised an eyebrow. "Do you really think Brock will pay that reward?"

I told her it was already in process. "I don't think parting with it will hurt him as much as finding out about Jenna. I don't feel right taking it, though. You need it more than I do."

She let this sink in. I'd never seen Billie thrown for a loop, but she certainly was at that moment, opening her mouth to speak, closing it again, opening it, closing it.

Finally, she said, "Know what, Chase? Maybe I will spend a few days in London after all."

That night, before getting into bed beside Mike, who was already sleeping soundly, I went into the bathroom to record the day's events in my journal so I didn't disturb him. Given the late hour and my waning energy level, I didn't write an extended record of my quasi-courtroom summation that afternoon. Mostly I attempted to put into words the incredible sensation of being in love, like a lovestruck teenage girl writing in her diary. The words, of course, barely conveyed what I was feeling; I am no poet. But they sure felt good to write down. When I crawled into bed, taking care not to disturb Mike, I put the drama of the day aside. All that I felt at that moment was the warm reassurance of a future brighter than I'd dared hope for.

Chapter 30

Saturday Morning
Broadmoor Hall

Charlie and Ramses were relaxing in the foyer the following morning when Mike and I came down with our suitcases. Charlie stood and handed me an envelope.

"Your next walk with Rovers North is on us, Mr. Chasen," he said. Looking down, I could swear his dog was also regarding me with gratitude. "It's our thanks for helping the police wrap up this unfortunate matter neatly and quickly."

I was as tempted to refuse his offer as I had been with Brock's, but Charlie would have insisted I take it regardless. "Thank you" was all I said, pocketing his envelope.

Billie joined us, toting her impossibly small carry-on. She wore a fuchsia, floral-patterned sweater I'd never seen before.

"I swear, Billie, how do you carry so many sweaters in that little suitcase?" I asked.

"The fine art of efficient packing, Chase," she said with a wink. "I think I'll do a TED talk about it."

"I can hardly wait!" Mike said. "I never pack the right way."

She leaned close and whispered to me, "I also want thank you again for your generous offer."

It took me a moment to realize she was talking about the

million-dollar reward. She went on to say, "But, if you don't mind, I've decided to only accept half of it."

"Nothing doing, Billie. I want you to take the whole—"

She held up her hand. "Hear me out. Half a million will certainly make up for what I've lost, and then some. There's someone else here who needs the money just as much as me."

She looked over to Pratt, knapsack over one shoulder and cowboy hat firmly in place, descending the stairs, carrying his suitcase. Parker followed, minus the hat, along with Carole, dressed demurely in a plain cotton shirt and jeans. Brock, I'd learned, had spent the night in the nearby town of Carlisle, where Jenna was being held.

Pratt set his case down, a broad grin on his face. "Did Billie tell you about the loan she made me?"

"It's not a loan, Pratt," Billie said. "I don't expect to be paid back."

"I am going to pay you back. Brock will split a gut when he hears that some of his money is coming to me. If I don't make good on it, I'll never live it down. I do have some dignity, you know."

Billie smiled. "Very well, then. For the sake of your dignity. I might return some of it to Brock, too, if I get some of my own money back."

Mike looked happy that I'd found recipients for the reward money, and I was pleased that it was helping people in need. Perhaps there was karmic force at work.

"I received another piece of good luck as well," Pratt announced, taking off his knapsack. He zipped it open and extracted a small cloth bundle.

"What is that?" Billie asked.

Pratt smiled as he unwrapped the bundle to reveal a large gold medallion strung on a gold chain.

"Is that—?" I asked.

He nodded. "It's my dad's necklace! I was passing through a

hallway on the way to my room last night and saw it in a case on the wall. Sure enough, Mrs. Cooper said it had been found in the river by one of her employees soon after our parents' accident. Nobody put it together with the accident, and somehow it ended up framed and on the wall. When I showed her photos of my dad wearing it, she knew it was the same one and let me have it."

Billie reached out to pick up the medallion. "The chain is very fine. It probably broke when the car hit the water."

"I could probably sell it for more than the money you loaned me," Pratt said as he wrapped the medallion and put it back in his knapsack. "But Dad always wanted me to have it. I'll get you your money back, Billie, one way or another."

"Have you heard what the authorities are planning to do with Jenna?" I asked Pratt.

"They're holding some sort of arraignment," Pratt said. "We're all going to Carlisle until that's resolved, which shouldn't take long, we're told. From there, she'll fly under custody back home."

I was certain her lawyers would argue that she'd acted out of some sort of mental delusion. It wouldn't be hard to prove.

"We want to thank you for all you've done, Chase," Carole said. "I've known Jenna for ages. She was always nuttier than a squirrel turd, but I never expected her to do anything like this."

Thinking about Joe, I said, "I . . . just wish I could have stopped her sooner."

She grasped my hand. "Hell's bells, don't be ridiculous." She nodded soberly and looked around. "I hope you don't think I'm heartless, Chase."

I asked, "What do you mean?"

"A man I loved and another lifelong dear friend have just been murdered. I should be totally destroyed, right? Well, I am . . . but I'm not. I haven't figured all of this out yet—after all, I'm not the sharpest knife in the drawer—but even though I miss Joe and Fiona like crazy, I still believe the best is yet to come. Is that nuts?"

I placed his hand on her shoulder. "No, you're not nuts. You're just human. In the best sense of the word."

"Human! God help me, how depressing is that?"

I bent and kissed her on the cheek.

We proceeded to the front desk, where Mrs. Cooper efficiently settled our accounts. A car beeped outside.

"That must be our taxi," Pratt said. He hefted up his backpack and suitcase and led us all outside.

After he and Parker put their bags in the boot of the taxi, I said, "Best of luck to you," and shook Pratt's hand. Turning to Parker, I said, "And to you as well. I hope you make it to the Taj Mahal someday."

He looked at me and gave me the first genuine smile I'd ever seen on his face. "Trust the groove. No speeding!" He got into the cab with the others.

Mike looked at me questioningly. "I'll explain later," I said, although I wasn't sure anyone could adequately explain Parker.

The Uptons' cab had no sooner driven off than Caldwell drove up in his Peugeot. He hopped out and strode toward us.

"I'm on my way to Carlisle to participate in the turnover of Mrs. Upton to US authorities," he said. "Because this was a case of a US citizen killing two other non-Brits, there's no need for me to be involved beyond that."

"Even though the second victim was Canadian?" Billie asked. "That's a British Commonwealth, isn't it?"

Caldwell dismissed that with a wave of his hand. "Perhaps there's a diplomatic hurdle in there somewhere, but it's someone else's headache now, not mine. What about you lot? Prepared to spend your million?"

I explained that the money was no longer my headache.

"Pity, Chase," he said. "You deserve to have it."

"It was a joint effort," I replied. "I should have given some of the reward to you."

"Couldn't accept it, unfortunately. There are rules against that sort of thing for blokes like me. Oh, by the way. Forgot to tell you what we'd found in Mrs. Upton's bags—a bottle of gamma hydroxybutate."

"Liquid ecstasy," Mike said. Caldwell nodded.

"That explains why Fiona got out of control so quickly," I said. "Jenna must have spiked her beer with it. And on more than one occasion."

"My work here is finished," Caldwell said. "And frankly, I want to get back to good old British criminals. They're much more conventional." He checked his watch. "Dear me. I'd better be off. I just wanted to stop by and wish you the best."

As he slid into the driver's seat, I told Caldwell that Mike and I were going off to spend a week or so together before I headed home. The inspector looked pleased and made us promise to look him up should we ever come back up north.

His Peugeot sped off, passing the taxi arriving to take Billie to the train station in Penrith. From there, she would proceed to London for a few days before going home. I wished her a good time.

"As much as I love London, I'm itching to go home and work with the authorities to find Marie and bring her to justice. Fortunately, thanks to your gift, I won't have to do that while living in a packing crate."

We hugged, and she got into the taxi. Through the window, she motioned me close and in a whisper said, "You must promise to tell me how things go with Mike. But only if you leave out the X-rated parts."

I laughed. "I promise. Let's do this again, okay? Another walk."

"Wouldn't miss it."

She waved goodbye as her taxi drove off.

"What was all that about bringing someone to justice?" Mike asked.

I took his hand. "I'll explain it all later, in detail. At the moment, however, I want to only think of you and our two glorious weeks together."

"There will be more than that, I trust," he said. He put his hand to my face and said, "I'm not ready to make any promises yet, Chase. But I'm having the devil of a time not telling you how much I love you."

"It seems like you just did," I teased. "I'm not going to be as cautious. I want to tell you that I love you . . . and I think I just did also."

We exchanged a quick kiss, picked up our suitcases, and walked to his MG. After managing to fit our bags in the car's small boot, I turned back for one last look at the fortress-like façade of Broadmoor Hall. I knew that I would never forget it and the secrets revealed within its walls. Those memories might haunt me for a while.

Best to put those thoughts in the past, I realized. I squeezed myself into the seat beside Mike, knowing I was about to create a lot more memories.

Far more pleasant ones.

Acknowledgments

Thanks to all the readers who took a chance on my first book and came back for more! I've enjoyed meeting many of you at book events this past year, and hope to connect with many more in the year to come.

Also, many thanks to my wonderful agent, Michelle Hauck, to my editor John Scognamiglio, Larissa Ackerman, Robin Cook, and the rest of the great team at Kensington.